The Turner Tomorrow Fellowship was created to encourage authors to write fiction that produces creative and positive solutions to global problems. Over 2,500 submissions were received. *The Bully Pulpit* was an Award of Merit-winner for this prestigious fellowship.

THE
BULLY
PULPIT

ANDREW GOLDBLATT

Turner

BANTAM BOOKS
NEW YORK • TORONTO • LONDON • SYDNEY • AUCKLAND

THE BULLY PULPIT

A Bantam / Turner Book / July 1992

ISBN 0-553-29906-9

Published simultaneously in the United States and Canada

Bantam Books are published by Bantam Books, a division of Bantam Doubleday Dell Publishing Group, Inc. Its trademark, consisting of the words "Bantam Books" and the portrayal of a rooster, is Registered in U.S. Patent and Trademark Office and in other countries. Marca Registrada. Bantam Books, 666 Fifth Avenue, New York, New York 10103.

PRINTED IN THE UNITED STATES OF AMERICA

RAD   0 9 8 7 6 5 4 3 2 1

This story is set in the future merely to allay suspicions the characters are based on current public officials, their families, or their staffers. It can happen much much sooner, if you want it.

I am deeply grateful to the following for their assistance, moral support, or both: Jean and Jim Andrews, Mary Jane Batson, Lisa and Don Benninger, Ted Bloom, Frances Cave, Paul Clifford, Claire Cortner and Steve Lesky, Jennifer Hershey, Janet Keller, Joan Kleinbaum, Mildred Kushner, Sara Leavitt and Marty Pollard, Glen and Jackie McClish, Adrienne Miller, Leon Nehmad, Jack Piltz, Mirka Prazak and Robert Pini, Janice Schachter and Audrey Kurland, Alan Simon, Stanley Simon, Lila Stevens, Robert Stevens, Sandy Yingling, and, most of all, Ms. Sweetness-and-Light herself.

THE
BULLY
PULPIT

1

I SHOULD HAVE been able to hear them celebrating as soon as the elevator opened, but all I heard was the heavy, slack-jawed breathing of Buford's guard. He gave a barely perceptible nod and let me pass, then stopped the other men in the elevator, a pair of unimposing tourists, with a hand to each of their sternums.

"Where you think you're goin'?" he asked.

"Is this the floor Jack Morgan's on?"

"Nope," the guard replied, and shoved them back so they tumbled like bowling pins against the back wall of the elevator. He pressed the down button and waved bye-bye as the elevator closed.

"They're comin' out of the woodwork tonight," he swore.

"Don't come down on them too hard," I pleaded. "They're potential voters."

He didn't bother to hide his disgust. "Next time I'll say excuse me first, okay?"

I headed down the red-carpeted, wall-papered hall-way to the executive suite. Three more of Buford's guards, posted by the double-door entrance, moved aside to let me pass. "Where's the man?" I asked. One of the guards nodded curtly in the direction of another corridor.

"Thanks." I always made a point to be polite to Buford's guards, mostly because I was afraid of them. With their ample black suits (the better to hide their massive biceps and high-powered rifles), ear pieces, reflector glasses, and contemptuous expressions they did an even better job of projecting menace than the Secret Service. Many times I wondered what kind of childhoods they must have had, to do their jobs so well.

The fact that Morgan had a private force protecting him elicited increasing interest from the press, especially as his delegate total approached the number needed for nomination. I explained that because there were three candidates during the primaries, the Secret Service was stretched thin. Morgan had received too many death threats to feel secure with the paltry contingent the Treasury Department allotted him, so he supplemented his protection with guards from his best friend Buford's firm.

It was a lie, of course. The Secret Service offered Morgan plenty of agents. The reason he surrounded himself with Buford's thugs was that he thought for sure someone would try to kill him, and he didn't trust the Secret Service to protect him. Perhaps his paranoia wasn't so farfetched; the Treasury secretary was the man he'd beaten for a Senate seat ten years ago. "Half a second, that's all they have to hesitate. Not so long that anyone would question their response, but long enough for some idiot to get me," is how he put it.

"Steinhardt!" Fallon hissed from a room along the corridor. "Where the hell you been all night?"

I was feeling good enough that even the portly Texan's impenetrable drawl failed to annoy me. "I set Jack up for an interview with Reed Gordin. Pretty awesome, huh? Two days ago NBC was hanging up on me.

Now they're sending us their star reporter. Hey, why so quiet? I expected the place to be drenched in bubbly."

"He's in one of his moods again. He'd grind his heel into an angel's balls, if he could find an angel in these parts."

"The man is finally getting what he always wanted, and he can't enjoy it?"

Fallon shrugged. He'd been on board only a year, and the boss's moods still mystified him. Not that Fallon had the tools to analyze Jack Morgan's inner workings in the first place. He was an old-fashioned operator who got by on sweaty handshakes and effusive promises. Make people happy whatever it takes—that was the sum of his political and psychological insight.

"I wanted to warn you before you went in there and made an ass of yourself," he whispered. "Follow me."

We headed down the corridor to Morgan's room. Ever since the Iowa caucuses the one constant in our harried, miserable lives was the nightly ritual of sprawling out in Morgan's room and talking strategy into the wee hours. The ritual grounded us, kept us a team, and usually gave us the courage to stick out the campaign another day. Except, that is, during losing nights or whenever Elena Morgan was in town. On those occasions the atmosphere was so foul that only cowardice prevented us from quitting. Tonight was a double whammy: It was primary day in six states, and Elena had flown in from Toledo.

The hotel had installed a bank of TVs atop the dresser so we could watch the returns on all the major networks. But Morgan had the TVs tuned to the game scenes showing in the Virtual Reality helmet that covered his salt-and-pepper hair and blue eyes. He sat on the bed with his back against the cushioned headboard, shoes still on, alternately looking one way, then the other, jerking the controls with each sudden appearance of a rival spaceship or gunslinger. The rest of the inner circle watched impassively as the action on the TVs changed.

Elena, whose delicate features had hardened over the years to show every wrong that had ever been done to her, sat to Morgan's right. To his left, on a chair by the bed, hunched his best friend in the Senate, Alonzo "Dingo" Hutson. Mel Buford leaned against the wall next to the window, looking out occasionally as if expecting a cab. Erika Mitchell the pollster, Ron Ishikawa the comptroller, and Lucy Casselwaite the speechwriter occupied chairs around the writing table. Molineaux the publicist flitted everywhere, taking snapshots with the cameras hanging from his neck. He was the only one the least bit animated.

"Dan-o, make Jack take off the helmet and smile, will ya?" he cajoled. "No one's going to believe I took these pictures on the night he won the nomination."

Fallon claimed the one remaining chair, by the desk. Lacking other options, I sat on the floor, back to the wall. "Congratulations, sir," I ventured.

"Where were you so long, Steinhardt?" Morgan asked, tearing off the blocky helmet after a thick, day-glo orange glove filled the screen, signifying that his boxing opponent had delivered a knockout blow. He grabbed a bottle of Jack Daniel's from the night table and gulped a swig.

"Toting up congratulatory telegrams—over six hundred as of ten o'clock. And holding the press at bay. They want to know when you'll make your victory statement. And Reed Gordin wants to confirm a date next week to do an interview."

"Fuck Reed Gordin." He debated which game to play next, then, apparently bored by them all, turned back to me. "I can understand why you're so happy. Your job just got easier. For the last year and a half you've had to buttonhole every dumbshit with a press pass and beg them to say something about me. Now they'll all be begging you. 'Just a fifteen-minute interview, Dan! You can name the ground rules. Fifteen minutes, please!' "

The rest of the staff squirmed silently. Hutson would become his attorney general, Buford his chief of staff, Fallon Democratic party chairman, and Ishikawa secretary of the treasury, yet none of them could keep him balanced. I feared that sooner or later word would leak that Morgan, miracle story of the 2008 campaign, was a chronic depressive, and his popularity would sink so low the Libertarian candidate would beat him out for second place.

Since I'd been with him all ten years in the Senate, I was accustomed to his low moods, and knew the best way to pull him up was to serve as his foil until he finished venting whatever vexed him. "Sir, you just won five of six states," I reminded him. "And with the second-place finish in Arizona, you've got the delegates to win the nomination. Want a boost? Go downstairs. Wall-to-wall admirers. And every one of them *believes* in you."

"Hah. They're even bigger fools than me."

"You're being maudlin, sir."

"Am I? You haven't worked it out yet, have you, Steinhardt? Well here, I'll make it plain. This magnificent triumph of mine was a setup."

"Excuse me?"

"What have I won? The chance to finish a humiliating second to that stupid bastard in the White House? No one else was fool enough to want the nomination, so they let me take it."

"Now, wait a minute, Jack," Hutson countered; what a relief to have someone else jump in! "Kirk put up a pretty damn good fight. So did Weldon. You mean to say they didn't really want the nomination?"

"Not bad enough. They didn't press me where they should have. They knew where I played both sides of the fence. If they had any brains at all, they'd have hammered at me till I had to take a stand and lose some votes. Hell, we've been waiting for them to do that for the last three months, and it never came. Kirk and Weldon may be assholes, but they aren't *that* obtuse."

"So why didn't they attack you?" Elena asked.

"It's simple, doll." He took another hit from his Jack Daniel's. "They saw that *New York Times* poll. You know, the one that rated all three of us against the President? I came closest, and I lost almost three to two."

"So they made you the sacrificial lamb. They'll try again in 2012, when there won't be an incumbent running," inferred Hutson.

"Exactly. It would have looked bad if they quit. So they stayed in long enough to boost their recognition for the next go-round and get matching funds to pay off their campaign debts. That's why I'm not jumping up for joy. This isn't the beginning of my career. It's the end. I'll be just another chump in the line that started with McGovern. I won't even be invited to the next convention."

"Don't ever ask for what you'll wish you didn't get," Buford uttered quietly.

"Wait, wait, don't tell me," chirped Molineaux as he pointed his camera at me, let the lens whir into focus, and snapped. I found him nearly insufferable at times; too much jewelry and cologne and open shirt. He even wore makeup, superfluous on his well-defined, Gallic features. "Judging by the tortured syntax, it must be one of the Greeks. Aristotle?"

"Seneca. A Roman," Buford corrected.

"But you know, it isn't over till it's over," I said to Morgan. "You can make the most of this."

"Thank you, Steinhardt. Buford quotes Greeks and Romans, you quote Yogi Berra. Oh, well. I guess it's no big deal to you if I lose. You can always get your job back with the Mud Hens."

"I'd prefer to be the White House press secretary," I said. "I've paid my dues in the bush leagues."

"Fine. Then tell me, how're you gonna get to *be* the White House press secretary? A Democrat hasn't won the White House since the bicentennial. Tell me how I don't go down in flames."

"I don't know, sir."

"Ah-ha, see? And beyond that, suppose I do win the election. There's no power in the presidency anymore—it's all been transferred to the private sector. The country's going to hell, the planet's going to hell, and here I am fighting for the office of chief eunuch to a dying empire. I must have been insane when I declared for that job."

"What you always said before was that the real power of the presidency is in shaping the national mood. Setting priorities, emphasizing certain values over others. Remember? You said it's not so much the bills you sign that gets things done as the actions you inspire in the people."

Morgan laughed sarcastically. "Oh, right, inspiring people—a Democratic specialty. What the hell do we stand for, Steinhardt? Does anybody here know what the party stands for? I'll bet you ninety percent of the people who voted for me don't have the vaguest idea what I'd do in the White House. I smile, keep my hair neat, spout generalities, and the cattle cast their ballots."

"If that's the way you feel about it, why did you even bother to declare? Why are you even in politics?"

"I ask him those same questions every day," Elena confided, visibly cheered to have me for an ally. Not that I wanted her to think me one.

"I did it for the reason everybody else does," Morgan explained. "Megalomania."

"Well, Jack, it seems to me the proper time to have these doubts has passed," interjected Dingo Hutson, reaching over to the table and taking a swallow of Morgan's whiskey. "You can't just up and quit after thousands of us have put in so much time and energy."

"And money," Ishikawa, the compact Sansei, added.

"No, I suppose not. That would be pretty flaky, wouldn't it?" His drunkenness was starting to show.

No one spoke for a minute, not even Molineaux, who continued taking pictures.

Fallon broke the silence. "Try looking at it this way. If it *is* a lost cause, this is your high point. You might as well go out and enjoy it."

"Go downstairs and accept the worship of the masses, eh?"

"Work that crowd."

"Goddammit, Fallon, I want to win this fucking thing!" Morgan thundered. Then, embarrassed by the outburst, he added more apologetically: "I'm tired of that joke about how Democrats and turkeys are alike—they both get carved up in November."

Silence again. Morgan snatched the Jack Daniel's by the neck, watched the brownish liquid quake—and threw the bottle in the trash. His facial muscles tautened.

"Lucy, you've got thirty minutes to write me a victory speech. The rest of you, your last assignment is to come downstairs with me. After that, you're on vacation until Monday. But while you're out cavorting on some beach or getting reacquainted with your families, I want you to consider this: How do we win November fourth? I want each of you to come up with a blueprint. And no working together. I don't want any groupthink."

"Anything goes?" I asked.

"Anything," said Morgan, "that gives me a chance."

2

WHAT I WROTE:

John Nathaniel Morgan was born in Toledo, Ohio, at 4:15 P.M. on November 22, 1963.

What I didn't write:

For all you shopping-mall mystics who believe in past lives, let me run that by you one more time: Jack Morgan was born hours after John F. Kennedy was killed. Anything significant about that? Not in my mind. Not in Morgan's either. But if you want to believe that Kennedy was reincarnated as Jack Morgan, that's more than fine with us. Why do you think he chose the nickname Jack? It wasn't just because his parents called him Bunky.

What I wrote:

Jack's father, M. Buckminster Morgan, was a stockbroker. His mother, Ann, worked as a nurse until Jack, their only child, was born.

What I didn't write:

In the late 1950s Buckminster Morgan invested heavily in Dow Chemical. He became a millionaire the day the Pentagon ordered napalm for the war in Vietnam. Six months before little Bunky (the sobriquet came from his earliest attempts to pronounce his daddy's name) started kindergarten, the family moved from a duplex in Toledo to a five-bedroom, split-level house in the wealthy suburb of Ottawa Hills. His mother hired a nanny to look after Jack while she spent afternoons with other housewives playing bridge and drinking Annie Green Springs.

What I wrote:
Jack was a bright, well-mannered child who found school an insufficient challenge.
What I didn't write:
Jack spent twelve hours watching TV for every hour he read or did his homework. In eighth grade he played baseball and touch football in the street, breaking car lights and, on more than one occasion, a neighbor's window, without ever owning up. A year later he was sucking gin and grapefruit juice from a flask he hid inside his locker, smoking marijuana every weekend, and feeling up girls in a car he drove using a counterfeit license.

What I wrote:
He was a popular student and standout football player in high school.
What I didn't write:
As a sullen adolescent Jack Morgan went to any length to prove he wasn't a soft rich kid. At Maumee Valley Country Day School, the local prep academy where he spent his high school years, he dressed in leather and affected a Puerto Rican accent, prompting his classmates to nickname him Jose. He joined the football team his junior year and played like a kamikaze pilot. The team was penalized so many yards as a result of his late hits that the coach eventually benched him, whereupon he quit.

What I wrote:
After high school Jack enlisted in the Marine Corps.
What I didn't write:

As part of an ongoing effort to spite his parents, deny his wealthy background, and vent his adolescent rage, Jack Morgan never took the SAT, despite having been named a National Merit Scholar based on his PSAT scores.

What I wrote:
His hitch included a tour in Lebanon, which ended tragically when he was wounded in a terrorist attack that left more than two hundred of his fellow soldiers dead.
What I didn't write:

That Sunday morning in October 1983 was the turning point in Morgan's life. He was lying half awake in his bunk on the top floor of Marine Headquarters in Beirut when a Muslim madman rammed a truck of dynamite into the building's flank. Morgan blacked out for he didn't know how long. When he came to and realized he was buried under tons of concrete, he screamed until he passed out again. The next time he woke he noticed a wire dangling inches from his head. He reached for it and pulled himself up, inch by inch, toward a ray of sun that beckoned through a crack in the debris. As he reached the top, rescue workers pulled him out and rushed him to a hospital, where it was discovered that except for severe lacerations filled with dirt and bits of glass (including one across his left cheek that later became the famous scar) he was unhurt.

He returned to the site of the bombing to help dig out his buddies. Wearing a mask against the smell, he picked and shoveled at the concrete boulders and twisted steel as others separated bodies and personal belongings from the wreckage. One time a sniper opened fire and they had to run for cover. He dived behind a heavy slab—and fell upon an oozing leg.

11

He celebrated his twentieth birthday in the mental ward at Letterman Army Medical Center in San Francisco.

After his release from Letterman he was given a promotion to corporal and a desk job at Camp Pendleton, where he spent the duration of his hitch. Evenings and weekends he headed for the public library in nearby Oceanside. He read every news account of the Beirut bombing and every book about the Middle East, and after he exhausted Oceanside's collection, he took the bus to L.A. and camped out in the big library downtown. His reading branched out until he knew more about American history than most college graduates, let alone Marines.

Beyond events and dates, though, Morgan learned of the futility of human action. He dreamed of somehow mitigating the damage humanity inflicted on itself, but because he realized fulfilling such a dream was near impossible, his mood thereafter always hovered near depression.

What I wrote:

After receiving his honorable discharge, Morgan enrolled at New York University. He supported himself by working thirty hours a week as a supermarket checkout clerk and graduated Phi Beta Kappa in 1989 with degrees in history and finance.

What I didn't write:

He wasn't always rich. For a few years he actually worked for a living.

After his mother died in an automobile accident, Jack's relations with his father deteriorated so much that at one point old M. Buckminster declared, "You should be grateful I don't have a favorite charity, because otherwise I wouldn't leave you fifteen cents." Although he originally planned to live at home and major in popular culture at Bowling Green, Jack moved to

New York on impulse. He paid $625 a month to rent an apartment living room on Greenwich Avenue (kitchen privileges would have been an extra hundred bucks) and worked at a Shopwell. He took the SAT, scored an almost perfect 1580, and was offered early acceptance by NYU.

He didn't fit in socially at NYU. Everyone else was Jewish or Asian or Catholic and thought Ohio bordered on the Mississippi River. That was all right, though; he didn't have much time for people. His fellow undergraduates referred to him as "the scar-faced dweeb."

What I wrote:
Morgan met Elena Barrett in 1990. They were married on April 27, 1991.

What I didn't write:
Elena gave birth to Wesley Barrett Morgan on September 15, 1991.

Elena was a theater major who aspired to a life on Broadway, but according to Jack her only theatrical asset was her willingness to sleep with anyone who'd offer her a part. She was moderately attractive—a skinny brunette who dyed her hair black and smeared rouge on her cheeks so she'd look right for New York—but possessed of the most sensual voice and body language Jack had theretofore seen. He wanted her from the minute he set eyes upon her, which was at a Help the Homeless rally in Tompkins Park. Within a month they'd moved in together. Within two months she was pregnant.

What I wrote:
Jack took a job on Wall Street with Dean Witter Reynolds.

What I didn't write:
The job was making cold calls to lottery winners and the heirs of deceased rich folk.

But he had another motive for taking work on Wall

Street. After he announced his marriage to Elena, his father made a bid for reconciliation. M. Buckminster had cancer. There were no tearful heart-to-hearts, no wistful recollections of Jack's childhood. Instead Jack flew to Ohio once a month and listened to his father reminisce about how he hoarded quarters during the Depression and kept the quarters in a big glass bowl for years and years until his wife forced him to roll them up and trade them in for paper money. That was 1963. Had he waited one more year he'd have had a fortune in silver quarters which, mark his words, in time would be worth infinitely more than those darned zinc-filled quarters they were minting now.

He survived long enough to hold the newborn Wesley. His last advice: "I still have your baseball cards in the attic. Don't throw them out—they're worth a lot of money." He left his estate, worth more than five million dollars, entirely to Jack.

What I wrote:
In practically no time at all the astute Jack Morgan built his father's nest egg into a fortune.
What I didn't write:
Dad had laid the groundwork, investing in all the right things: biotech, communications, natural gas. After moving back into the Ottawa Hills estate, Jack took his earnings from those stocks, got in touch with two of M. Buckminster's old broker buddies, and with them launched an import/export firm that sold local goods, such as Vernor's Ginger Ale and Bob Evans Farm Sausage, to Eastern Europe, where the products were coveted as status symbols. In two years the Wholly Toledo Trading Company was worth forty million dollars and employed three hundred people in work-starved northwest Ohio.

The *Toledo Blade* ran a front-page story on the local wunderkind. The article was picked up by the *Cin-

cinnati Enquirer, the *Columbus Dispatch,* and the *Cleveland Plain Dealer,* giving him statewide exposure. He bought a tuxedo and began attending high-brow social functions. Politicians jostled to be photographed with him and courted his endorsement. He and Elena had a second child, a girl they named Eleanor Brooke Morgan.

What I wrote:

Disgusted by what he saw as congressional complacence in the face of growing problems, Jack declared his candidacy for the U.S. Senate on November 22, 1997, and after a hard-fought campaign won election the next year.

What I didn't write:

He didn't know a thing about politics and won by the skin of his teeth. Without his own money and the endorsement of the popular, retiring incumbent, he wouldn't have come close.

I had to teach him media relations starting with the basics. He didn't know that at press conferences you talk directly to the microphones, not to reporters or the imagined crowd at home, and that you don't start speaking until you're standing squarely on the podium. Nor did he know that he should keep his hands out of the way of his face. Or that he shouldn't address reporters by name, because rival stations might not run the subsequent remarks.

But he learned quickly. By March he spoke fervently of bringing jobs to Ohio and breaking the hammerlock the special interests had on Congress while offering no concrete proposals for achieving either. Potential rivals for the Democratic nomination dropped out once they realized he intended to finance his campaign out of his own pocket, which meant he could stump the state for votes while they groveled at one fund-raiser after another. His Republican opponent in the general election scored him repeatedly for vagueness, but Morgan relied on his youth and reputation as a man of action to pull him through.

What I wrote:
He quickly established himself as a skilled and honest legislator.
What I didn't write:
His first day in office he attracted national attention by introducing a bill to change the national anthem to "America the Beautiful." By summer, however, he was so disillusioned with senatorial procedure that he concluded nothing could ever be accomplished through Congress, and therefore stopped trying. He served without distinction on two committees: Environment and Public Works, where he cosponsored many successful bills but authored none; and Agriculture, Nutrition and Forestry, in which his main activity was asking higher subsidies for products grown on Ohio farms. His bill to change the national anthem was introduced in each new Congress and died in committee.

As for being honest, power offers the chance to satisfy desires. For some senators that meant making money; Jack Morgan never took a bribe. For some that meant controlling other people's destinies; Jack Morgan always strove to minimize oppression. For Jack Morgan, power meant the chance for sex. One of his staffers (all right, it was *me*) estimated Morgan bedded over sixty women his first term in office, among them Lucy Casselwaite, a student at American University who interviewed him for her journalism class and wound up on the payroll as his speechwriter. He never told Elena of his wanderings, nor did his staff betray his secret. But Elena knew that he was up to *something*.

What I wrote:
He was reelected with an unprecedented seventy-six percent of the vote in 2004.

What I didn't write:

He hadn't added one job to Ohio's economy or changed congressional behavior, but he had so much money no one could afford to oppose him.

What I wrote:

Morgan declared his candidacy for president of the United States on July 4, 2007.

What I didn't write:

Elena Morgan left him before the press conference ended.

Over the years she'd grown tired of his moodiness and argued against his running for president on the grounds it would only aggravate his psychic lows. "If you think you feel hopeless now, wait until you're president," she warned. "It'll be like dragging a pyramid across the desert."

When he told her he'd decided to run anyway, she pulled out all the stops, saying she knew he was sleeping around. She threatened to leave him, which would kill his campaign in its cradle. He laughed and said she was bluffing.

He found her the next day at Dingo Hutson's house. He promised to stop philandering. She waffled. He promised to build a new wing on the Ottawa Hills house. They made up. An hour later he flew off to Iowa to start his campaign.

What I wrote:

The central theme of his campaign—"America: Together We Can Bring the Greatness Back"—is that America must look to the future and make the hard decisions about where it wants to go, rather than continue standing still, which means it falls behind.

What I didn't write:

We racked our brains for weeks to come up with a slogan that (a) capitalized on popular anxiety that the nation was in decline and wasn't dealing with its problems; (b) offered no specific ideas or proposals that portions of the electorate might object to; and (c) stressed our faith that solutions could be found and implemented painlessly.

The winner, coined by Lucy Casselwaite, had the added advantage of implying Morgan was the unity candidate. The early endorsement of Dingo Hutson, the country's sole black senator, along with Morgan's subsequent naming of Hutson as campaign chairman, greatly reinforced the perception that Morgan could unite the party's disparate elements, and proved a big boon in the early primaries.

What I wrote:
Jack Morgan intends to be the most hopeful, visionary, and inspirational chief executive since John Fitzgerald Kennedy.
What I didn't write:
If only he had an inkling how to do that.

3

FROM SAN FRANCISCO you take the Bay Bridge to I-80 East, heading beyond Berkeley, Richmond, and the refineries to suburbs such as Hercules, which were too small for the map when I was a kid but have since grown into sprawlopoli. With any luck the traffic won't cost you more than twenty extra minutes. The congestion usually clears up by the time you cross the Carquinez Bridge, and you can shoot to Vacaville in less than half an hour. When we were kids and relatives would visit from L.A., my folks would point to the sign in Vacaville for the Correctional Medical Facility and say, with the hammy foreboding of Vincent Price, "That's where Charlie Manson lives."

East of Vacaville you exit onto 505, which knifes through the golden hills of the western Sacramento Valley to the automotive backbone of the West Coast: Interstate 5. It takes you up, up the valley, past Arbuckle and Willows and Orland, villages that have hardly changed since the seventies when I first saw them.

Two hours later you're still in the valley. Little thrills, like a hawk sitting on a fence beside the road, cease to excite you, and you yearn to either stop or reach your destination. You're feeling vaguely hungry, your bottom is numb, and the irritability that always comes on during endless drives has you thinking vengeful thoughts about the other people in the car.

But as you approach Red Bluff the sides of the valley finally begin to converge. The mountains to the north, once indistinguishable from low clouds, gain definition. You're going uphill now—a slight but steady climb—and by the time you hit the Red Bluff city limit you're three hundred feet above sea level.

If you started out from San Francisco in the morning, by all means push on through. If you started any later, though, Red Bluff is the place to pull in for the night. Find the tourist strip off the exit for California highways 36 and 99 and check into one of the motels by the road. Avoid places that hang AAA signs from their office: too expensive. Among the rest of the motels prices vary only by a few bucks, so base your choice on how many cable stations you want. Get a room in the rear if one's available, so you don't have to contend with the freeway noise all night.

The next morning take State Road 36, a weaving two-lane blacktop, east into mixed woodland forest. Ancient volcanic boulders dot the golden forest floor. Gaining altitude in earnest, you climb into a pine forest, and soon go over one ridge after another. At Mineral there's a long break in the trees: Battle Creek Meadows. There's a campground at the west edge, a ski hill at the east, and a poor excuse for a town in the middle. But this is not your stop. You join with Highway 89 and travel onward, your engine chugging because you're a mile above sea level, and where 89 forks toward Lassen National Park you bear right. You course past the mom-and-pop resorts at every roadside meadow until you come to Chester.

This is your last chance to pick up supplies or sit on a toilet that flushes, so make the most of it. East of

Chester the highway bridges over the north tip of Lake Almanor, which would be more beautiful if you didn't know it was created by a dam, and five miles later you're at the exit for Road 10.

Road 10 is a Forest Service route, designed for logging trucks and rugged four-wheel drives, not wussy city cars. It's a washboardy dirt track on which you take the chance of ruining your suspension every time you better fifteen miles per hour. At mile intervals or so an even rougher road with a name like 30N11 trails into the forest. As you head in, a fine layer of dust settles on everything and makes it impossible for you to see out your back window. You sneeze, and get tired of the vibrations that anesthetize your feet and rear. You start to fret about a breakdown and realize you're three hundred miles from your mechanic. You round a bend and find a herd of cattle loitering on the road, swinging their tails in utter disdain as you try to shoo them from your path.

But don't let all that make you turn around. Persevere a little farther, past Shotoverin and Betty lakes, to a fork in the road just east of Silver Lake. Stay to the right, and cheer up! Only another mile now. The road curls around to the west, taking you over even narrower and bumpier terrain. At the next fork you leave 10 and head left, and there it is at last—Silver Bowl Campground.

Congratulations. You've arrived at the edge of the Caribou Wilderness, elevation 6,400 feet, one of the few remaining places in the state of California where the hand of humankind is minimally discernible—and where regardless of the time of year you won't have many neighbors. Under the aegis of the Deficit Reduction Program, at the turn of the century utilities in search of geothermal energy bought much of the public land north of Lassen and the Caribou, but this terrain

was poor in exploitable resources and thus escaped corporate engulfment.

Maybe in the Mojave Desert or Sierra or Lost
Coast areas you can find another spot in California
where the nearest phone, washbasin, store, or police-
man is eighteen miles away, but this, I think, is the most
hospitable climatically, at least in summer. Nights get a
little chilly, but not so bad that you need a winter sleeping bag. Days are sunny and mild, usually cloudless. It
rarely rains. In practical terms this means you don't
have to overload your car or pack with contingency
clothes such as rain gear, heavy sweaters, and thermal
underwear.

If you're tent camping, I recommend sites five
through ten. (If you're RV camping, I recommend you
don't come here at all. Down with Wreck-Creational
Vehicles!) There's a water pump among the trees inside
the campground loop. The latrines are about a hundred
yards away, closer if you're at a lower-numbered site;
thanks to light use and the mild weather the aroma is
minimal. The Forest Service posterboard at the campground entrance announces that the camping fee is ten
bucks a night, and a brown mailbox contains envelopes
to enclose your payment. But I've never seen a ranger
here, and suspect that if you never pay you won't be
hassled.

This is where Kaya and I go for soul repair and
contemplation. She heads to the lake and watches ospreys hunt for fish. I sit out and read or, if the mosquitoes are abundant, do my reading in the tent. After
giving ourselves a day or two to get accustomed to the
altitude, we cross the gentle ridge separating the campground from the Wilderness and hike.

Not that the hikes are any kind of challenge. For
the most part the Caribou consists of wooded, rolling
hills dotted by subalpine lakes. Real hikers can easily
cover the area's maintained trails in just a day. We more

casual types can amble by a few lakes over the course of a morning and bask in the tranquility of a world without humans.

People like Molineaux and Fallon think I'm nuts to spend my time off in places like this, amid the dirt and dangers of the wild, but I feel infinitely more clean and secure here than I do with them, with the human race in general. Because nature doesn't lie or cheat, manipulate, betray, or strive. True, its rules are harsh, but they are knowable and evenly applied. That is the real value of the natural world to the human race, and why it is my grand passion: It reminds us that there *are* such things as honesty and fairness.

How much easier to defend against the brutal frankness of the wild than the honeyed falsehoods of society! This year bears and wolves and snakes and lightning bolts will kill only a handful of Americans, and those the foolish and unwary. By contrast, prevaricating money managers and politicians will kill undeserving thousands and embitter millions more. So you tell me which you should be more scared of. And you tell me where your guard should be up most, here or in so-called civilized society. Here I can sing at the top of my lungs, raise my arms to the sky, and twirl around until I drop from dizziness if I want to, and no one cares. I know, I've done it. Try that in your office sometime and see what kind of reaction you get.

As usual it took but five minutes to set up our A-frame tent. We had cheese sandwiches for lunch, then Kaya grabbed her binoculars and walked to Silver Lake, intending to catch up on those ospreys. I crawled into the tent and got my first good sleep in five months. Since the start of the campaign I'd slept in two hundred different places, but this was the first in which I felt at home. The fresh high-country air, the ray of sunshine warming up the tent, the squawking jays, the snap of twigs and needles as the squirrels and chipmunks scur-

ried by—all combined to lull me into sweet unconsciousness.

We arrived midmorning, so the sun on the tent pro-
gressively grew stronger. Before long I was sweating. To
no avail I turned one way, then another in quest of a
cool, dry spot atop my sleeping bag. Then I heard a
persistent pawing and snorting outside the tent.

I sat up and looked through the mesh door. Not ten
feet from me a buck nagged at something in the hollow
of an old tree stump. He was so close I could see the
flies on his back and the veins inside his mulish ears. He
didn't notice me until I reached to zip the tent door
open. His head rose in alarm, ears and eyes locked in on
me. I didn't dare move; up close deer are much bigger
than you imagine, and look especially formidable when
you're sitting down and gazing up at them. As there was
nothing but a layer of weather-beaten nylon to protect
me from the creature's pointed rack and muscle-rippled
legs, I filled with the sort of primeval terror the cavemen
must have felt when a wildcat or pack of wolves surprised them. It was thrilling.

We had a standoff going, watching one another for
at least a minute, when a loud crack like a tree bough
snapping caused us both to bolt around in shock. Only,
after the buck bolted, he collapsed into a heap, his head
lolling as if suspended on piano wire. He tried to stagger
to his feet and had almost straightened out his front legs
when, muzzle straining toward the sky in agonized be-
wilderment, he fell upon himself once more.

"Yo!" I heard a warning to my right as I crawled
out the tent. "Yo! Stay back! He'll kick you if he ain't
dead."

Two men in khaki hunter's garb hurried up the
campground road toward me, each bearing a rifle.

"Didn't mean to scare you, buddy," the older one
huffed as they crossed into my campsite. They were evidently father and son. The father was of middle height,

heavyset, with a broad, thick-skinned face and short, graying blond hair. The son, much thinner and about the same height, had long hair, acne, and a receding chin; a black baseball cap emblazoned with a heavy-metal band's insignia hung low over his eyes. Judging from the smell of their breath and the slack look on the son's face, they were drunk. "Gotta make a little more noise here," the father apologized as he handed his rifle to his son, pulled a pistol from his shoulder holster, and finished off the buck.

It was then I noticed the half-watermelon wedged inside the hollow tree trunk.

"You used that as a lure," I accused, pointing at the fruit.

"Um-hmm," the father acknowledged as he placed the gleaming silver pistol back inside its holster.

"That isn't legal."

The two looked at each other and laughed like teenage girls with a secret.

"In fact, I don't even think it's deer season," I pressed. "And if it was, it still wouldn't be legal to go hunting on this land."

The father inspected the coal-black barrel of his rifle as if looking for specks of rust. "Hear that, Bill? This fella's quotin' us the regulations."

The kid, who'd been on a knee toying with the buck's rack, looked up at me with an open mouth and dilated, watery-gray eyes. "Bet he's gonna teach us how to shoot a rifle too," he smirked.

It was then I realized they might hurt me if I went too far.

"Now look, fella," the father warned, his thick, cal-loused fingers thrumming the rifle absently, "we don't mind havin' folks up here, so long's they don't get into our business. Fact is, this *is* deer-huntin' season, and this *is* a legal place to hunt. Besides," he pointed with his gun, "that's just a buck right there. His doe'll have a fawn, and there'll be plenty Bambis to go cooin' on when you come back next year."

He looked me in the eye, demanding I accept his truth. My return stare, composed of equal parts submission and disdain, riled him, but also let him know he didn't have to press his point. "Where ya from?" he asked.

"San Francisco."

"Probably a fag," the kid said, jumping up from the buck and walking over to inspect my car. The father laughed, as if to say "Yeah, but it ain't proper to embarrass him by sayin' it," and then said, "Take his license number, Bill."

"Don't got a pen."

"Aw, shoot. We'll just have to memorize it, then. You take the first number and the letters, I'll take the last three numbers." He turned to me again. "Not that we don't trust you, bud, but we got to protect ourselves, you see? Sometimes people get a little carried away. I got this friend's a CHP dispatcher. Someone gives us trouble, he calls up the license number, and we head to that person's house and give the trouble back—and doubled."

So you admit you broke the law, I wanted to say, but was too afraid. The guns had something to do with it. More intimidating, though, was the man's crude bulk and menace. Although I'm no weakling, and was at least ten years younger than him, I knew with the same primeval pulse that made me frightened of the deer that I could never take him in a fight. Even if I unleashed all my anger (and sustained it while I asked myself what the hell I was doing), I could see him pinning me, a smile curling on his face, and I could see him slapping me lightly once, twice across the cheek and taunting me before delivering the final, crunching blow.

"Eight, *A, A, L,*" the son quoted. "That's mine. You gotta remember seven, seven, five."

The father nodded. "You go get the truck, Bill. Seven, seven, five. Seven, seven, five." He ran his fingertips along the rifle barrel, cleaning off a little dust. "Get here often?" he inquired, as if the contention was now past and we were friends.

"Often as I can," I murmured.

"Beautiful, ain't it?"

I nodded.

"Go fishin' in the lake?"

"Hiking, mostly."

"Mm. Good place to hike. Once hiked from the trailhead over the ridge here all the way to Warner Valley. Know where that is?"

"Yes, I do." I know these parts, you bastard. "That's quite a hike."

"Did it in a day. Me and my wife and our two little kids. You married?"

Kaya. I'd forgotten all about her. My body tensed at the thought of her running into this man—or his leering son. I nodded—didn't want to give this guy more reason to think I was gay—but added nothing.

"Got kids?"

"None," I murmured.

"That's too bad. Every man should have a son."

I heard a motor in the distance, and discouraged further conversation by turning away to get a glimpse of the approaching vehicle.

"Seven, seven, five," the hunter said.

A blue Chevy pickup rumbled past the Forest Service posterboard and around the campground loop toward us.

"Mind doin' us a favor and movin' your car so we can pull up closer to the buck?" the hunter asked.

I don't think anything more than angry words would have ensued if I'd refused; at worst the kid would have kicked a dent into a door or shot a tire out. But I felt myself enthralled to this man's strength and artless

27

Andrew Goldblatt

will. Might always makes right, and he was mightier. That's why he could act so friendly: He'd won that elemental struggle between us, and he knew it. And so I acquiesced, revving the car and making way for the pickup.

In my side-view mirror I watched the two men drag the buck along the ground, then lift it into the flatbed of their vehicle. They giggled about something, then got into the truck and pulled away. The father, in the passenger seat, waved good-bye: a hand held straight out, palm down and fingers splayed. A salute, really, a masculine display of solidarity, respect.

I pressed the index and middle fingers of my right hand to my temple, but if they saw the gesture it was only in their rearview mirror.

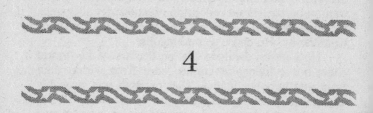

4

MELVIN BUFORD IS my closest friend in the campaign. He shouldn't be, because he is impossible to trust, but nonetheless he is. And I think I finally understand why.

No one knows Buford's real story, since he volunteers only the broadest outlines and the most disembodied details from his past. The mythology we've synthesized from years of separate conversations begins with him and Morgan meeting as Marines. Buford was an officer, but took such a liking to Morgan that they became good buddies and stayed that way after Morgan was discharged. As Morgan floundered in New York, Buford climbed the promotional ladder and was eventually assigned to a plum post in the National Security Agency. In time he became a specialist in Eastern Europe, analyzing reams of economic and political data collected by the CIA. The results of his analyses often went directly to the president—and, more than one well-placed wag has speculated, to the up-and-coming Morgan, whose export corporation blossomed during the economic downturn of the 1990s.

Buford, who thanks to his Marine Corps training knew twelve ways to kill a man with his bare hands, went on to absorb the tradecraft of intelligence inside the NSA. With that much training and the government's protection, he once confessed, it was nearly impossible to resist coercing others at a whim. The only thing preventing him and his colleagues from descending into wanton barbarism was adoption of, and strict allegiance to, some moral code. Most of them chose patriotism or Christianity. He chose something else.

He's never divulged the particulars of his moral code, but evidently it comes more from within than from any lumpen dogma. That by itself was probably enough to provoke consternation in his fellows. But something else happened—judging by his hints, a row over how to interpret some fresh data, perhaps connected (I'm just guessing) to the rise of ethnic violence in the Balkans—and he was on the outs. At first he fought his broomcloseting with a barrage of memos. That didn't work, so he decided to stick things out, figuring he'd be vindicated as events unfolded. When events turned out as he predicted and his status didn't change, he finally got the message and resigned.

Morgan made him a partner in the Wholly Toledo Trading Company. Within a year Buford bought a riverfront mansion in the Toledo suburb of Perrysburg and started his own enterprise, Anti-Social Security, which specialized in protecting the lives and property of celebrities. He enjoyed a moment of fame when he personally disarmed a psychopath trying to shoot a female rock star. His first "serious" client was tycoon and senatorial candidate Jack Morgan.

Buford was very good at what he did. His bodyguards were better trained than the Secret Service. And he personally kept an eye on those of us in Morgan's highest echelon. Periodically he'd engage us in what started out as friendly conversation but soon took on a nervous edge. Just as you realized he was scrutinizing you, Buford would smile, say something flattering, and break off, giving no clue as to what his purpose was or whether you'd betrayed yourself.

Not that he looked so menacing. At six feet two, he was the tallest of the inner circle, but slender. With his gold-rimmed glasses, his salt-and-pepper, wavy hair, and his softish features he could easily be mistaken for an academic, maybe even a perpetual grad student.

His hellacious bookishness only reinforced that tweedy image. He didn't read newspapers, magazines, or popular novels but rather the classics: from Plato and Aristotle to Ovid and Horace and Cato. The seat next to him on the campaign plane was always piled high with red- and green-jacketed Loeb Classics. When he tired of those, he lightened up with Shakespeare or a Russian novel. He was fond of quoting what he read, which prompted Lucy Casselwaite to dub him the Greek Chorus.

I felt totally inadequate in Buford's presence, not even close to matching him in physical and intellectual prowess. Nor was I the only one to feel that way; you could sense the anxiety in the other members of the inner circle whenever he approached. Doubtless they wondered how Morgan could be best friends with such a monster. Did Buford know where Morgan's skeletons were hidden? Did Buford control Morgan, and was he the real power in this campaign? The latter possibility made us sick, because if it were true it meant we were working to make Mel Buford one of the biggest puppetmasters in the history of humankind.

But nothing in Morgan's behavior indicated he was scared of Buford. Indeed, we got almost the opposite impression, that the only man on earth Buford would defer to was Jack Morgan. That could have been all show—at most a minor tax on Buford's talents—but none of Buford's actions gave us cause to doubt his loyalty. And so we swallowed our misgivings and accepted him.

Nevertheless, you can't trust someone like that; you can't even *like* someone like that. That is, provided you are normal and possess the standard self-protective sensibilities. If you're me, you do trust him. I have told Mel Buford more than I've told anyone except Kaya. And for the longest time I didn't have any idea why.

For the most part he treated me the way he treated everybody—like a temporary ally. But there were times, often late at night, after the rest of the inner circle had straggled off to bed, when he would take me into his confidence. He'd invite me to his room, sit backward on a wooden chair, and ask me what I thought about some governmental action—intervening in the Middle East, say. Like a Socratic teacher he'd use my answer as the basis for a deeper, more philosophical question, until pretty soon we'd be mulling elemental problems and getting mired in the swampy ambiguity between absolutes. This, I think, was where Mel Buford really lived, and I took these midnight sessions as his acknowledgment and reciprocation of my trust.

If he'd had a bit to drink he was liable to dispense with the Socratic method and rail for upward of an hour. He'd encourage me to rail as well, nodding like a pleased teacher at my recitals of disillusionment. I believed what I was saying, because I do get disillusioned, but I was also telling him what he wanted to hear. I couldn't help myself; I'd fallen into his intellectual orbit, and I guess I was so scared of him I had a childish compulsion to please.

"Americans are schoolyard bullies," he said. "Don't laugh. They're a bunch of kids who aren't very smart, who get their rocks off pushing smaller kids around, and blame someone else the minute they're in trouble. Think about it. Think about the defects in our character. The greed. The demand for freedom without responsibility, service without payment. The way the polls go up each time the troops invade.

"You know why the Republicans win and we lose? Because they exploit the psyche of the bully. The Democrats think that's some sort of moral wrong. They've been standing for the weak ever since the civil rights movement, and it's just killed them. And it will continue to, because the Republicans have convinced the country that liberalism is the philosophy of wimps, and that the Democrats are liberals. And the Democrats play into it —they *act* like wimps. You don't believe me."

"It's such a sweeping pronouncement. I need time to think it over," I protested.

"I'm telling you, Americans are bullies," he insisted. "I know, because I was one myself."

"And still are."

"And still am. That's right," he acknowledged with a smile. A tingle of alarm shot up my spine.

He had a bit of the sadist in him, and at moments such as those I wondered why I even talked to him. And yet, so good was he at judging my exact level of discomfort—and, I suspect, so great was his need for company —that he always backed off just as I considered flight.

"Ah, hell. You're from the bleeding-heart Bay Area. What would you know about bullies?" he excused me in conciliatory tones. "That was a blessing and a curse, to grow up in such an enlightened city. You came up the way everybody *should*, all egalitarian and tolerant and innocent. But you're how old now? Thirty-six? You're too old not to see them. Just from flacking for that baseball team you should know how good midwestern churchgoers can get on a guy for being funny-looking, or for going in a—what do you call it?—a slump."

What I should have done, instead of letting him go on for an hour trying to convince me that Americans were bullies, was to concede at once. Yes, you're right, and you know what, Mel? We San Franciscans don't have to go as far the Midwest to find them. They're right here, in northern California, shooting deer. In fact, they're even closer still. They're in Hayward. In Orinda. In the frat houses of Berkeley and single-family houses of the Sunset District. They work in offices and restaurants and repair garages. American bullies by the millions, and if those of us west of San Francisco Bay and east of the Hudson River seem at times to have successfully escaped them, we are nonetheless aware enough to know that outside our havens the prevailing sensibility is fuck the law, fuck other people, fuck the whole of goddamn nature, we have a right to anything we want because we *want* it. Everywhere. A nation full of bullies.

In fact, Mel, far from feeling sheltered, I feel like my whole life has been a fight against the bullies. I don't know where or how the loathing started; although I wasn't a big or strong kid, neither was I sickly or inept, and I don't remember anybody picking on me. The one unjust event I recall occurred in third grade, when my teacher accused me of stealing her pen. Another kid did it—I watched him filch it from her desk, slide it up a sleeve, and carry it back to his seat—but for some reason she felt sure I was the culprit. With my every denial her voice grew louder, shriller, until I started crying. Only then did she let up.

Furtively I wiped my sleeve against my face. Then I glanced at the kid who'd stolen the pen—the kid I'd just protected. I expected gratitude, or at least a look of ain't-the-teacher-stupid solidarity. But instead he leered at me, screwed his face into an exaggerated bawl, and after mouthing the word *crybaby,* leered at me some more. The kids sitting next to him snickered behind their hands so that the teacher wouldn't notice, and for the rest of the day I sensed them stealing looks at me and laughing.

I thought about fighting the pen stealer after school. I imagined myself sitting on top of him in the asphalt schoolyard while my classmates, circled around us, taunted him as they had taunted me. And though I bragged about how much I hated girls, I envisioned my-self winning admiration from them with my triumph. In my head the scene was glorious.

All I had to do was challenge my opponent—which I never did. He was burly and a couple inches taller, and back in third grade in Pacific Heights a kid who stole a pen from a teacher was reckoned pretty tough. I wasn't that tough. I was just a normal kid who got along and thought that when you took the rap for someone else that person owed you more than his derision.

I don't think that by itself the pen-swiping episode turned me into a bully hater, but after that day I'm sure I became more sensitive to injustice. That sensitivity in-creased as I got older and emerged as a smart kid. Schoolyard wisdom holds that a smart kid is a nerd un-less he proves with his fists that he's not, and in junior high, before I even realized it had happened, I was branded a nerd and generally shunned by everyone ex-cept the real nerds. This despite the fact that I was an ace baseball player and held my own in basketball and football. I remember going home and complaining to my parents about how unfairly my peers treated me. "So what do you want me to do?" my father asked. "Go to school and tell all the kids to be nice to you?"

Then I got to Lowell High, a world totally apart, where cool was determined by how good your grades were. Everyone was smart at Lowell, the magnet school for high achievers, and though most of my classmates showed zeal only for their studies, I fell in with the mi-nority involved in politics. We were flaming liberals and proud of it. The more outrageous the stand, the more ardently we advocated it. And Buford was absolutely right in this regard: We were wimps. We considered it an honor to be the last ones picked for teams and ex-erted ourselves as little as we could in gym class.

I wish Buford had been with me as the hunters strode past my tent to inspect their kill. At the very least

I wouldn't have been scared to give them trouble. And at the best I'd have had the pleasure of watching Buford hurt them—badly. Because Melvin Buford, I understood now, still lived by that private honor code that caused the NSA to purge him. It was the code of the medieval knight: his strength reserved for foes of equal dint, his contempt aroused most hotly by a strongman's use of force against the weak—the modus of the bully. No tool for the ruler he; Buford was the champion of the disadvantaged, humanism's warrior.

And that was why, despite the fact that I shouldn't trust him, Buford was my closest friend in the campaign. He was my noble knight, the ebon-metaled arm who'd drive his lance through my oppressors. With him on my side *I* was strong. I could not be beaten—or at least I could more easily deceive myself into believing that.

5

I'D COME TO the Caribou Wilderness with two ambitions: to relax after the primaries and to complete the assignment Morgan gave his staff. Now that the hunters thwarted the first ambition, I hoped to use the anger they provoked to spur fulfillment of the second. Right after breakfast the next day I took my wife and pocket dictaputer into the lake-filled wilderness for a brainstorming session.

Starting at the trailhead on the southeast side of Caribou Lake, we walked about a mile along the Wilderness's level, pine-forested border until turning west and switchbacking four hundred feet up an ancient granitic bluff. Except for occasional gentle slopes that hardly ever exceeded one hundred feet, that was the sum of our ascending. The trail itself was forgiving—firm, dustless, occasionally blanketed in yellow-brown pine needles.

I periodically fell behind to watch Kaya prowl the woods. I was awed by how much this leggy, freckled blonde walked like an Indian, her every step balanced, sure, and silent. And her alertness! She'd come to an abrupt halt, raise an arm, and point, and when I looked

I'd see a woodpecker, a rabbit, or a marten I'd have missed had I been by myself. Other times she'd pause to admire shelf fungus on a dead log, beetles lumbering across the trail, or chipmunks running off with morsels in their mouths, until I caught up and we went ahead together.

We strolled at a mile-an-hour pace through the gap between Jewel and Eleanor lakes into the heart of the empty country. A couple miles in we hit a junction with a north–south trail and headed up to Turnaround Lake, where we did just that—turned around—and proceeded in a southerly direction past Black Lake and on to the Divide Lakes.

The entire way I pondered strategies for winning the election. I started with a list of our man's advantages and disadvantages.

"Advantages," I whispered into the dictaputer at a rest stop by Black Lake. "One, youthful vitality and can-do image. Two, shining military record, purple heart. Three, successful entrepreneur. Four, not pinned by ideology. Five, genuinely smart.

"Disadvantages. One, facing an incumbent. Two, economy is shaky but okay. Three, they've got the slick PR machine. Four, they'll outspend us three to one. Five, the solid South and West.

"The trick is to make best use of our advantages and neutralize our disadvantages. But how?"

The biggest obstacle, it seemed, was the built-in edge the other side had in the electoral college. The South had risen again, controlling presidential politics by voting as a bloc for the Republicans. Carter was the only Democrat since the civil rights movement to break that bloc, but that was because he was a native son. So even if Morgan out-Republicaned the Republicans, a strategy attempted in the nineties to no avail, there was no way he could wrest the South away from the incumbent.

The West, too, was solidly Republican, which meant that, excluding California, we were spotting our opponent one hundred fifty electoral votes. And if the Republicans won California, which they almost always did, they'd need less than seventy electoral votes from among the three hundred thirty-five still up for grabs. Victories in New Jersey, Pennsylvania, and Illinois, where Republicans traditionally ran well, would wrap up the whole thing for them.

So most likely that would be their strategy: Make token showings in the strongholds to rally the faithful and concentrate their formidable resources in California, New Jersey, Pennsylvania, and Illinois. Even if we conceded the South and West, making only half-assed, low-cost efforts there, we wouldn't have the money to match them in the crucial states, and thus our loss was guaranteed.

At the northwest end of North Divide Lake we hit a junction with a trail that led east and looped back to the campground. We found a pair of relatively flat boulders by the shore and stopped for lunch. Some clouds had unexpectedly come up, a thin layer of white wisps with holes of blue sky showing through. As I watched them blow eastward, in the direction we'd be going next, they were suddenly burnished by two swaths of color crossed against each other—like a T laid on its side.

I took off my sunglasses, thinking maybe it was some effect caused by the tint. But no, the rainbow T was really there. The bottom of the stem was purple, the rest of the stem blue; the left side of the top glowed orange; where stem met top was yellow; and the right side of the top line looked a reddish blue. "Do you see that?" I asked Kaya.

"Oh my God," she gasped, reaching for the binos. "That is the weirdest rainbow I have ever seen."

"If it even is a rainbow. I half expect a UFO to swoop down from it," I said.

I'd hiked and camped all over California, spent weeks in wilderness and parks around the country. I saw rainbows every morning on the big island of Hawaii. I saw huge ones after rainstorms in the Colorado Rockies. I nearly had my retinas burned out from the intense light of an arching rainbow north of Santa Fe. Yet in all my time in nature I'd not seen anything remotely close to this, and I lapsed into the primal awe of a Stone Age tribesman. We watched, mouths agape, as the lines of colored vapor gradually faded.

"Do you think anyone else saw it?" I asked.

"I don't know," Kaya replied. "It may have been our private rainbow."

"And no one would believe it if we told them about it."

She kicked at the tiny waves lapping against the boulder's base. "I'm kind of glad it was just ours. I don't know if anyone else would have appreciated it as much."

"That's us," I teased, "the last of the red-hot nature lovers."

"Sometimes I think that's just about the truth. You think those guys who shot the deer would give a shit about a rainbow?"

"Nah. They couldn't kill it."

She screwed the top off her green plastic canteen and took a long pull on the water. "Stupid assholes. I'm so sorry you had to see that and have your vacation ruined. You've worked so hard."

My first reaction whenever Kaya made me the object of her sympathizing was denial—in this case, no, my vacation isn't ruined, and the work was kind of fun. On an immediate level I found her compassion embarrassing. But she knew how much I needed comfort, pure and simple comfort, and one of the many ways she bound herself to me was by providing it in abundance.

Every time I considered playing around (and in my

line of work the temptation arose at least three times a week) I asked myself, Once the infatuation wears off, will this sweet thing ever read my mind as skillfully as Kaya? And if she does, will she be as sympathetic and protective? I had two girlfriends before Kaya, and a few months into each relationship they started laughing at me, calling me a baby, pouring on the mock sympathy in toddler talk. Perhaps I did act like a child—I was a lot younger then—but I was doing the very thing women were supposed to want, showing my emotions, and the response was ridicule. The memory of those humiliations, even more than the look I imagined creasing Kaya's face at news of my betrayal, was usually sufficient to dissuade me from pursuing nookie on the sly.

So Kaya had her hooks in me, all right. But I don't think she did it out of any insidious motive. Rather, it was just the way her parents taught her to treat other people. Her folks were hippies from Arcata, the village of far-out brothers and sisters at the north end of Eureka Bay. They named her Kaya because to her Jewish mother it meant "life" and to her stoned-go-lucky father it meant "good herb." They were poor ("My dad works mainly as a sinsemilla sampler," she explained when we first met), oblivious to middle-class protocols of appearance and manners—and very happy. They had no TV or other high-tech gewgaws in their wood-stove-heated cabin except a CD player and a couple hundred discs of reggae, rock and roll, and classical. They spent their time together reading, talking, or playing a game that one of them would invent on the spot.

Her folks would often take her out of school and go to the Marsh and Wildlife Sanctuary, where the town's effluent was naturally detoxified. They'd pack a lunch and spend the day observing wildlife, especially the birds. She fell in love with nature, counted herself among the anti-logging crowd in high school, and spent a lot of late afternoons and evenings at the Co-op asking passersby to sign petitions for some cause or other. She made National Merit Scholar without studying for the PSAT, got into Berkeley, and enrolled in the Environmental Studies program. And so it was more than sympathy that provoked her to call the hunters stupid assholes and to feel sorry that I had witnessed their barbarity.

"And now I have to convince assholes like that to vote for Morgan," I said ruefully. "I just don't see a way. We're going to get creamed."

"Then why even bother trying?" she asked.

"Good question. I was thinking of resigning."

"That would be okay with me."

We'd spent a lot of time apart during the past ten years. She detested Washington, refused to live there. According to her there weren't any birds except pigeons, sparrows, and starlings; the only grass was in the park across the street from the White House; and the only trees were cherries planted in a row along a highway. Rock Creek Park was a joke, about as untamed as the Marina Green. No wonder Congresspeople didn't care about the environment, she'd said; from such surroundings they could easily conclude there was no such thing.

Then there was female society. Washington women wore makeup and perfume. Many of them smoked. Worst of all, with an almost medieval fanaticism for hierarchy they ranked themselves according to their man's position. Kaya had never shaved her legs, much less worn a formal dress, and was scornfully ignored by other wives, even those within the Morgan camp.

So it would have been great for her if I gave up my job and moved back home. But there was just one hitch: I loved the work.

More than loved it; I thought it was important, too. Although Morgan hadn't distinguished himself in his decade as a senator, he almost always voted on the right side of the issues, and so by working for him I engaged in what the Buddhists called Right Livelihood. And there was potential to do more, much more—if we came up with something that would make him president.

She took my silence for what it was, a no to the idea of quitting, and, despite her disappointment, decided to be helpful. "Remember when we were in college," she asked, "and we knew the only way to save the world was to change how people thought about it? Not as something to exploit, but as something to love the way we love ourselves?"

"Deep ecology. We were going to be such eco-warriors. Ah, we were so pure back then."

"And some of us, in that respect at least, still are. When did you become so soiled?"

"When I realized that I had to make a living, and life was nothing but a series of compromises."

"But that's no reason to abandon those ideals. Don't you remember all the talks we had in my dorm room, with my stupid roommate Pam from Rolling Hills Estates? Trying to convince her that the one thing we could never compromise on was the environment, because we depended on it for our very lives?"

"Yeah, and her saying that the one thing she could never compromise on was her second serve, because she'd rather double-fault than give her opponent a chance to smash a great return."

She sighed with exasperation; sometimes I could be so dense. "Look, Danny. If it's really true that Morgan can't win, why not go down fighting for what you believe in? When you got nothin', you got nothin' to lose."

"You're right," I conceded. "Hold on, I'm turning on the dictaputer."

"No, don't. It makes me so self-conscious. I don't know how you stand to use it."

"For trips like this it's necessary. You didn't think I was going to lug a laptop out here, did you? Let's get

43

back to it. So you're saying that we stand on principle. That alone would be an innovative strategy."

"No one else has ever tried it."

"That's for sure. Morgan comes out four-square for the environment. The whole gamut. Clean air, clean water. Public transit."

"Uh-uh, not public transit. Too communistic."

"Right. I forgot that on the eighth day God created General Motors. All right, then. One, come out four-square for the environment. Two, play down the sacrifices. Three, accuse the other guys of sucking off polluters. The Republicans are soft on grime!"

"Oh, Danny."

"All right, we'll find a better slogan. But they're vulnerable on the environment. They've been saying they're environmentalists for years but haven't done a thing unless they're forced to by the grassroots. That's what we've got to do, have Morgan point out all the lies. Trumpet the statistics and say pollution's killing people by the thousands every year."

It just might work. Erika Mitchell, our pollster, repeatedly told us that even in the West and South she found apprehension over the environment. It was a potentially explosive issue, and Morgan had said all the right things during the primaries. But there was a reason no one had ever come out as an environmental candidate and meant it. "It won't work," I muttered, picking up a stone and winging it into the lake.

"Why not?" Kaya asked, taking umbrage at my abrupt turn of mood.

"All the money disappears."

"What money?"

"Corporate and PAC donations. The mother's milk of politics."

"But the candidates get money from the government, don't they?"

"Not enough."

"Well, however much you get, it'll have to do."

"But it can't. The government only gives you something like a hundred million bucks. Last time out the Democrats spent fifteen million a week just on TV between Labor Day and the election. Add in direct mail, travel, salaries, polling and research, rent for headquarters, phone banks, bumperstickers, buttons, pennants, a million incidentals. You need a ton of greenbacks, and the only place to get it is from the corporations and the PACs."

"But I thought Morgan didn't want to run the usual campaign."

Sometimes, when I'm in a state of half-alertness, the fragment of a memory will flash across my mind and vanish just as quickly, and I'll desperately try to recall that memory for the next few minutes, usually to no avail. As Kaya's meaning registered upon my brain, a vision of Excalibur suddenly burst up from the lake, and I jumped.

"You all right, love?"

"Fine," I said, waving so that she'd know I didn't want distraction. Because this time I had nabbed the memory. Gomer Wilson, manager of the Toledo Mud Hens, short and stout and reeking of tobacco, was telling me his hitters were so bad they couldn't hit the outfield fence if they ran into it, but the other teams were smacking four home runs a game.

"So what are you going to do about it?" I asked.

"Promise you won't tell no one?" he asked.

I nodded.

"You gotta swear to it, 'cause I could get my ass into a stew if this gets out."

"You have my word," I swore.

He leaned a little closer. "I did it already. Moved the fences back ten feet. Had the grounds crew do it on the last road trip, when nobody was watching." I looked at him in admiration. "Boy," he said, more loudly now, spitting a brown chaw from his mouth, "if you're losin' and you can't change players, then you got to change the game. Remember that. *You got to change the game.*"

SIX

Plan for Winning the White House
by Steinhardt

1. Introduction

Presidential politics is a Republican game. We're never going to beat them at it unless we change the game so *we* have the advantage.

What follows is a plan for drastic changes in the three arenas of the game: issues, money, tactics. The plan exploits these public anxieties: that presidential campaigns have become tasteless battles between advertising agencies; that wealthy special interests control government; and that we aren't dealing with the most urgent problems.

2. Issues

I'm starting with this because last Tuesday night you asked what the Democratic party stands for. The answer, as we all know, is nothing. That has to change if we expect to win. I propose we stand for the environment.

I picked environment because it's most likely to help us forge a new, enduring Democratic coalition. Environmental problems cross all political, ethnic, and class lines. Conservatives are just as vulnerable to the poisons in the air as liberals, whites as vulnerable as blacks, rich as vulnerable as poor. Environmentalism plays well in suburbia, where there are lots of votes and the Republicans normally win comfortable majorities. Usurping suburbia could be a key in breaking up *their* coalition as well as building our own.

With the metropolitan suburbs in particular going our way, we swing a lot of states into our camp, big ones such as New York, New Jersey, Michigan, and Illinois. Then there's the Pacific coast, including California, where environment is *the* big issue. If we sweep the big states and the Pacific coast, that puts us more than half-way home. Throw in our traditional strongholds in the East (Massachusetts, D.C., West Virginia, Georgia), Midwest (Minnesota, Wisconsin, Iowa), and your home state, and we need at most forty more electoral votes.

Mitchell keeps telling us she's found anxiety about pollution, toxic waste, solid waste, et cetera in every region, even the South and Southwest, where environmentalists are considered commies. The country trusts the other guys for leadership on economics and defense, but they worry that the environment is something the Republicans have lip-serviced for years.

You can neutralize the Republican edge in economics by pointing early and often to your success with Wholly Toledo. You can neutralize their edge in defense with the scar. When the bad guys try to neutralize *your* advantage on environment, probably by saying it's bad for the economy, you say *au contraire,* it's actually good, for reasons that follow.

The popular impression is environmental legislation impedes business, too many regulations and all that, and smacks of socialism. But you will grant that the system works; no one's come up with a better motive for economic progress than profit. *What you're going to do is change the rules, so that the profit's now in saving the environment instead of destroying it.* Not only will that preserve the environment and keep us all healthier, but it will put American industry in the forefront of sustainable technology, which will be a long-term boon to the economy.

In practical terms, changing the rules means mandating that sixty percent of all packaging be made from recycled material. It means subsidies for solar energy and fusion research. It means tax breaks for developers who infill urban areas rather than exacerbate suburban sprawl. It means subsidizing farmers who grow crops organically. It means we stop selling public lands, especially the forests (selling off some BLM land might actually be okay) to cover the federal deficit.

A more specific example: a tax-rebate program based on mileage per gallon for all new automotive vehicles sold in the U.S. Less than twenty city MPG: $10,000 tax. The tax goes down $400 per mile thereafter, until tax on a vehicle that gets forty-five city MPG is zero. Thereafter the rebates kick in, $300 for every MPG up to sixty-five. The biggest rebate, $7,500, goes to vehicles that don't use fossil fuels at all. This (a) still gives Detroit the right to sell gas guzzlers, undercutting their "free enterprise" argument; (b) ends the need for MPG regulations and EPA smog standards, neither of which is ever enforced; (c) reduces smog and carbon dioxide emissions; (d) reduces dependence on foreign oil.

This warning, though: I wouldn't make this public until after you're elected. It'll kill your chances in Michigan and could cost Ohio also. All those Toledo Jeep workers voting against the favorite son would embarrass us no end. What will voters elsewhere think when they see you can't carry your home state?

The key is that we're the biggest single-country market in the world, so if we set strict environmental standards for products and pollution, the rest of the world will have to go along. The Japanese in particular would rather change their way of doing things than lose their market share. Also, other governments would be encouraged by our example and raise their own product and pollution standards.

Again, though, I wouldn't elaborate too much, especially where jobs or a perceived decline in the standard of living is concerned. Americans are all for saving the environment, but not at the cost of economic displacement or restrictions on their usage of convenience items. You can say you're against further sales of federal land or off-shore drilling, because that doesn't take away existing jobs. But if you talk about the auto-tax-rebate proposal, there go your votes in the industrial Midwest. When their livelihoods or comforts are at risk, people aren't going to philosophize that economic displacement happens all the time, but that this time it's for a healthy purpose they should go along with.

Your environmental voting record in the Senate is solid. No major embarrassments, nothing indefensible. You can underscore your commitment and integrity by publicizing your votes in favor of stronger acid-rain restrictions, since you cast them despite heavy pressure from Ohio coal miners. Hasn't the League of Conservation Voters given you at least an eighty percent rating every session? And I bet it would be a cinch to get endorsements from environmental organizations, or, if their charters don't allow it, from prominent environmental leaders. Also from Hollywood celebrities; lots of them are greens.

3. Money

The biggest drawback of a commitment to the environment is that the corporate money will stop rolling in. Before the media can make an issue of your fundraising problems, you must announce that you *refuse* donations from polluters and their PACs. Take the high ground with a screw-the-special-interests attitude.

To some extent we can counter the expected fall-off in contributions by obtaining the mailing lists of environmental organizations and sending out direct-mail appeals. My guess is the response will be excellent, because you'll be the first genuinely pro-environmental candidate to make a run for president. Even the Edward Abbey fringe may send you money.

Still, most of the contributions will be small and won't make up for the loss of corporate donations. Federal funding plus private donations probably won't come to more than $125 million, at best a third of what the other guys will have at their disposal.

But even if you don't take a principled stand on the environment you won't get much from the corpos, not against a heavily favored incumbent who'll leave them alone. So I don't think you'll be losing much in practical terms. Besides, what you lose in financial capital you may gain in moral capital, and that may win you more votes than the TV and radio spots you won't be able to afford.

Just in case that sounds like rationalizing, I have a strategy for conducting the campaign that not only keeps you within budget but should also defuse the Republicans' money advantage. More on that under "Tactics."

No doubt at some point the media will accuse you of rejecting the moneyed interests before they can reject you. The connotation will be that you're a loser, the smart money knows it, and this is just a desperate attempt to make yourself look good, that is, make misfortune look like virtue. That's true, of course, but a couple other things are also true and should be stressed instead. First, that you're running a completely different kind of campaign, one you think the people have been wanting for a long time (again, see "Tactics"). Second, that you've never been in anybody's pocket and don't want to start now. You can also attack the other guys, especially if we can match a list of big Republican contributors with a list of stands that suggest a payoff to those donors.

4. Tactics

This is where the other guys are strongest. They make superior commercials, manipulate the press more deftly, target their direct mail more effectively, and so on. But Mitchell's polls (and Harris's, and Gallup's, and Yankelovich's, and almost everybody else's) have detected deep dissatisfaction with the way campaigns are run. So we change the game to make their tactics an embarrassment. No commercials, except for a few ten-second spots I'll describe in just a second. Total accessibility to the media. No staged photo opportunities or angling for maximum-impact sound bites.

Basically you play on the public's growing disillusionment with conventional campaigns, where candidates are sold like soap. Announce you're going to run an issue-based campaign that will never insult the intelligence of the voters. And then stay home.

That's right—*stay home.* A front-porch campaign, like McKinley's. There's no need to fly hither and yon anymore, not when the overwhelming majority of voters get their news from TV. The media *have* to cover you, so make the most of the free time. Instead of exhausting yourself (and your faithful staff), set up camp at home in Ottawa Hills. Talk to the press candidly every day in extended, freewheeling sessions. Let them watch you welcome visitors (ordinary citizens) into your home for coffee and impromptu exchanges.

I think a homespun campaign will play well with the press. They'll be grateful they don't have to fly around the country, having to keep track of deadlines across time zones and all that. They can set up base camp in a nice room at the Commodore Perry Hotel, drive out for the daily press conference, and after putting together their stories have the rest of the day to themselves. Given the additional time, accessibility, and rest, they may do more favorable pieces on you, and once you get them on your side, the other guy's on the defensive.

Another advantage of the front-porch campaign is that it saves a ton of money that would normally go for travel.

Big departure number two: Instead of spending a fortune on a PR agency, production expenses, and air time for commercials, put together a few ten-second spots listing toll-free phone and fax numbers the public can call to order videos in which you explain your stands on various issues.

This will take a lot of time and effort to put together (basically we have to start yesterday), but it may work better than commercials because the videos will be tailored to each voter's special interest. Each video will start with some standard spiel: "Thank you for your interest in my candidacy, together we can make America a better place to live, blah blah." Then you splice in a header speech for the general topic requested, for example environment, biotech, defense; the speech shouldn't run more than three, four minutes. Then you have a standard closer, along the lines of "Thanks again, if you're interested in videos on any other issues, call or fax these numbers toll-free and we'll be glad to send them to you." Total length of presentation: twelve minutes at most.

Filming all these blurbs and setting up the hardware and software to combine them into videos will cost a lot of money, as will the payroll for the staff that sends them out. The postage won't be anything to sneeze at either, probably two bucks a shot. But the materials will be cheap, and after all is said and done, I think this will be a lot more economical and effective than buying air time for commercials, which ran to over $15 million a week for the last guy who got trounced.

If we've got the money, we can send issue-specific follow-up letters thanking voters for requesting a video and including your comments on relevant events that have occurred since the time of order.

Another thing we can do is put your position papers (revised to reflect the campaign's new environmental agenda) on line with Prodigy and other national data bases. This isn't as big a deal as the videos, because nobody except Buford reads anymore, but it can be done cheaply, and the people who care enough to call up your position papers are almost certainly going to vote. We'd be fools not to provide them with the data they desire.

Every two weeks or so you can run those ten-second TV and radio spots with your phone and fax numbers, to remind people how to order videos. No saturation advertising! We don't want to annoy. And if the videos aren't moving, we should send them out unsolicited, for example the spiel on coastal oil drilling to California members of the Sierra Club.

The new strategy will put you on the offensive. The Republicans will have to react to you somehow, either ignore you or attack you or adopt your methods. If they take the first route, you deconstruct their strategies in front of the press every day, as in "His latest commercial says X, but here's his record on that issue, and this is just more cynical rhetoric, an insult to America's intelligence." If they go the second or third route, you've got them, because at that point they've dispensed with their own game and have started playing yours. Someone in the media will write an op-ed piece pointing that out (I'll make sure of it), and the national impression will be that you're calling the shots.

The daily meetings with the press should be informal, full of give-and-take. There won't be room for error, but since you won't be exhausted from traveling, you'll probably have sufficient self-control to keep from blurting out something stupid. When something happens in the news, comment on it the way a sitting president would. And always, always, lay bare the enemy's campaign strategy and label it cynical, condescending, insulting, propagandistic, et cetera.

Another good gambit is to challenge the incumbent to a debate. There's a debate every election, but it's carefully staged, with reporters asking questions and no direct exchange between the candidates. This time you'll insist on a no-holds-barred confrontation with only a moderator between you. Direct questioning, direct rebuttals. *Mano a mano,* as it were. Once you throw down that kind of gauntlet, there's no way you can lose. You're smarter than him, so if he accepts the challenge, you'll make him look bad. If he doesn't take the challenge, he's a coward. And if he dickers for the standard format, you accuse him of hiding behind his image makers. That's one thing we ought to harp on ad nauseam: The President's a creature of his image makers, not nearly as sharp or forthright as the White House PR machine proclaims him.

5. Conclusion

I don't have a feel for numbers, so maybe Fallon, Ishikawa, and Molineaux could do some calculator tapping to find out how much my plan would cost. My guess is a lot less than a conventional campaign, considering how much less traveling and advertising there'll be. And you'll be more effective, drawing attention not just to your stand on the issues but to the type of campaign you're running. In fact, if you want, you can say this is not just an election between you and your opponent but rather a plebiscite that will determine the nature of future campaigns. Risky, but there's nothing to be gained by playing this election safe.

If you adopt this plan, I suggest keeping as much of it from the National Committee as possible until the convention, because they'll have a cow when they find out. Also, we don't want any leaks. In your acceptance speech you can announce how you'll conduct the campaign, claiming you were prompted to it by your high-minded concern that we've trivialized the democratic process. Have Lucy come up with something stirring.

We can get loans against forthcoming federal financing in order to start the video project rolling. We'll have to come up with a list of issues, to ensure that the blurbs address most of the voters' concerns. We can bring in your issue advisers to help on this. I'd be happy to assist Lucy in writing scripts. With six weeks until the convention, we ought to have time to write everything out, film your presentations, and get production started, so that we can flash the toll-free numbers on the screen during your speech and have operators standing by.

7

THERE ARE TWO Jack Morgans. The first, whom you've already met, is despondent, snappish, prone to indulging his vices; not a sympathetic sort, and probably not someone you'd want as president, even though men of more objectionable character have held the job successfully.

The second Jack Morgan radiates so much genuine midwestern charm that you just can't help but like him. He treats you like an old friend, listening earnestly to your most disjointed ramblings and responding in a sympathetic manner that indicates he's heard you fully. A gentle humor leavens his discourse; he often breaks up tedious sections of speeches with little jokes and a disarming twinkle of the eye. He remembers people—not just congressional colleagues but everyday constituents—and after not seeing them for months can recall with stunning accuracy what they talked about the last time they crossed paths.

You watch Jack Morgan operate and swear this has to be an act, that no one, especially in politics, can really be this nice. That's certainly the media's opinion; for months reporters plied me for the story of the "real" Jack Morgan. But it is no act. The Dr. Jekyll side is every bit as unfeigned as the Mr. Hyde. And if that uglier persona goes unreported, it's because the candidate and his staff have sense enough to keep it hidden, not because the nice side is in any way a put-on.

We live in dread of word about his darker side emerging. The main fear is he'll be perceived as schizophrenic: "Well, now, which Morgan has his finger on the button *today*?" The quickest way to kill a candidate is to wrap a pejorative so tightly around him that he smothers. *Liberal* has worked in recent decades; now, just as its effectiveness is wearing off, we have to watch lest Morgan's depth of character be labeled *lunatic.*

I first met Morgan while working for the Mud Hens. I majored in mass media at Berkeley, and then, because I couldn't find a job and wanted to hang around until Kaya finished school, got a master's from the Graduate School of Journalism. I studied media theory (lots of McLuhan and Ong) and public relations, so when the time came to get a job I was neither qualified nor inclined to start out as a cub reporter for some boondock daily. I sent out nearly two hundred résumés, but the nation being in an economic slide, received only two offers: from the National Tobacco Institute and the Toledo Mud Hens minor-league baseball club. I talked it over with Kaya, and we decided to move to Ohio.

The hard times of the nineties were a boon to minor-league and college baseball. Cable stations broadcast games; magazines about the lower leagues gained thousands of subscribers; and perhaps most importantly, prices were affordable at a time when tickets to big-league games went through the roof. Whereas previously fans from northwest Ohio would drive an hour or more to watch the Detroit Tigers, now they came to see the local Mud Hens, and as the franchise prospered it hired extra personnel, including a PR guy, to keep the money coming.

Once in Ohio it took Kaya and me two, maybe

three minutes to feel homesick. Instead of the hilly, windswept, clean and scenic coast of California, we had the plowed flatlands and brown, sluggish rivers of the Midwest. We rented a red-brick, split-level house ("They make houses out of *brick*?") two blocks from the Maumee River. The gnomish, alcoholic landlord, who clearly didn't trust us to obey, warned us not to bring niggers on his property. The ceiling was falling in one of the upstairs bedrooms. The bathtub leaked. The carpet in the living room stank of cat pee. Then we went to a nearby Kroger's, and when we saw the pale, anemic produce we cried.

Formally my job was to supervise advertising, write articles for the scorecard, edit and update the media guide, and supply the press with statistics, trivia, and general information. Informally I was to entertain season ticket holders and talk up the Mud Hens wherever I went. That was the hardest part of my job: approaching total strangers, sticking out a hand, and, after introducing myself, asking if there was anything I could do to make the ball game more enjoyable. Several people suggested I go out and get some decent pitchers and a shortstop who could hit. More often I'd be handed a couple bills and sent to fetch hot dogs and beer.

And then there was Jack Morgan. Not yet a candidate for senator, he held four season tickets. The first thing I noticed about him was the shiny, thick red scar that crossed his left cheek in a jagged line.

"Pleased to meet you, Steinhardt," he said, grasping my hand. "Maybe there *is* something you can do. I was just telling my wife Elena here that I would pay five thousand dollars to the guy who can make the ball club switch from playing the 'Star-Spangled Banner' to 'America the Beautiful.'"

"Come again, sir?"

"It's such an ugly song. You've got to go to Juilliard to sing it. But take 'America the Beautiful.' Perfect title, eh? It's all about the land—the fruited plains, the purple mountains. That's something you can really *sing* about. And even I can sing it on key."

"Don't mind him," Elena apologized. "He's only kidding."

"Actually I'm not," he said. "Five thousand bucks if you can get your boss to change the song."

"The boss is pretty conservative, sir."

"Horseshit. I've met Dubermann. Strictly a bottom-line type. Tell him this idea will bring his team a ton of free publicity and he'll do it. Go ahead, give it a try. Let me know how it turns out."

That was my first job for Jack Morgan. I went to Dubermann and argued for the change, and, as expected, he said no even after I promised we'd get lots of free publicity. But I persisted. "America the Beautiful" was just as traditional as the official national anthem, I said. It even mentioned God.

"I don't care," he huffed. "I'm not gonna start no ball game with a song by some commie hobo folk-singer."

"You're thinking of a different song, sir." And then I made my clinching argument: If he made the change, I could persuade one of our season ticket holders to donate five thousand dollars' worth of seats to high school students who received all *A*'s on their report cards.

"How'd you do it, Steinhardt?" a plainly surprised Morgan asked the night the change was made. True to his word, he whipped out his checkbook.

"Never mind. Just make it out to the Toledo Mud Hens, and go ahead and take a tax deduction on it," I replied.

He instantly figured out what I had done, and was both aghast and awed. He was a businessman; I doubt he'd ever run across someone who would take that sort of risk with his employer on behalf of a stranger and then refuse reward.

"Tell you what, Steinhardt. I'll make the check out to you, then you make one out to the team. That way you can take the deduction."

"Believe me, I don't need that big a deduction."

He shrugged, then handed me the check and invited me to watch the ball game in his box. We spent the evening talking baseball, reminiscing about San Francisco and Cincinnati teams of the recent past—who was better, Matt Williams or Chris Sabo? He offered to buy me a beer. I told him I'd get a couple cold ones for us gratis. "No way," he objected, and hailed a vendor and paid full price for two sweating, flimsy cups of Stroh's.

As the season wore on I found myself stopping by his box more often. Some nights Morgan's employees or clients occupied the seats, and I'd skulk away. Although we never saw each other anywhere except the park, I came to look upon him as a friend, and without him there I felt like I had gone to see the game alone. Of all the people I'd met in the Toledo area, he seemed most ready to dispense with that patina of midwestern blitheness and reveal his inner thinking. We talked about California and Ohio, the economy, whatever made the news that day. His intelligence and grasp of history impressed me.

Occasionally he dragged Buford to a game. Buford didn't care for baseball, reading while we debated the advantages of bunting versus hit-and-running. Other nights Morgan brought his wife. At first Elena tried to understand what went on between the lines, but by August decided the game was too arcane for a "normal" person to care about. She squirmed in her seat like an eight-year-old on a long ride and whined when Morgan wouldn't leave before the seventh inning.

His best companion at the games was Wesley, not yet six but already sharp enough to boo and cheer at the right moments. I was terribly uncomfortable around the kid, not knowing what to say after asking who his favorite player was, and I admired Morgan's naturalness with him. A sad yet persevering man who raised his child gently. What more could commend him?

And so without hesitation I suggested myself when, the following summer, he confided that he'd be running for the Senate and wondered whether I knew anyone who could handle media relations.

It was the first time I made a major decision without Kaya. She went apoplectic when I told her what I'd done. The only thing she liked about Toledo was the *unk*ing twangs the nighthawks made during their courtship dives. Now I expected her to move to Washington, D.C.? Well, Morgan's a novice, he probably won't win, I said. She sincerely hoped not, because then I'd be out of work and we could move back to the coast.

But Morgan did win, and we moved to Washington, and it was even worse than Kaya feared. Elena Morgan, her one friend during the campaign, abruptly became Queen Elena on arrival in D.C., enveloping herself in all the trappings and perquisites that befit a senator's chief consort, and after that Kaya had no one to talk to. She cried every afternoon.

For me the problem was that ugly side of Morgan. I'd seen him in bad moods during the campaign and gradually came to realize that his soul dwelt mostly in the dark. But I was shocked by the depth of his despair in the months after his swearing in. He'd realized that three quarters of his fellow senators were petty potentates too frightened to allow the others to accomplish anything, and in his disappointment he took to floozies, alcohol, and loud, prolonged tirades at staffers (myself included). More than once while the Senate was in session we heard his office sofa creak under a gasping groupie. I thought the man was going mad and might even resign.

I decided I would quit before he did. Kaya volunteered to return to San Francisco and find us a flat near the Presidio. The day she found one I handed in my resignation. But as I cleaned out my desk, Morgan, bursting from his office and practically shoving his latest bimbo out the door, threw my letter down and said abruptly, "I'll have none of this. Come into my office."

He missed two floor votes while we talked. In the end I agreed to stay in exchange for an eye-popping raise and assurances he would stop his persecution of the staffers.

I dreaded telling Kaya that I'd changed my mind. Although she didn't have a temper, I expected she'd protest loudly enough that I'd be able to hear her from San Francisco without a phone. But when I broke the news, all I got was a startled "Oh," and a prolonged and chilly silence.

"You're mad at me," I finally choked out.

An indignant "Mm-hmm!" followed by another stony silence.

"He offered me a huge raise. Kaya, let me do this for a couple years. If we're really careful with the money, we can buy ourselves a place in the woods, like we've talked about."

She considered it. "I'm not moving back to Washington."

Chasms opened at our feet. Ours had been a happy marriage; nothing ever threatened it before. To my ever-lasting relief and gratitude, she stepped back quickly from the brink.

"You'll have to fly home every recess and long weekend," she insisted.

She had a deal—one that saved our marriage but, because of two rents and countless airfares, didn't save us any money toward that dream home in the forest. After two years we grew accustomed to the arrangement. I never brought up my promise to quit, she never held me to it, and for the last ten years we've been apart as often as together.

My front-porch campaign had, at root, a selfish motivation. Our stay in the Caribou Wilderness convinced me that I needed someone with me all the time. I figured if the campaign had a single base in a place that Kaya could tolerate, we could live together for the four months prior to election day. As we bounced along the dirt road back to civilization, I dreamed of having everything I wanted: a great job *and* companionship.

We stopped off at the mall in downtown Redding and faxed my proposal both to Morgan's house in Ottawa Hills and to his office in the Hart Building. We took the long ride down I-5, braved the traffic on I-80 to the Bay Bridge, and arrived home, exhausted, around eight P.M. As I had a reservation on a morning flight, I showered and went straight to bed. Kaya petted our cat Nimby, opened the mail, and listened to our phone messages. I was just getting warm beneath the blanket when she jumped into bed beside me. "Danny, you've got to hear this!"

I wasn't asleep—in fact was overtired from the drive—but I rubbed my eyes just so she'd think she woke me up. She apologized, then dragged me to the phone, rewound the tape, pressed play, and watched for my reaction.

"Steinhardt, this is Morgan calling around six-thirty your time Sunday evening. I've looked at your proposal. I've got some problems with it, but I like it. Unless someone comes up with something better by tomorrow, we may go with it."

8

"ALL RIGHT," MORGAN called to order, and the separate conversations ceased. We were sitting at his long, walnut dining table, our papers scattered everywhere.

"I'm sure you've seen the polls. I'm starting off behind by anywhere from ten to sixteen points. Weldon's trying to lure my at-large delegates away so he can steal the nomination. He won't succeed, but he's gonna make me look real bad. So we've got our work cut out for us.

"We've got to gamble big. You've had a chance to look at Steinhardt's program. It's not the soundest one submitted, but it's the boldest. Now it's time to play destroy-the-press-secretary." He looked my way with a malicious grin. "I imagine everyone has problems with the plan."

"I know I do," Fallon interjected.

"All right, then. Let's bat this thing around, see if it's worth the risk. Poke your worst holes in it—Lord knows the other guys are gonna probe for soft spots till they find them."

"If we poke enough holes in it . . . ?" Fallon queried.

"We drop it," Morgan promised.

"So you didn't like any of the other plans?" Lucy Casselwaite asked, too obviously peeved.

"None were as innovative or comprehensive as Steinhardt's. You recording this, Molineaux?"

"I am indeed," the PR chief acknowledged. "And may I add for the record that I object to this proposal. You can draw whatever conclusions you want from last week's polls, but I've got eighty years of market surveys to prove that people only care about two things: status and money. Environmentalism doesn't offer either. It doesn't *seduce.*"

"Hold it," Morgan scolded. "It's my campaign, I get to raise my problems first. Two things, Steinhardt. First, after the convention there's no *oomph* behind this plan. I just sit home and chatter with the press. How am I supposed to keep excitement up?"

I've never been real good at thinking on my feet. I need time to think my answers through, to get the wording right so that they're consistent with my larger strategy. At briefings I almost always read directly from a script, and I respond to questions as succinctly as I can. I had addressed the few objections I was capable of anticipating in the proposal itself. So I sat there tongue-tied until Buford came to my rescue.

"Well, obviously you could string out major policy announcements over the length of the campaign. This week Morgan's bold initiative about this. Next week a pronouncement about that. We can be flexible, too, going by whatever's in the news."

"This raises a larger concern of mine," Molineaux broke in, "namely that this campaign is going to be *boring*. You got to remember, Dan-o, a national campaign is theater. If you can't be entertaining, you haven't got a prayer."

The battle lines were forming: Buford and myself against Fallon, Molineaux, and possibly Casselwaite, with the others piping in occasionally to show they were alert but otherwise waiting to see which side prevailed before taking a stand.

It figured that Fallon and Molineaux felt most threatened. Fallon was the old-school, nuts-and-bolts politico, the guy who'd shaken hands with every minor party functionary from Maine to San Diego. He was in his sixth presidential campaign, this time as manager of the whole show, and this was a departure from the back-slapping, baby-kissing, Happy-Days-Are-Here-Again electioneering he'd cut his teeth on.

With Molineaux the problem wasn't a lack of imagination but of income. Although he was probably sincere when he claimed the environmental theme would be a tough sell, what really splintered his behind, no doubt, was that his role would change. Instead of creating and booking commercials and print ads he'd be producing Morgan's videos, and with that change would come a huge cut in commissions to his firm. Heretofore it seemed he was more interested in Morgan the client than Morgan the candidate. I wondered whether he would stay on without the financial incentive.

"But that's the thing I like the most about this plan," Morgan answered Molineaux. "It *is* theatrical—the play within the play. Steinhardt put the emphasis on environmentalism, but look at all this other stuff. Where is it?" He went thumbing through his copy of the proposal. "Here it is, page eleven. 'And always, always, lay bare the enemy's campaign strategy and label it cynical, condescending, insulting, propagandistic, et cetera.' You see, Molly? Not only do we campaign on the issues, we *campaign on the campaign*. Great theater."

"I don't know," grumped Molineaux.

"Let's take this down to a more basic level," Fallon said. "Will it play well in Peoria? Or Abilene, or even San Francisco? People aren't looking for a gimmick from their candidate. They're looking for an upright, solid citizen. You run this way-out kind of campaign and you'll be the country's laughingstock."

"Perhaps, but perhaps not," said Erika Mitchell. "Our focus-group research is turning up such disgust with conventional campaigning that even a halfway honorable race will win us points."

"I think Molineaux may have a point," Buford offered. "We should think about whether environmentalism is really the issue we want to make our centerpiece."

"You have a better idea?" I sputtered defensively.

"I guess none of you saw my plan. What the Republicans do every year is play on insecurity. They take the big stand on crime, the big stand on the death penalty, the big stand on gun control, and we get killed because we think they're bogus issues. They *are*, but they matter more to people than environment. Environment doesn't frighten people like a hoodlum prying at their window with a crowbar. So the first thing we have to do is co-opt those stands and cancel the Republicans' advantage. Send Jack down to the local rifle range and have him hold a press conference while taking target practice. Then, maybe, we talk about environment."

"Makes a lot a sense to me," chimed Fallon.

"Except my record will betray me," Morgan answered. "I vote with the softies. I'd be too vulnerable to charges that I've flip-flopped. No. I think we default to Steinhardt's strategy. You pointed out the kernel of the argument yourself, Mel. The Republicans *always* take those stands. They've been taking them for twenty years, and nothing has improved. In fact it's gotten worse. You've got four times as many people in jail and the streets are still a war zone. We argue that the tough-on-crime approach is a sham they use to frighten people into voting for them."

"But," Fallon blustered, really worked up now, "we can't get through the next five months with just one counterpunch. If we say it's cynical campaigning every time they attack us, they'll get wise and say you're being evasive, and then we'll be in one hell of a fix."

"But we won't be. We'll have counterproposals. Besides, I don't intend to be on the defensive much. This plan is offensive by nature."

"You can say that again," Molineaux sniffed.

Morgan pressed his hands together as if in prayer and stared into his fingertips. "I don't know, Fallon, maybe you're right. But we'll cross that bridge when we come to it. If the popular perception is that I'm avoiding issues, we'll have to change our tactics. Until then we stick to deconstructing their rhetoric."

"I think you're better off on the hustings every day, energizing crowds and hitting them with everything you've got."

"But that style is outmoded, damn it! How many people can I possibly shake hands with between now and the election? How many will hear me speak? Let's go high and say ten million. That's ten percent of the voters, Fallon. A total waste of time and money in the broadcast age."

Fallon put up his hands, looked away, and slumped back in his chair. It was clear that little would sway Morgan from my plan, and though he had encouraged disagreement, now that he'd come out so forcefully in favor I could see the uncommitteds swallow their objections. Molineaux, sighing, stared at the wall resignedly.

"When you go on the attack," Dingo Hutson cautioned, tacitly acknowledging that my plan had been adopted, "do it just the way we're doing here, like it's the Republicans, not the President himself. Because if you lose, you're going to have to deal with him, and if you attack him personally, he's going to nail you when you're up for reelection in two years."

"If I lose," Morgan said, pressing his fingers to his

mouth, "I'm not running for reelection. I'm out of politics entirely."

"In that case," Hutson replied, "go for the neck."

We laughed perfunctorily, which gave Morgan the chance to put the meeting back on track.

"My second problem, Steinhardt, has to do with money."

"I went into that in detail."

"About campaign funds, yes. But I'm looking one step down the road. Where's the money gonna come from for the subsidies and tax breaks I'm proposing? How'm I gonna keep the deficit down with all these new expenditures, plus end the sale of public lands? You see what I'm getting at? Am I gonna be another tax-and-spend Democrat?"

On this one I had more of an idea. "Not at all. You're not just opening new subsidies and tax breaks, you're closing old ones that are anti-environment. For instance, in Alaska the Forest Service spends a hundred bucks to build roads for every dollar it receives in usage fees from logging firms. The BLM spends millions administering the western grazelands and gets almost nothing from the cattlemen who use it. The nuclear industry? Billions in subsidies a year. There are water subsidies to close. And big oil—boy, if you're looking for a target, when's the last time an oil company paid taxes?"

"You think we can close enough loopholes to compensate for the new spending?"

"Probably not. But it's the perception that matters. If you mention examples like these without getting into numbers, you'll convince people there won't be any rise in spending."

"I hope you're right. Ron," he turned to Ishikawa, the comptroller, "I'm assigning you that job. Go through the budget looking for environmentally abusive subsidies, the bigger and more blatant the better. And another thing I want you to do: Take out a loan against our federal funding. I don't know exactly how much yet, but get together with Fallon and Molineaux and figure out how much it's gonna cost to make those videos, set up a phone bank and processing center, and pay staff."

"If I can backtrack a bit, I have a question about campaign funding," Ishikawa piped up. He was the other Californian in the inner circle, a muscular, square-jawed accountant from Fresno, about my age, who grew up picking vegetables in the San Joaquin Valley. "The Democratic central committee isn't going to like that you're renouncing special-interest money. That's where most of their funds come from. If you discourage contributions, that's going to hurt the state and local Democrats and really piss them off."

"And you need those state and local people," Fallon reminded him. "That's your grassroots. Your canvassers, your envelope stuffers, your voter-registration volunteers, the folks who put your sign in their living room windows."

"The central committee's free to raise money however it pleases. I'm running my campaign my way, they run theirs their way. Besides, I'm the nominee, I run the party now. If we get trouble from the bureaucrats, we fire 'em and put our own people in charge."

"In the middle of the campaign? No way," Fallon snorted.

"And picture this," the suddenly hopeful Molineaux said. "Best-case scenario. You get elected without help from the special interests. Your allies in the House and Senate get elected *with* the help of PACs and special interests. How are you going to govern? I thought part of our assignment was to find a way for you to govern once you win."

"If I upset the incumbent, that's a mandate. And I'll have plenty of ways to punish opponents within the party."

"Still, it looks bad," said Ishikawa. He frowned as

he spoke, as if apologizing for uncovering the biggest weakness in my scheme. "The state and local efforts are by definition going to help you, and it'll seem like a sneaky way of accepting PAC money."

"The Republicans do the same thing, don't they?" I asked.

"Yeah," Molineaux sneered, looking like a Buckley in high dudgeon, "but they're not the ones making an issue of it. And you can also rest assured they'll bring up Buford's PAC. Everyone inside the Beltway knows it's just a front for Jack and that he used it to lay the groundwork for his presidential run."

That one struck its target; Morgan looked like he was beginning to doubt. "Well, we'll dodge that somehow," he said, convincing no one.

"Now, where was I?" he resumed. "Dingo. You and me are going back to the Senate to accept some well-deserved congratulations. Your job for me is threefold. One, to handle the convention. Coordinate with Fallon on this. I want Kirk and Weldon in line with no promises. Hear that? No promises. I mean, don't rule out the vice presidency or any other post they want, but no affirmative commitments. Maybe we can toss them a few bones in the party platform, and that'll satisfy 'em. And do what you can to bring their better staff on board.

"Two, you and Ishikawa are my liaisons to the party central committee. Not a word of this to any of them. If they have questions about the campaign, tell them we're working things out and we'll call them as soon as they can be of service.

"Three, you're going to help me narrow down a short list for vice president, and conduct interviews.

"By the way, that's our cover. We make a big deal out of looking for my running mate. While the media are focusing on that, we secretly construct our alternate campaign. It ought to be a breeze. With me in Washington there won't be anybody in Toledo snooping on arrangements. And you can bet the *Blade* won't be alert enough to figure we've got something special going."

As we laughed he stretched his arms out, yawned, and smiled. "Erika, I want polls done on specific environmental issues, especially in states that can go either way. What frightens them? Which of their concerns have the Republicans ignored? Is there anything besides the job-displacement issue that I should soft-pedal? And another thing. I want to know what doubts people have about me. We'll address those issues right up front, maybe even on the videos.

"Lucy, you're writing up my video scripts. I want a good draft of the opener and closer by Thursday morning. You're also writing my acceptance speech. You've got to outline everything we're doing in the most dramatic terms, without spilling over into pathos. I want good, clean phrases, warmth and righteousness together, lots of evidence I love my country and all that standard shit.

"Fallon. You've got a hundred things to do. First, I want two weeks of meetings with my policy advisers. Bring in the foreign-policy advisers first. Then the economics people. Then domestic issues. Lastly the environment. Let's make it almost like an afterthought. Then in the next few days we have to make a list of running mates. I want your input on their assets and liabilities."

Fallon tried to make as if he wasn't appeased, but his pouting air of resignation stank of superficiality. Fallon was the sort who grumbled continually about the numerous overwhelming loads placed on his shoulders, then bristled at suggestions he disburden himself. He *needed* the sense of oppression that responsibilities brought with them; they were the source of his self-worth. When he first joined the staff we worried that given his experience and pugnacity he would push us around. But Morgan, tipped off by colleagues to the beefy Texan's nature, made a point of emphasizing the campaign's dependence on him, and that kept Fallon as loyal and obedient as the family dog.

"I want you firming up the state campaigns," Morgan went on, eyeing Fallon squarely. "Let me know how they're shaping up, whether there are any fires I can put out. You've also got to make arrangements for the convention—that by itself should be a load. In fact, I think we'll keep the campaign plane for another month so you can get around. And you and Ishikawa figure out how big a loan we need to get the videos set up.

"Molly"—he turned now to the genuinely put-off Molineaux—"you've got to get the video production into gear. Be discreet. No heading down to Tower for a million blank cassettes. I want you giving Ishikawa input as to how much it'll cost. You've also got to get your people working on ten-second spots. We won't be able to finish them until we've got a few 800 numbers, but I want the concepts down by Thursday.

"Steinhardt, you're helping Casselwaite with the video scripts. I want one or the other of you sitting in on all my policy meetings. Grab those people, have them outline positions on specific issues, stuff that's picayune but of concern on state and local levels. Go hard on the local angle. Jeez, if we could have a separate video for each congressional district, that would be terrific."

"Dream on, boss. A four-minute presentation on each issue, plus four hundred thirty-five miniscripts on top of that? Impossible. It would take forever," Molineaux derided. "You're bound to do a bad job on a lot of them."

"Just a goal to shoot for, Molly. Anyway, Steinhardt, you're being inundated with requests for interviews, I'm sure. Don't you have one cooked up with Reed Gordin? Fallon's in charge of my schedule, as usual. Have him block an hour every week for interviews. Don't overexpose me! The line I'm taking, and the line I want all of you to take, is that we know it's gonna be an uphill fight, but we have some surprises in store, and we'll talk about them at the convention. Got that? No leaks. You each have a hard copy of Stein-hardt's proposal. That and the transcript of this meeting will be our working documents. No additional copies, either on disk or on paper. The element of surprise is crucial.

"Buford. You're gonna have to split yourself in two. The first thing I want you to do is secure a space for the video operation. Set up the phone bank, screen workers, all that other stuff. Then you've also got to do the background checks on my vice-presidential choices. I won't be brought down by my second fiddle.

"Is everybody straight on their assignments? Good. I'm going back to Washington. We'll have a secured-line conference call at eight P.M. each night to keep tabs on each other's progress. Any major problems, call me earlier. Otherwise, that's it."

9

Of all the oxymorons I have heard, my favorite is *objective reporting*. The daily media—by which I mean the TV networks, wire services, and national newspapers—piously claim to produce fair, balanced, value-free news. But that's impossible. Someone has to decide which stories to cover. And within each story someone has to decide which facts to emphasize. Those are subjective decisions, and nothing constrains reporters and editors from indulging their biases except this rule: Keep the public coming back for more. And business sense is hardly an objective criterion.

From the start of a presidential campaign through the end of the primaries, the daily media control the political agenda. They determine who gets covered and how, and their decisions make or break the candidates. So mighty are the daily media at this stage that they can make *and* break a candidate, manufacturing political dramas that not-so-coincidentally raise news consumption. In 1984 an underfunded, understaffed, obscure politician named Gary Hart gained the media's collective eye by proclaiming himself the candidate of new ideas. He won the New Hampshire primary in a stunning upset and became a national celebrity. Then the same media that exalted him began to ask about his new ideas, and when Hart couldn't produce any, he was trashed, finishing the primaries a weak and worthless second.

Had the daily media asked Hart *in New Hampshire* about his new ideas and closely examined his response, they'd have pegged him as a charlatan and he never would have had an impact. (As it was, his emphasis on new ideas helped ruin the November chances of the party's nominee, Walter Mondale, who implicitly had old—read that "discredited"—ideas.) But that's asking for something closer to the true meaning of *objective:* a dispassionate investigation of the facts. Owing to niggardly news budgets, tight deadlines, and limited space (print) or time (TV and radio), the daily media rarely engage in anything so useful to the voter. What they do instead is take whatever's handed them by the candidate, usually a press release or speech, weigh its provocative potential (really good stories are called *sexy*), and, after sifting out the most outrageously self-serving statements, pass the message on, suitably abbreviated and sensationalized, to the public.

The result is that unless you read more nuanced accounts in periodicals like *The New Yorker*, you'll be misinformed about the campaign for the presidency. You'll miss important developments because, unless there's a press conference or leak to publicize them, the daily media won't cover them. Conversely, insignificant events such as a slip of the tongue will become turning points precisely because they occur in front of the microphones. And everywhere the details, hundreds and hundreds of telling details, are divorced from context, simplified, or overlooked entirely.

Until I sent out a press release announcing he'd hired veteran campaign consultants Fallon, Molineaux, and Mitchell and had formed an exploratory committee to study the feasibility of a candidacy, no one reported Jack Morgan's intention to run for president. But the clues had been accumulating for years. Even a moderately assiduous reporter could have seen the pattern and found sufficient evidence to break the story earlier.

Shortly after persuading me to stay on, Morgan started his own political-action committee, or PAC. PACs are the money arm of special-interest groups, contributing the maximum allowable amount to campaigns of candidates they support. They make for very grateful politicians, many of whom tacitly repay their debt with votes. Public officials are not allowed to run PACs, but Morgan got around that by having Buford organize the operation. And so Citizens Against the Trade Deficit was born, underwritten mostly by the Wholly Toledo Trading Company (Morgan's interest having been put in blind trust to avoid any hint of impropriety). Other export firms participated, but never gained majority control, giving Buford, and through him Morgan, a free hand to dole out money where he pleased.

The purpose of CAT-Dee, as we came to call it, was not so much to lobby for favorable legislation as to build Jack Morgan's power base in Congress. Whether they supported CAT-Dee causes or not, Morgan contributed to House and Senate Democrats facing tight elections. In addition to rescuing old hands in peril, he played a role in bringing many new Democrats to Capitol Hill. The recipients of his largess looked up to him as a political as well as a financial patron, and frequently followed him on the major issues.

By his fourth year in office Morgan was a force within the party, with a reputation as a generous team player. So generous was he that he often lent out staffers (myself included) to help with the election efforts of his allies—a sly way of preparing his people for a national campaign. After his reelection by an overwhelming margin in 2004 he became a power broker, as his fellow Democratic senators appointed him to run their Congressional Campaign Committee, the panel that disburses the party's election funds.

The party leaders in each house of Congress receive a lot of attention, as do the party whips. But by and large the guy who holds the purse strings is ignored, again a failure by the daily media to report what is really important. As chairman of the Campaign Committee, Morgan was in a position not just to reward his friends, but, by cutting their share of the party's war chest, to punish his enemies. By the election of 2006 he was one of the ten most powerful Democrats in the country and optimally positioned for a White House run. But because there wasn't a single bill or issue to associate him with, none of the pundits put him on their list of potential candidates.

In the early part of 2007 Morgan criss-crossed the country, meeting with governors and state legislators. The ostensible reason was to improve coordination between state and national campaigns, but the real reason was to introduce Morgan to men and women whose organizations would be of help to him in caucuses and primaries. By then Kirk and Weldon had declared their candidacies, however, so what little attention the daily media paid to Democratic politics focused on those two.

Thus when, nine years after Morgan started working toward the presidency, I sent out that press release, the daily media characterized his candidacy as a surprise and the prospective candidate as a dark horse.

In one respect they can be forgiven. The Republicans have held the White House for twenty-eight years, a lock on executive power that sometimes happens in democracies—witness the Christian Democrats in Italy and the Socialists in Sweden. The quarter-century of supremacy has discouraged all but the most quixotic Democrats from making the big run. Consequently Washington insiders, including the print and broadcast people on the national beat, assume that base builders such as Morgan are merely consolidating their power in the party, not laying the groundwork for a presidential bid. Why would anyone risk becoming another George McGovern, Jimmy Carter, Walter Mondale, Michael Dukakis?

For Jack Morgan the answer was simple. As his feelings of powerlessness and frustration grew and his bouts of depression increased in frequency, he had to either quit or make his move. After weeks of agonizing over whether to challenge an incumbent president, a stretch during which any minimally curious reporter could have walked into his office and obtained a confession from staffers that the man was going bonkers, Morgan decided to go for it.

Within a week the exploratory committee concluded he had a chance to win the nomination, and on July 4, 2007, he declared his candidacy.

Perhaps to punish Morgan for not cluing them in to his aspirations, the media lambasted his thin legislative record. But mindful of the Birch Bayh debacle of 1976, we ignored the charge. Bayh, a senator from Indiana, based his presidential candidacy on extensive legislative credentials, boasting that he'd added more words to the Constitution (through authorship of amendments) than anyone since Jefferson. Not only was he wiped out in the early primaries, but the next time he came up for reelection to the Senate he was beaten by Dan Quayle. If ever there was proof that voters didn't care about lawmaking skills, that was it.

So instead of going on the defensive by answering the press's charges, we had CAT-Dee beneficiaries from both houses of Congress vouch for Jack's sincerity, integrity, and toughness. Most reporters didn't buy the line, which of course they shouldn't have, but their skepticism was neutralized by the rush of more credulous journalists to brand Morgan the most intriguing personality in the campaign.

Now that the primaries were over and Morgan evidently had the nomination sewn up, the rules would change. We no longer had to vie for coverage and be grateful for whatever we got; the daily media were *obliged* to cover Morgan. But with the exponential increase in attention came a corresponding increase in the danger that a misstep might cost everything. From his choice of running mate to his choice of clothing, Jack Morgan would be scrutinized like a potential lover.

With Morgan, Hutson, and Fallon back in Washington, reporters fell all over themselves in their haste to follow, leaving us free to carry out our campaign preparations unnoticed. While Morgan speculated coyly about his choice of running mate (in our evening conference calls I advised him to draw out his decision until Independence Day), Buford found a warehouse for our video operations and hired staff. Fallon recruited Weldon's computer whiz, an Angeleno named Kathy Cheng, and sent her to Toledo to revamp our data bases and networks. Molineaux, in New York, put together a number of potential formats for the videos, and Mitchell tested them on focus groups around the country.

Casselwaite and I alternated between D.C. and Toledo, three days on, three days off, to attend Morgan's conferences with policy advisers. Here again the daily press overlooked a valuable opportunity to reveal what kind of president Morgan would be. A candidate's policy experts are likely to become officials in his cabinet. Knowing them—their credentials, their temperaments, their ideologies—gives you more idea than any number of speeches what his administration would be like, as well as what kind of man he really is. Does he surround himself with technocratic yes-people? Old political hands? Mavericks? Some combination thereof? These are solid clues about his character, much more telling than his television image.

And the media missed another clue when several of us moved our spouses to Toledo. I rented the same dilapidated, red-brick house that we lived in when we first moved to the area ten years ago, and Kaya joined me by the end of June. This time she brought Nimby, our little gray cat. Of all the signs that something peculiar was in the offing, the press secretary settling his cat near the candidate's hometown had to be among the surest. Why would he do that if he meant to spend the next four months on the road?

"The cat's okay," assured our short and shiny-pated landlord, tongue thickened and belly bloated by another decade of booze. "He can kill the mice in the garage. But that guy you work for, don't let me see him on the premises," he warned, shaking from laughter or the DTs or both. "I'll shoot the bastard in his tracks." Reeling around the yard, he looked into my eyes for just a second, then curled his mouth into a sneer. "He don't have a chance, you know. You'd think them Democrats'd had enough of runnin' liberals, after the whippin' they been takin'. They ain't never gonna learn, are they? Oh well," he laughed, slapping my arm and immediately recoiling. "It's a livin' for ya, ain't it?"

"America speaks," said Kaya once he left. Inside, the fallen bedroom ceiling was still unfixed, the bathtub leak had turned into a stream, and the living room carpet stank even worse of cat pee, prompting Nimby, normally the mutest feline in existence, to let out a plaintive, prolonged yowl.

At least no one from the press was there to notice.

10

I WENT TO the warehouse Buford was setting up for the video operation and ran into Kathy Cheng. She was gorgeous: silky hair down to her hips, almond eyes, high but not immodest cheekbones, and full red lips beneath a button nose. She stood much taller than the average Chinese woman, probably five foot eight. Most of the extra height was in her legs; her sheer black stockings, worn beneath a plaid, knee-length dress that could have passed for a parochial-school uniform, showed off slim ankles and a sturdy pair of calves.

But what most aroused me was her knowledge, in spite of her few years (I doubt that she was twenty-five), that nothing intimidates a man more thoroughly than female desire. Not the breathy, pouty helplessness of Hollywood and network writers, but the I-hope-you-took-your-vitamins-I-wanna-do-it-six-or-seven-times carnality that tells you right up front she has her own ideas when jumping into bed. In a country where sex is portrayed as the man's prerogative and a woman's job is to lie down and submit, her attitude was nothing short of subversion—and I have always had a fondness for subversive women.

When Buford introduced us and she aimed her breasts my way, showing them off like Olympic medals, I lost every pretense of command, barely squeaking out a "Welcome aboard" and sweating through my shirt. I shook her slender, long-fingered, immaculately manicured hand gingerly, as if entrusted with a priceless jewel. God—with barely more than a hello she controlled me more completely than Mel Buford. Had I stuck around much longer I might have been tempted to sink to my knees and kowtow, but Buford, sensing the threat to his primacy, took my arm and guided me down the vast and empty warehouse, regaling me with details of the project's progress as construction workers sawed and hammered up a din. I heard everything he said, but remembered nothing. All I thought about was Kathy Cheng.

"You like her?" Buford asked. "Well, you wouldn't if you knew her better. She slept with every guy on Weldon's staff. Not only that, but she's an airhead."

I didn't want to talk about her—not with him, anyway. I suggested we go out for dinner and persuaded him to join me at the one decent restaurant in Toledo— that is, unless you prefer taste-free American cuisine— an Indian place on Reynolds Road called Mahatma's.

Where I come from there are Mexican, Peruvian, Brazilian, Chinese, Japanese, Korean, Indian, Thai, Vietnamese, Cambodian, Afghan, Ethiopian, Italian, French, Greek, and Middle Eastern restaurants, dozens and dozens of each, and only the tourist-oriented are shy about their spicing. But in Toledo people prefer their meat red and their bread white and their beer as clear and tasteless as a glass of water. To them a culinary adventure is dining at a local fast-food chain instead of at a national one. The hometown favorites are the Big Boys, where the interstate buses stop to feed their passengers, and Bob Evans, which serves basically the same constipative fare as Big Boy, only against red-gingham decor.

Given the local gustatory preferences, it's a miracle Mahatma's survives. It has four booths, six tables for two, and a bar, but only twice have I seen the booths full. I've never yet seen anyone at the tables, and the only person ever at the bar is the owner, who, given the volume of patronage, can hardly be blamed. The menu lists three other franchises, so maybe they keep this one afloat. For whatever reason Mahatma's remains open, I'm grateful.

Buford took one look at the menu and blanched. For the first time in my life I think I had the advantage over him. "Where the hell do they eat this food?" he asked. "The black hole of Calcutta?"

"The curries are usually hot," I chirped.

"I just want something normal." Haplessly he watched a waiter deliver dinner to the only other patrons. "You know, something that isn't smothered in an orange sauce."

We went through the menu looking for something he would find palatable and settled on saag paneer, which I disingenuously described as creamed spinach with chunks of mild cheese. When the order came, in gleaming metal bowls on metal trays, Buford rolled his eyes.

"This is called a *thali* dinner. It's how Indian food is traditionally served," I explained.

"Oh, right. I suppose the Buddha ate from steel cups too."

Although at that point I suspected it was mostly put-on, or sublimated jealousy of Kathy Cheng's impact on me, I got a kick from Buford's petulance. It wasn't often that I felt myself top dog. Wanting to prove that I could be magnanimous, I decided to play up to him a bit. "Hey, dinner's my treat," I said, and then "you know, I never thanked you for supporting my campaign plan."

"I didn't support it," he said, taking a bite of a chapati, which he seemed to like. "I think it's the stupidest idea I've heard in ages."

"Why did you help me, then, against Fallon and Molineaux?"

"Because I hate those guys. And I wasn't helping you. I was putting forth my own idea. Remember?"

I realized now I'd made a mistake. Buford despised flattery, because it was a tool he often used to gather information from the vain and unsuspecting. He'd be damned if he would let himself get sucked in that way. I could attempt to save myself by changing the subject— but it was too late.

"You know why it won't work? Because change comes from the bottom up," he started, after averring that the saag paneer was pretty good. "Especially in democracies. No government will go out on a limb proposing bold new programs unless there's already a consensus for the move among the people. What have we got here? Granted, we've got people worried for the environment. But we've also got people totally unwilling to do what must be done to save it, because that means change, and they don't want to change. At least not *that* way."

"How do you know?" I challenged, but my voice was as weak as when I shook hands with Kathy Cheng.

He wiped the corners of his mouth with a napkin, leaned toward me, and asked, "Do you know the town of Ephesus?"

"O little town of Ephesus?"

"Ephesus. Heraclitus's hometown."

"Oh, that Ephesus. Sorry. Doesn't ring a bell."

"How about as in Paul's Epistles to the Ephesians?"

"Okay, I've heard of that."

"Thank God. Then you know that it's an ancient town on the Aegean Sea."

"Well, no, I don't, but go ahead."

"It's in Turkey now, but back then it was part of greater Greece. The legend is the Amazons settled it, which is probably a remnant from the times of matrilineal societies. Anyway, it was a very prosperous town, built on hills along a river mouth. When it was first settled, four thousand years ago, the hills were full of oaks.

"Then it became home port for the trade routes into Asia, and the population grew. They cut down the trees for boats and fuel and houses, and grazed cattle on the hills. A thousand years later the hills had changed to shrub and grassland. But still the town kept growing. They built a temple to Artemis that seated twenty-four thousand people. The Lucas County Rec Center doesn't seat that many! After a while the cattle didn't provide enough food, so by the time of Saint Paul they were planting wheat on the hillsides."

He stabbed a cube of cheese from the saag paneer, meditated on it briefly, then consumed it. "You're the naturalist, or the one whose wife is. You tell me what happened next."

"It faded into history."

"Right. But why?"

"You can't be forever blessed, I suppose."

"Oh, come on, Dan. Don't play the fool. Don't you get it? From forest to grazeland to farmland. What do you think happened to those hills?"

"Soil degradation?"

"That's right." He wiped his mouth again and gestured at me with the hand that held the napkin. "The trees held all the soil. When they chopped down the oaks, the soil ran off to the river. The river silted up so that the boats couldn't dock. To keep the town alive they had to move the whole thing west, to the edge of the new delta. Then, when they transformed the grasslands into farmland, more soil ran off, and the river silted up again, and they had to move the goddamned town *again.* And then again, and then again. How many times can you do that and stay prosperous?"

"Evidently not many."

"Evidently not," he acknowledged coldly. "The town was just a podunk by the year 900. But the phenomenon goes back even further than Ephesus. When the Egyptians built the Sphinx, it was in the middle of rich farmland. And remember the Fertile Crescent? Not so fertile anymore, eh?"

"What are you getting at, Mel?" My throat was dry and I didn't feel like eating anymore.

"The same thing Heraclitus said: Man's character is his fate. We can't help what we are, Dan. We're degraders. Always have been, always will be. Give us bounty and we'll use it up as fast as population and technology permit. You're trying to impose an antidegradation ethos from the top down. Get Morgan in the White House, change the agenda, change the law, and that will change the public mood. And then everyone will come around and we'll live happily ever after. But it doesn't work that way. Quite the opposite, in fact."

By now I think Buford was beginning to feel a little sorry for me. "Look, Dan," he said more soothingly, "you're a smart guy. You grew up around smart people. You graduated from a top-flight university. Except for the time you put in with that goddamned baseball team, you've always worked with people smart just like yourself. So you can be forgiven for assuming everyone is capable of seeing things as clearly.

"But the fact is, most people are cretins. Downright, irredeemably dense, and proud of it to boot. Remember those numbers Mitchell quoted us a couple months ago? A quarter of American adults are functionally illiterate? Two thirds never read another book after they graduate from high school? A third can't figure out the change due from a twenty-dollar bill when they buy groceries at the store? Well, every one of those dumb fuckers gets as many votes as you."

"Now I understand why the Greeks despised democracy," I murmured as a growing despair disrupted my digestion.

"Think about the guys building the warehouse. They're in construction. You know what they aspire to? Steady work. Enough to keep the kids fed and the wife's mouth shut and a night's supply of six-packs in the fridge. The pinnacle of existence is to make it to foreman, unless you're really ambitious, in which case you spend your life gunning for project manager. Now look at us, Dan. You know what we aspire to? A place in history. We're gunning for the White House. How much do you think we have in common with those guys?"

I thought about Kathy Cheng, how I looked at her as a subversive. What did those guys think of her? Did they think about where she was coming from, what was behind her free and easy manner, or did they call her cunt and take turns boasting what they'd do to her?

"I guess we don't have much in common," I conceded.

"Damn straight. I congratulate you on making your agenda Morgan's. That's what politics is all about—influence—and you influenced. But the fact is your plan means fewer jobs for those guys, and even if it doesn't, they're going to think it does. And they'll be damned before they cast a vote for someone who thinks birds and trees are more important than a steady job or making foreman."

"But if my plan is ass-backward, why is Jack so square behind it?"

"Why do you think? Because he's going loony."

"You are just kidding, aren't you?"

Buford was the innermost member of the inner circle. If something had gone seriously wrong in Morgan's head, he would know before the rest of us.

"I don't know. I just don't know." He turned his sweating water glass inside the puddle that had formed around it. "He's not insane, if that's what you're asking. Maybe just a little mad."

"Did you tell him after our meeting that you didn't like my plan?"

"Me and almost everybody else, except Elena, who thought staying in Toledo was a great idea. But you couldn't sway him with a cradle."

Hmm. I had thought that after the primaries things would go more slowly and become more comprehensible. For the first time it struck me that perhaps the opposite would be the case.

11

Casselwaite and I alternated three-day stints at Morgan's policy seminars in Washington. I longed to find out whether she was as bored by them as I was, but as our schedules were exactly opposite she became the one member of the inner circle I never saw. While in D.C. I also did a lot of foundation building with the press corps, promising they would enjoy covering us this fall, although not explaining why.

It was of utmost importance to maintain the daily media's morale. Traditionally reporters covering the successful candidate become White House correspondents, and with the White House beat comes big money and a chance to rise into the ranks of media celebrities —network anchors, syndicated columnists, million-dollar authors. Over the past twenty-eight years those opportunities went to reporters covering the Republicans, to the point where drawing the Democrat became a sure sign of disfavor within a news organization. The resultant bitterness spilled over into stories, with disastrous consequences for the candidate. As so many Democratic press secretaries had done before me, I tried to reassure the pack that this time we would run a great campaign and win, bringing them along. I doubt I was convincing, but for the time being, anyway, they treated Morgan kindly.

On July 4th Morgan named his running mate: Joe Perez, the governor of Florida. As a political gambit the move made sense, because Perez could pull Florida's electoral votes into our column. He was popular, had a good organization, and, according to Fallon, who went back with him a long way, "would swim naked through a gator pond for a vote." He was also Hispanic, which would help us with the liberal and minority wings of the party and be an asset in New York, Texas, and California.

On a personal level, though, Perez was a risk. He was headstrong and impulsive. Given their differing styles, clashes between him and Morgan would be inevitable and might prove embarrassing to the campaign. Morgan acknowledged this at the press conference, saying that he was looking for "No-people"—people who had ideas of their own and who, in championing those ideas, would prevent a Morgan White House from becoming insular. "I welcome disagreement within my own ranks," he said cheerfully, a statement also meant to mitigate possible damage from discord at the upcoming convention. "With a diversity of minds we're much more likely to come up with innovative answers to our problems."

That evening I flew back to Toledo and, curious to gauge the impact of naming Perez, called Erika Mitchell. She was in the midst of a tracking poll, so we agreed to meet at Mahatma's for lunch next afternoon.

Erika Mitchell was by all accounts the best pollster in the party. A trim, athletic-looking sixty-year-old who tied her long gray hair into a ponytail, she was the daughter of Chicago college professors persecuted by McCarthy. The family was exiled to Cedar Rapids, Iowa, a town, she bragged, distinguished by three things:

It was home to Grant Wood, painter of *American Gothic;* it had the largest oat-processing plant in the world; and, like Paris, its city hall was built on an island in the river running through the town.

Mitchell herself was distinguished by three things. First was that she pioneered the polling method known as NABR (Neighborhood Attitude Breakdown Research), which used direct-mail data, magazine subscriptions, and census-bureau information to sort the country into thousands of distinct neighborhoods. On the basis of its education level, religious leanings, ethnic makeup, consumption patterns, and the like, each neighborhood was then grouped into one of fifty superheadings. My neighborhood in San Francisco, for instance, was grouped into *Yuptown.* A pollster could walk into the heart of New York City's West Side, take a comprehensive sampling of the local attitudes, and know what people thought in my neck of the woods as well.

Mitchell had done comprehensive surveys of every superheading in the country. She knew which issues were the key ones where and, through a marvelously complex computer program, could accurately estimate the number of votes won or lost with each move a politician made.

Her second virtue was dedication. No one worked harder or got less sleep, not even Morgan. To my consternation Morgan had come to take that for granted, increasing her assignments and shortening her deadlines as the campaign progressed. Yet she hadn't once complained. She formulated her questions overnight, dictated them to her office manager in Cedar Rapids the next morning, and input the data gathered by her phone canvassers or test takers into a portable computer by dinnertime, coming up with comprehensive, easily interpreted results before the evening meeting of the inner circle. Then Morgan would give her another set of assignments, and she'd repeat the process.

Her dedication was also evident from the quality of her questions. The toughest part of polling was posing the right questions. You could ask about things the public didn't care about and inflate the importance of an issue. Or, conversely, you could overlook an important issue by failing to inquire about it. Then, too, you could slant your questions, prompting respondents to tell you what you wanted to hear. Mistakes like that could be fatal to a candidacy. So she spent hours honing her questions, sometimes running them by us to make sure she'd winnowed out the biases and presuppositions.

Her third virtue was perhaps her greatest: She hardly ever said a word. In a typical political campaign everybody pushes a personal agenda from dawn till midnight and beyond. Pollsters in particular have a reputation for advocacy, because they are convinced they have their finger on the national pulse. But Erika Mitchell didn't seem to have an agenda. Of all the members of the inner circle she was the only one who failed to submit a campaign plan. At our nightly confabs she rarely talked unless a question was directed to her, and even then she never ventured far from the security of her numbers. Such discretion elevated her beyond the squabbles that mar all campaigns and made her the one universally respected member of the Morgan team. It was also the reason she earned more money than anyone except maybe Fallon and Molineaux.

Kaya, missing me after my three days in Washington and not having had Indian food in more than a week, badgered me into taking her along for lunch. Erika was already there, in the rear booth—my favorite because you can see through a window into the kitchen —and after introductions we got down to business.

"So," I asked, "will Perez help or hurt us?"

Erika rubbed her hands together absently and smiled. "Won't make one bit of difference," she pronounced.

"That's what your tracking polls say?"

"That's what I say. The choice of running mate never makes for more than two points' difference in November. And it's only that much in extreme cases, like when one candidate runs with a prince and the other with a toad."

"I'm sorry," Kaya interrupted sheepishly, "but what's a tracking poll?"

"Doesn't he explain these things to you? Danny, shame on you," she scolded amiably. "A tracking poll is when you ask a few questions about a specific event to a limited number of people immediately after the event occurs. It's not as reliable as a standard poll, which is broader and samples more than a thousand people over two or three days, but it gives an indication of how things are going."

"And so you took one to find out how Perez went over with the public?"

"That's right. There's a tiny blip in Morgan's favor. He's still ten points behind."

"Ouch," groaned Kaya.

"How many undecideds?" I asked.

"Nineteen percent. And they're all across the spectrum. No one group's sitting on the fence waiting for the candidates to say the magic words."

"This is fascinating, how you find these things out," Kaya said. "On the way over Danny was telling me about NABR and how you're a pioneer in it."

"Mm-hmm," Erika nodded, smiling without parting lips.

"What other kinds of polling do you do?"

"Well, there's one kind the Republicans are good at, but lately we've been doing more and more of it. That's called TRACE. You get sixty to a hundred people in a room and give them each a joystick. Up on the joystick means 'interest' or 'like,' down means 'boredom' or 'dislike,' and the middle is for neutral responses. Then you show images you want reactions to, like TV commercials, and you get people's visceral impressions."

"How do you make sure they aren't lying or pushing the joystick the wrong way?"

"We have hidden cameras that record their ocular reactions," she smiled conspiratorially. "The eyes don't lie."

"That's so interesting!" Kaya exclaimed. "Next time you do one, let me know. It's okay if I take one, isn't it? I'm not ineligible because my husband's an employee of the company?"

"We usually do our TRACE work in midsize cities with centrist politics. Kansas City is a favorite. Pittsburgh. San Jose. We used to do some in Ohio, in Columbus and Akron and Dayton, but I don't think we'll do it this year because of the favorite son."

"Why will we be doing *any* TRACEing?" I asked. "It doesn't seem there'll be much need."

"Actually Molineaux has stuff he wants TRACEd, and Fallon gave the go-ahead."

"This is news to me." Those bastards! Were Molineaux and Fallon trying to outmaneuver me, covertly preparing a conventional campaign for the day they talk Morgan out of following my plan?

"Most of it is video-related," she said, the usual cautiousness returning to her voice. "But he did give me a couple of commercials."

"What were they about?"

"Mood stuff, mostly. Aimed at aging baby-boomers like me. One's of toxic-waste dumps, belching smokestacks, dying forests. The other's people playing with their grandkids, happy stuff like that. The voice-overs are different, but the background music is the same— 'America' by Simon and Garfunkel."

"Oh, God, remember them? I keep forgetting which one is the short one and which one has the frizzy hair," Kaya interjected. Within a minute she and Erika were swapping memories. I had never heard Erika talk so much before. Kaya was really drawing her out—what a stellar journalist she would have made.

Erika had two sons, a doctor in Chicago and a graduate student in history at Princeton, and had been married twice, the last match ending seven years ago. She recalled taking the kids to the Great Midwestern Ice Cream Company, and what it was like to eat a heaping dish of French Silk, a rich chocolate with a smidgen of vanilla flavoring, on nights the stench came up from the hog-rendering plant. Kaya bragged about Double Rainbow, the San Francisco gourmet ice cream of our youth, but couldn't top the story of the burning pork.

It was clear I wouldn't get a chance to ask further about Molineaux's commercials; stealing conversations was one of Kaya's specialties. Not that I minded. Except with workmates and longtime friends (the latter of which I never see anymore) I'm not comfortable talking, so it's a relief to have my wife carry the load of interaction. It gives my mind a chance to wander. Was Kathy Cheng like this? Could she waste an afternoon discussing chocolate, children, shopping? How much I longed to get to know her. What were her secrets? I pictured us in heart-to-heart confession. I'd reel with empathy for all she'd endured and hug her till her monsters went away. But I couldn't picture making love to her. Part of that was having Kaya by my side—she was my number one. But there was also the specter of a worldly Kathy laughing at me as my first two girlfriends did. I had little doubt that she could be that cold.

"I'm sorry," Kaya apologized. "You guys came here to talk business and I've monopolized the conversation."

"It doesn't matter," I said quietly.

"So what do you think of Dan's campaign plan?

Pretty clever, eh?" Kaya beamed, patting me on the back.

"I like it," Erika declared with a conviction I didn't think her capable of mustering. "If anything, it doesn't go far enough."

"Are you serious?" I gasped. "Everybody else thinks I went too far."

"Not me. When I was a kid and we moved to Cedar Rapids, the thing that made me like it was the red admiral butterflies that came out every summer—right around this time of year. Millions of them! They would land on you, sit on your shoulder. I was a city kid. I'd never seen anything like it before. Now"—she sighed wistfully—"maybe a dozen in a day, if you sit out long enough and really look for them."

"But the change involved scares people way too much," I said. "Your own polls must tell you that a strong stand on environment won't win us the election."

Erika Mitchell waved her hands contemptuously. "Fuck the polls," she said.

12

WHERE I COME from the weather never gets too hot and vexing. Maybe four, five days a year the thermometer pokes above ninety, but when it does the humidity is usually below fifty, so you don't feel like you're wrapped inside a moldy blanket. In the evening the fog rolls in, meaning you don't sweat up your bed and roll around in twisted sheets all night. And the Pacific winds keep the mosquitoes and other buzzing scourges from your ear while you're asleep.

Although I've spent the better part of the last twelve summers in Ohio and D.C., I still haven't gotten used to the muggy, insect-ridden swelter. What makes the eastern summer even more oppressive is its light. A fuzzy layer of high clouds refracts a cranky, drab glare on the landscape. In San Francisco, after the fog burns off the sky's a dazzling, cheerful blue. And on cloudy days the clouds are thick and dense, admitting a shadowless illumination that intensifies the floral greens and adds muscle to the pastel paint on the Victorians.

The two weeks before the convention were the hottest and most enervating I've ever experienced. The whole eastern third of the country was a blast furnace. I would drive with all the windows down to our warehouse on the North Side, mere blocks from the clammy, frothless sump Kaya called Lake Eerie, and nearly choke on the stench coming off the water. Because a glance up would require too much effort, I would flash my ID badge to Buford's gatehouse thug without looking at him, and wheel into the compound.

I was also suffering from a torpid grouchiness that had nothing to do with the heat. This entire operation was my brainchild; *I* had called the biggest shot in a national campaign and persuaded a potential president to take up my great cause. It was the stuff that dreams are made of. But that very victory undid my peace of mind, because now that I had something to defend, I fretted constantly. What were Molineaux and Fallon plotting? Mitchell had said we were still ten points behind; would Morgan scuttle everything if the numbers went unchanged through August? And what about what Buford said?

Inside the warehouse the construction workers, shirtless and slick with sweat, went doggedly about their tasks. I walked along the row of offices set up for the inner circle, wondering whether my deputy, Tim Avery, would be in, but stopped dead in my tracks at the office door of Kathy Cheng.

She sat before a monitor intently typing in commands, strands of thick and silky hair draping her shoulders and white sundress. The first button of the dress had been undone, revealing more than I should have seen. There was no denying it, at least not in her presence: I was in lust. I was happily married, more than ten years older, eternally wary of southern Californians, and in a rotten mood, but just the slightest whiff of her pheromones transformed me into an adolescent.

Perhaps it was my heavy breathing that distracted her from work. "How's the weather treating you?" I asked as she looked up.

Her eyes, wide open when she stared into her monitor, narrowed into slits as she broke into a smile. She drew a hand across her forehead and flicked away imaginary sweat. "I must have visited the mainframe room a dozen times today. It's the only room with air-conditioning, you know."

"Not at all like where we come from, huh?"

"You from L.A. too?"

"San Francisco."

"Oh. Then to you this must be even worse. You're used to such coolness."

"No, I suspect it's worse for you. Everybody back east thinks it's always ninety-five degrees in southern California and that you should be accustomed to this."

"God, I'd give anything to be on the beach right now. I'd even settle for a window."

She grabbed the straps of her dress and fanned her body with the fabric, and though that might have cooled *her* down, it sent my temperature beyond the boiling point. She was half exposing herself to me; each time she pulled the dress away, I glimpsed her perky breasts almost to the nipples. How much I wanted to close the door, wrap my arms around her, and bury my face inside that airy little dress! Had she only said the word, nothing would have stopped me.

"Had lunch yet?" I asked.

"Can't go out today," she said. "Too much work. Bummer, eh?"

"Yeah. I know this Indian place that's air-conditioned."

"Indian food? You mean like curry? I'm not too keen on that."

"How about Mexican? You must like Mexican."

"Yeah, but how can anyone eat Mexican in *this* weather?"

"True. Oh, well. The Mexican food in these parts is

101

pretty awful anyway. Maybe some other time? When the temperature's a little cooler?"

"Sure." She smiled, leaning forward and going back to her computer.

I didn't want to leave. "Have you seen Lucy Casselwaite?" I asked.

"The speechwriter? About an hour ago. Or was it two? She was in her office."

"Thanks. I'll see ya."

I was supposed to meet with Casselwaite to divvy up script assignments, but wandered down the hall unable to concentrate on anything but Kathy. You know what you just did, asshole? You asked her on a date! You've already taken step one on the pathway to adultery, and there goes the trust you've built with Kaya all these years. But she said sure! You wait until the weather cools—if it ever does—and you'll go out with her, and you'll go out with her again, and *you'll make love to her before the campaign's over.* My God, to be in Kathy Cheng—

"Danny! I've been waiting for you." It was Lucy Casselwaite. "Come into my office—or what passes for it. I've got wires coming out of every wall. One wall's got a hole the size of Cleveland in it. There's a layer of sawdust on all my furniture. These carpenters work slower than the legal system, don't you think? And you'd think they could have put in air-conditioning! I guess it costs too much, right? And it doesn't fit in with our brand-new ecological theme. I can see the headlines now: 'Environmental Candidate Lavishes Air-Conditioning on Mere Underlings.' "

The dig brought me out of my daydreams. I was no big fan of Casselwaite's. Morgan was potentially a dynamite speaker, but the lines she gave him carried all the explosive potential of mud. She wrote in full sentences, which would have served admirably in Lincoln's day but make for disaster in the era of the ten-second attention span. Nor was she terribly original. Consequently Morgan came off as sincere, mild-mannered—and uninspiring. On several occasions Fallon, myself, and others implored her to put more crackle into Morgan's speeches, but she demurred, saying she didn't think Jack capable of delivering a fiery peroration. We suspected the real reason she refused was that she knew she couldn't write that good a speech.

To our continuing frustration Morgan stood by her. While still an undergraduate she had walked into his office asking for an interview—an assignment for her journalism class—and wound up on his sofa. Before long she was "interviewing" him every afternoon, swishing by us in her peasant skirt and sandals. She wore her blond hair in a perm, had a little, unobtrusive face, and a sturdy build. We didn't know what Morgan saw in her, but clearly he adored her, because for her graduation present he put her on the payroll as his speechwriter. After Elena's tirade brought the affair to a close, we figured he'd let Lucy go, but out of loyalty or gratitude or something else he kept her on.

I followed Casselwaite into her office, settled into the folding chair in front of her desk, and, looking at her sternly—she'd yanked me from a happy daydream—waited.

She stared back at me sadly. "Can I say something that will stay between just you and me?" she asked.

"I guess."

"Yes or no?"

"It depends on what you're going to say."

She began to cry. This was the last thing I needed on a day like this. I squirmed against the hard back of the chair, trying to unstick my shirt, and looked away as she wiped at her face with a tissue.

"Why can't you say yes? Why are you being so hard on me?"

"I'm not being hard on you, Luce." PMS, I thought

103

—unfairly. I was hot and irritable and unwilling to entertain someone else's insecurities when I had so many of my own.

"I should have expected as much, now that you're Jack's boy. You've outmaneuvered everybody. How does it feel to be first among equals?"

"I didn't outmaneuver anybody, Luce. Jeez. We all came up with plans, and he chose mine. That's all there is to it, I swear to God. And as for being first among equals, I sure as hell wish *I* felt that way."

She was plainly disbelieving and resentful.

"Look, Lucy, I don't want to get into an argument, not on a day like today when I'm hardly in the mood to work, much less fight. Morgan calls the shots in this campaign, not me. If he has more faith in my plan than I do, that's not my fault. Now, what is it you have to say?"

The tears cascaded freely. "I don't know where to start."

For years Casselwaite had put up with the barely concealed disdain of Morgan's staff. So long as Morgan protected her she could hold her head high, but alienated from his affections, as she had been for a year now, she must have felt increasingly vulnerable. And so I sensed that what I was about to hear would be more than just a confession; it would be a plea to save her job, to put in a good word with the boss.

"I think I'm going to have a nervous breakdown," she began. "I'm serious. I've got to do a million stinking scripts plus the acceptance speech in fourteen days, and I'm not going to make it."

"Tell Jack. Tell him that you need assistants." I forced a laugh. "Just don't tell him to put any of your load on me, 'cause I'm backed up as much as you are."

"Except, and you'll excuse my French, he's really pissed off because we haven't narrowed down the themes of the acceptance speech. We can't agree on whether the environmentalism or the no-b.s. campaign or something else should get top billing, and he's taking his frustration out on me. You understand, don't you? He's never been mad at me before. I don't know what to do. I think he's going to fire me."

"He won't fire you."

"That's all they talk about in Washington—a purge. Fallon's sure he's gone because he bad-mouthed your ideas. You know what he told Jack? That your plan won't work because it relies too much on the media to give us favorable coverage. 'Even if that Steinhot charactuh was any good, we cain't expect the press to treat us squayuh,'" she mimicked the infernal drawl, so precisely I broke out in laughter. "I swear that's what he said," she giggled through the tears. "And Molineaux. Molineaux thinks that after all the videos are made he's a goner too."

"I haven't heard a thing about a purge. Jack is not that kind of guy. You know that, Luce."

"Yeah. But I also know we're ten points down, and things get shaken up when you're in that position."

"But if anyone has to worry it's me, because it's my plan that he's following. Besides, the campaign hasn't even started yet. Write him a good speech and the gap will close, and you and Molineaux and everybody else will forget you ever worried about this. Okay?"

"You're sweet to say that, but you aren't getting the big picture."

"What big picture?"

"Me and Jack." She paused and dried her face again. I waited for her to continue.

"I feel so sorry for her now," she finally volunteered.

"Who?"

"It serves me right, I guess. When you're twenty-two, you don't realize that the biggest sin a woman can commit is getting older."

"Who are you talking about?"

"Elena. Have you met the new programmer?"

"Kathy Cheng? Buford introduced us."

"Beautiful, isn't she?"

"She caught my eye," I confessed. Hell, Buford knew, and that was much more dangerous than Lucy knowing.

"Well, don't plan any midnight rendezvous with her. You're a couple weeks too late."

The flash of sweat that coated my skin I could blame on the heat. But the sudden tautness in my muscles and the inability to swallow or look Lucy in the eye —they had their source in a different kind of burning.

"His eyes popped out when he first saw her," she recounted. "That was when I understood. He doesn't need me anymore. He pays attention to me out of kindness, not out of interest. And when he yells at me about the speech? He's really saying I should quit, get out of his life. Do you understand now, Dan? Can you put yourself in my shoes long enough to understand?"

"I can," I said rather dazedly. It became imperative I leave the room at once.

13

THE DEMOCRATIC NOMINEE-APPARENT spends the fortnight prior to the convention preempting potentially embarrassing challenges from opponents and special-interest blocs. It's a battle he can't win. If he chooses to compromise with the discontented factions, whose complaints always get wide media attention (the quadrennial "Disunited Democrats" story culled from the archives and updated), he comes off looking weak. If he doesn't compromise, the convention is disrupted for the world to see, and the endorsements, money, volunteers, and votes the spurned factions might have otherwise provided are withheld.

Morgan assigned Fallon and Hutson to smooth out the convention. Thanks to our unorthodox fall strategy, which we'd succeeded in keeping secret, the two had leverage no nominee's agents ever had before: We didn't *need* the spoilers' volunteers and money. And so Fallon and Hutson spread the word that if the dissidents didn't fall in line, they'd get nothing. No platform concessions, no party posts, no White House appointments in the event of victory. And if they didn't like that, they could go to hell; their public whining would only succeed in making Morgan look more resolute, a quality Americans wanted in their leader.

Dingo Hutson was especially effective. A tall, heavy black man with a forceful manner and authoritative voice (the James Earl Jones of politics, the pundits dubbed him), he had started out a prosecutor in Fulton County, Georgia, a patronage appointment from the mayor of Atlanta. The D.A. took an immediate dislike to him and assigned him high-profile, sure-loser cases. But through a combination of cleverness and bluster Hutson won his share of those assignments, garnering headlines in the process, and two years later ascended to the D.A.'s post himself.

In the hometown of Martin Luther King he stirred enormous controversy over his zeal for prosecuting blacks. One prominent civil rights leader called him "a black man only the Klan could love." But Hutson stuck to his modus operandi. The vast majority of crimes by blacks are committed against other blacks, he said, and if this is what it takes to stop us from preying on each other, so be it.

The result was unprecedented popularity among whites. In 1998 he ran for state attorney general and won. Four years later he tried for the U.S. Senate. His prospects were doubtful until a PAC called Citizens Against the Trade Deficit replenished his coffers. Closing with a saturation blitz of television advertising, he won by less than twenty thousand votes, becoming the first black senator from the South since Reconstruction.

Knowing to whom he owed success, Hutson became Morgan's fast ally, readily accepting the invitation to serve as campaign chairman. It was a smart move for both men. Time had healed the black community's bitterness toward Hutson; in fact he had become one of its most prominent spokespeople. By appointing him, Morgan sewed up black support and also precluded opposition from his left. As for Hutson, his prominent role in the campaign would gain him stature in the party and put him in line for attorney general if Morgan won.

Hutson was up for reelection this year, so after the convention he'd cease playing an active role in the presidential campaign. But in the meantime he did Morgan's business with a messianic fervor, cowing the malcontents into stunned and bitter silence. "Let them hate, provided that they fear," Buford reassured him when Hutson worried that he'd hit some fellow Democrats too hard. The quote, Caligula's motto, did nothing to ease Hutson's apprehension, but in spite of the misgivings he kept his iron fist clamped firmly on the throats of Morgan's rivals.

The hard-line strategy paid off: Kirk and Weldon, after initial pouting, closed ranks behind Morgan, as did organized labor and the bleeding hearts. The mainstream media noted that the Democrats were going into this convention more united than at any time since Franklin Roosevelt was president. Much of the credit was attributed to Morgan's staff. We were developing a reputation as crack political operators.

While Fallon and Hutson did their thing, the rest of us, working in Toledo and New York, put the videos together. The process started with Molineaux creating several introductions from the footage and photographs he'd collected during the primaries. (The conclusion would be composed of visuals from the convention.) Mitchell took the introductions to Jacksonville, Buffalo, Omaha, and Fresno to do TRACEs. There was no clear winner, so Molineaux combined the most favorable images into a brand-new introduction. Mitchell TRACEd that, turned up acceptable ratings, and we were on our way.

After the introduction the personalization of the video began, with a general statement tailored to the concerns of each NABR classification. Under Mitchell's supervision Cheng set up a directory of NABR districts by nine-digit zip code, so that each person requesting a video would get the pitch appropriate to his or her neighborhood. The task of writing the fifty scripts fell to Casselwaite.

Casselwaite also did the sixty-odd scripts on major issues. This latter task wasn't quite as onerous as it sounded, since she could cannibalize material from Morgan's old speeches and position papers. The issue spots, as many as the caller requested, would follow the NABR pitch.

To me fell the task of putting together statements on local environmental issues. The local statement was the most specific in the video and would come just before the conclusion. Although the statements would be shorter than the NABR and issue presentations, I had to do one for each congressional district, and so my work was cut out for me.

I was greatly aided by Ishikawa, who in buying the Sierra Club's mailing list also obtained from them a chapter-by-chapter leadership roster. Using that roster as a guide, I had Avery and his underlings call at least two environmental activists in each district. The activists would identify the biggest local environmental issue, outline the pro-environmental stand, and tell us who the main opponents were and where the local Democratic office holders stood. From there I would compose a ninety-second blurb for Morgan.

When going good I could knock off ten an hour. "As part of my commitment to preserving the environment," I opened, "I will see to it that [local issue] is [desired action]. [Desired action] is vital to [name of community] if it is to [remain or become] a safe and healthy place to bring up children. In the Senate I have [sponsored, voted for, advocated] [name of legislation], which [if it lost: would have gone a long way toward accomplishing that goal] [if it won: is a good start toward accomplishing that goal]. I join with [local Democrats sharing the position, or, if none, "farsighted members of the community"] in calling for [desired action], and will make it a top priority in my administration."

Once Casselwaite and I finished a script it was faxed to Molineaux's studio in Manhattan, where Morgan read it off. He often needed several takes to get it right, particularly on the longer speeches Casselwaite had written, and as time wore on it took him longer to read the spiels to Molineaux's satisfaction. Along about the eighteenth take of one script his midwestern equanimity deserted him. He bolted from his chair, knocking over the nearest light fixture.

"I'm promising the sky to everyone!" he shouted. "Are any of you geniuses cross-referencing this stuff, so we know if I'm contradicting myself? Is Steinhardt consulting local Democrats before he writes? How do I know I'm not getting myself neck-deep in some neighborhood morass I shouldn't take a stand on?" The first time he exploded, Buford calmed him down, but after blowing a fifth take on script three hundred forty-something, Morgan bolted from the studio.

Buford and a pair of Secret Service men caught up with him as he slid into the backseat of a cab. They piled in as Morgan barked a Little Italy address. "Where you going?" Buford asked.

"To a whorehouse," Morgan answered. "At least there was one at that address fifteen years ago."

"You can't go to a whorehouse."

"The hell I can't."

"What if the press finds out?"

"You see any reporters here?"

They talked him out of going in. Instead he took them on a tour from Little Italy to Chinatown to SoHo up to Chelsea, pointing out the brothels and bars he'd frequented in student days. They ended up at Washington Square Park in Greenwich Village, where Morgan ordered Buford to pay the driver and popped out of the cab. The Secret Service hurried to catch up as he joined a crowd beside the fountain listening to a scruffy street performer.

Morgan and the sunglassed, scowling, business-suited Secret Service agents melded into the crowd about as inconspicuously as Einstein at an astrology convention. The street people, junkies, and NYU students took immediate notice, and a few even recognized the guy sporting the scar. A murmur rose as word got around. The Secret Service goons stuck their chins in their lapels and whispered Maydays into their transmitters. Buford tugged at Morgan's lapel.

"Let's get out of here. You could be killed," he hissed.

It was too late. "Hey, man, there's only one comedian allowed here at one time," the performer in the center of the circle taunted.

"Then get off the stage," Morgan retorted, elbowing his way into the middle of the circle. And then, in the street patois he'd learned here years before: "You mus' be a Republican, blud. You ain't knowin' how to tell a joke, you just knowin' how to be one."

Out of embarrassment for Morgan, or maybe out of realization they'd be on the news that night, the crowd tittered.

"I brought your probation officers along," Morgan added as the Secret Service agents flanked him. "They tell me it's a while since they seen you."

"Yeah, well, I be goin' now," the street performer bowed, reaching deftly for the coin-filled cowboy hat at his feet and dashing off. The crowd applauded, then watched Morgan expectantly.

"Damn, I forgot to bring my hat," he said.

Someone handed him a Mets cap. "All right. Where you wanna start?"

For fifteen minutes he bantered with the crowd, sharing cigarettes with bearded burnouts, dancing with fat black women to bass lines thumping out of boom boxes, and putting on a couple of Hispanic kids in muscle shirts by clenching a fist and shouting "Puerto Rico libre!" He stopped only when Buford pointed out the presence of reporters and police. "Oh-oh, party's over," Morgan announced, casting an exaggeratedly rueful glance at the men in blue. "Well, I guess they gonna put me in my cage again. I see you people. I see you in the White House!" he proclaimed.

The cap filled up with bills and coins. Buford stuffed the money in his pockets.

Safely back in Molineaux's studio, Morgan whipped off six straight issue speeches on the first try, then read with brio sixteen of my local scripts. News reports that night and the next morning indicated that his surprise appearance caused a positive sensation. In our nightly conference call it was suggested that he make an unannounced appearance every day until the videos were done, but we nixed the idea after Erika said that it would diminish what we'd gained.

But not even Morgan's romp, and the upward blip it brought us in the polls, could mitigate the tension as the pace wore on. Casselwaite broke into tears each time Morgan ordered a rewrite of an issues script. Cheng suffered cognitive failure when it came to programming both NABR and congressional districts by zip codes, causing Fallon to berate her constantly. Erika, maternal instincts aroused, helped Kathy iron out the problem. Ishikawa, in the office next to mine, slammed his phone down with a seething "dildo brain!" each time he talked to someone from the party about money.

As for me, uninterrupted it would have taken a week to complete my scripts, but my concentration was constantly broken by calls from reporters. The correspondent from *The New Yorker,* a smart, thorough veteran of countless national campaigns, visited one afternoon in person. Considering how much respect she and her magazine commanded, I didn't have the option of refusing an interview. But I did have the option of withholding our true plans, which I exercised when she inquired about the construction going on in the warehouse.

Another reporter pestered me about Morgan's height. "What the hell does that pertain to?" I snapped. "I'll tell you when I get the information," came the coy reply. We went around and around until I finally called New York and asked Morgan how tall he was. "Six feet on the nose," he said, which I dutifully relayed to the reporter. "On the nose?" he asked. "No fraction?" No, no fraction, I said. "Too bad. The taller candidate has won the last twenty-six elections. The President is six feet and a quarter inch."

"Six and three eighths! Morgan's six feet and three eighths!" I spluttered into the receiver. Too late, though; the bastard had hung up.

Somehow everything got done. Casselwaite and I wrote scripts. Morgan read them. Molineaux edited the tapes. Cheng prepared the automation program to produce the finished videos. Buford hired workers to handle orders and mailings. We had Molineaux express-mail several segments back to us and made some test runs of the program. Not only did it work, but the product looked half-decent, hardly like the rush job it actually was. We sent sample copies back to New York, where Fallon, Molineaux, and Morgan gave approval. Everyone was satisfied.

Except for Lucy Casselwaite. After she handed in her final script Fallon fired her, saying Morgan had decided to compose the acceptance speech himself and wouldn't need a writer for the fall campaign. In keeping with the status generally accorded speechwriters, no reporters followed up after I sent out a press release attributing Casselwaite's departure to "creative differences."

14

"... AND SO, LADIES and gentlemen, it is my honor to introduce to this convention the next president of the United States, Jack Morgan!"

(Morgan strides to the podium, stands erect, smiles, and waves both hands. Thunderous applause. Balloons. Confetti. Waving placards. The P.A. system blares George Harrison's "Ding Dong Ding Dong," repeating the lyrics "Ring out the old ring in the new/Ring out the false ring in the true." Network cameras focus on vigorously applauding Senator Hutson talking with fellow members of the Georgia delegation.)

"Thank you . . . thank you . . . thank you very much."

(Crowd noise slowly subsides.)

"My fellow Democrats, I accept your nomination for president of the United States."

(More thunderous applause. More balloons. More confetti. Placards wave again. Sound of screechy plastic horns. Morgan nods acknowledgment. Noise slowly subsides.)

"Ladies and gentlemen, acceptance speeches are intended to be galvanizers. I get off a couple wisecracks

116

at the other party, you applaud. I reaffirm our traditional commitment to the little guy, you applaud. I remind us that we have to work together, you applaud.

"That's been the standard Democratic acceptance speech since Vietnam, and I need not remind you that the last seven times we used it, it didn't work.

"So tonight, and for the rest of this campaign, I'm trying something else. It may not make you break out into cheers. It's not designed for that. But I hope it makes you break out into thought. Thought about what kind of nation we're becoming, and what kind of future we all have if we continue down this road.

"My fellow citizens, I will put it to you bluntly. A pair of threats loom over us. Threats that we are not addressing, because the perpetrators of the threats are working night and day to take our minds off them. And perhaps, too, because we'd rather that we *didn't* think about them.

"They aren't secrets. In fact they've been well known for years. But since the advent of Republican control in 1981, we haven't done a thing to stop them. Quite the opposite in fact. And as a consequence they've gotten worse.

"If we don't stop them now, we never will. We will forfeit our democratic way of life. And we will forfeit the great bounty God has given us.

"The overriding purpose of a Morgan administration will be to stop these threats dead in their tracks. To stamp them out and build safeguards against their return, so that our children and grandchildren will never know they once existed."

(Muted applause. Network cameras focus in on anxious faces in New Hampshire delegation.)

"Ladies and gentlemen, if you've got a bar of soap that isn't any different from the other bars of soap, except perhaps for its perfume, how do you make the public buy it?

117

"*Ad*vertising.

"If you've got a soft drink that's essentially the same as other soft drinks, how do you make the public buy it?"

(Crowd joins in.) "*Ad*vertising.

"If you've got a boxy little car that isn't very different from the other boxy little cars out on the market, how do you make the public buy it?"

(More of crowd joins in.) "*Ad*vertising.

"And, ladies and gentlemen, if you've got a politician who isn't very different from the other politicians, how do you make the public buy him?"

(Entire crowd joins in; some laughter.) "*Ad*vertising.

"Yes, advertising. The same way we sell soap and soft drinks, we sell politicians. We all know why it's wrong. Politics is real life. It's money, it's jobs, it's war, it's peace. It's basic human rights. It is survival. But we've reduced it to a war of propaganda. Whose commercials are more clever. Fifteen-second sound bites. Photo opportunities. Gut-wrencher slogans.

"That, fellow Americans, is the first threat that we face. It imperils our democracy, because it turns the most important issues of our time, as well as our leaders, into commodities. Simplified. Sensationalized. Trivialized.

"Think about it this way. Do you think that in this time of hundred-dollar haircuts, thousand-dollar suits, and million-dollar smiles we'd elect as president a stooped, plain, bearded, moody hayseed with a high-pitched voice and a wife who's insane? Much as we might like to think we would, you know we wouldn't. And yet I've just described our country's greatest president, Abe Lincoln.

"Imagine the insult to that man's dignity if he were forced to campaign like we do today. Can you see him forcing a smile and making a thirty-second pitch for himself on a TV commercial, knowing, as he did, what lay ahead for the United States? Can you see him explaining his position on slavery and secession in fifteen seconds? When he debated Douglas, they went on for seven hours! Seven hours, ladies and gentlemen! And people paid attention! The only things we spend that much time doing these days is working, sleeping, and watching our TVs.

"Again, this isn't something we became aware of just this year. We've been decrying the decline of public discourse for almost forty years. But no one does a thing about it. They're afraid the other guy will gain advantage if they don't play along. Well, fellow Americans, someone has to brake the skid. I have thought about it long and hard, and I've decided, come what may, that *I* will be that man."

(Applause.)

"I am not a bar of soap or soft drink. The things I have to talk about are of the utmost importance, not just to me but to every one of you. I respect you too much, and I respect myself too much. And therefore I will not reduce my campaign to a made-for-TV sales pitch."

(Applause.)

"I will not careen across the country searching out the perfect photo opportunity. Instead I will stay home. I will meet reporters every day on my front porch and talk about the issues, and if they do their jobs responsibly, what I say will be faithfully passed on to you, without distortion. And all of you are welcome to visit. If you've got a question, come on down! If circumstance permits, I'll answer you in person.

"But if Toledo in the summer isn't your idea of fun—"

(Laughter. Cameras zoom in on Ohio delegation.)

"—I've got another plan. Even as I speak, my staff is in the final stages of assembling videos that outline, in

119

detail, my stands on all the issues. Not hype, issues. You should see numbers flashing on your television screen."

(Two eleven-digit numbers appear on screen.)

"Those are toll-free numbers you can call to get your free Jack Morgan videos. The top number, 1-800-ASK-JACK, is for phone orders. An operator will come on the line, ask your address, and ask which specific issues you want to hear from me about. The bottom number is for fax orders—1-800-FAX-JACK. Give us your full address, including zip code, and note the issues you're most interested in.

"In a couple of days your video will arrive, and you can watch it at your leisure. Remember, this is at no cost to you. And, except to publicize these numbers in simple ten-second spots, I will not bombard the airwaves with commercials. I will not spoil your evenings with offensive and misleading ads.

"This election, then, isn't just a contest between myself and my opponent. It's a referendum on democracy."

(Cautious but prolonged applause.)

"It's up to you, ladies and gentlemen. How seriously do you take the democratic process? If democracy to you is no more important than the brand of soap you use or soda pop you drink, then by all means vote for my opponent. But I will not be part of that. I will not put out a feel-good image as a smokescreen while I reward the rich, deprive the disadvantaged, and ruin our environment and common heritage."

(Sustained applause.)

"I will not be a fascist with a smiling face, showering you repeatedly with half-truths, until you can't help but believe them."

(Louder applause.)

"I love America too much. I love democracy too much. . . ."

(Morgan yields to roar of crowd. Standing ovation.

Waving placards. P.A. system blares "Ding Dong Ding Dong" again. Morgan smiles broadly.)

"And I say to my opponent, Mr. President, I dare you to come out from behind your protective wall of PR men. Let's go one-on-one against each other in a no-holds-barred, freewheeling debate—"

(Another uproar. Morgan waits.)

"—where we question each other directly, with follow-ups, and the sole job of the moderator is to make sure that we don't exceed our time limits."

(Shouts and cheers of approval. Morgan looks hard at the crowd, then at the camera, until noise wanes.)

"Let me go on to the second threat. This one threatens not just us but the entire world. It is environmental holocaust.

"I say holocaust, even though it's not as horrible as gas chambers or mushroom clouds, because if we continue to ignore the global fouling of the earth, the cataclysm that we face will make a world war look like mere annoyance by comparison.

"Half a billion refugees from flooded coastlines, including millions from our own East Coast. Famine from unending drought in farmlands, including the Midwest. A drinking-water shortage, as aquifers dry up and ocean water infiltrates freshwater reserves. A tenfold increase in cancer, cataracts, and respiratory disease. And then, as a consequence of the political and economic upheavals these disasters will inevitably cause, real violence and war.

"If this is not a holocaust, nothing is.

"We've known about the problem for a quarter century. Terms like *global warming, acid rain, ozone depletion,* and *toxic waste* have been a part of our vocabulary since the nineteen-eighties. Words like *pollution* and *extinction* go back much, much further. But under twenty-eight years of Republican rule we've done only the most token things to stave this threat. Instead of

121

curbing causes of the coming holocaust, they occasionally pass legislation that keeps destruction at its current level, which is the equivalent of saying to your teenaged daughter, 'We don't mind you're pregnant, so long as you stay just a *little* pregnant.' "

(Laughter. Scattered applause.)

"Yes, there's always an excuse to go on fouling our nest. Reagan said no nation conserved its way to greatness. Bush said he wouldn't stop the country to clean the air. Great slogans, eh? Simple, sensational—and stupid."

(Laughter and nods of agreement.)

"Then came the debt crisis of the nineties, and the subsequent recession—all of it, I might emphasize, a product of the opposition's harebrained economics—and the trumped-up charge that environmental safeguards are a drag on the economy.

"My opponent says we can't restore environmental regulations, we're on the verge of full recovery. But that's another advertising line. The assumption is we must go on polluting to make money. It's a big lie my opponent and his predecessors have been repeating for so long that most of us believe it.

"But it isn't true, my friends. It isn't true at all. You can have prosperity and preservation. And that will be the overriding object of a Morgan administration. We will put the *eco* back in economics."

(Applause.)

"Ours is a wondrous economic system. It follows profit with the unerring logic of a computer. Today profit lies in exploitation of the planet earth. In pollution. In destruction.

"But we can change that. We can put profit into preservation. We can put American industry at the forefront of sustainable technology, which not only will save the environment but will be a long-term boon to our economy."

(Mild applause.)

"It will take a lot of detail work. Many short-term sacrifices. And it will take a willingness to absorb a few political hits. Not everyone is going to be happy with what we propose. But that's a president's job: to make the tough decisions. I won't just *talk* about them. I will *make* them."

(Applause.)

"I will put a stop to the boondoggles. The dam building, the highways to nowhere, the high-tech energy plants that never work. It's time to put a lid on the pork barrel. To end this welfare for the wealthy that costs taxpayers and environment alike so dearly."

(Mild applause.)

"We will create a market for recycled products, reducing our demand for raw materials and the flow of solid waste."

(Applause.)

"We will give tax breaks for research and development of practical, environment-friendly products like hydrogen-fueled cars and substitutes for harmful chemicals."

(Applause.)

"And we will cease the witless giveaway of our priceless natural lands."

(Vigorous applause. Sound of plastic horns. Cameras focus in on California delegate wearing GREENPEACE button on lapel.)

"All this and more, my friends. We will make environmental health, along with human rights, the cornerstones of our foreign policy."

(Applause persists. Morgan has to shout.)

"We won't afflict the Third World with grandiose construction projects that destroy their ecosystems. No longer will we ship them pesticides we've outlawed in our own land. We will encourage them to preserve their wildernesses and endangered species. And we will help them put a lid on population growth through equitable resource distribution and family planning rather than through famine, drought, and civil war."

(More cheers. Minority delegates shake fists in air.)

"We will reassert the worldwide leadership in human rights that we lost back in the eighties—this time as a force for everybody's long-term good."

(Long, clamorous ovation.)

"In closing, my fellow Americans, I would like to point out that the two threats I've described here intersect. Advertising tells us to consume, consume, consume. And it is the overconsumption of resources that endangers the health of our planet.

"Where did the consumption ethic come from? Certainly not from our Judeo-Christian heritage. The Bible warns repeatedly against extravagance, from Ecclesiastes' 'He that loveth silver shall not be satisfied with silver' to Matthew 19:24, 'It is easier for a camel to go through the eye of a needle than for a rich man to enter into the kingdom of God.'

"Nor did it arise from the American tradition. Our founding fathers and mothers were renowned not for their consumerism but for their thrift and industriousness. Think of old Ben Franklin. 'A stitch in time saves nine.' 'Early to bed and early to rise makes a man healthy, wealthy and wise.'

"This, ladies and gentlemen, is our heritage, not the wasteful buying-frenzy advertisers whip us into. I say the time has come to repudiate the hucksters, to take America back from the flimflam men. The time has come to bring back thrift and industry as American ideals."

(Applause.)

"The Morgan administration will be a thrifty administration. No more of the penny wisdom and pound foolishness that measures success purely in terms of quarterly bottom lines. We will redefine the term *effi-*

ciency to mean what does the most good for the most people over the long term."

(Applause.)

"We will be a farsighted administration, willing to infuriate the special interests so that America might prosper down the road."

(Applause.)

"So that a generation from now, two generations from now, our children and grandchildren will have a land cleaner, fresher, and richer than the land we have today. For the children, ladies and gentlemen, for the children."

(Cheers. Sustained applause. Over the noise:)

"God bless America. Thank you all very much!"

(Morgan steps back from the podium. Convention-eers rise as one and shout and clap and sing. Elena Morgan comes onstage, kisses and embraces Morgan. He holds her hand up in the air. They wave. Perez and his wife come out. The four link hands and wave.)

15

THIS IS WHAT you saw and heard if you watched the leading network:

"Well, there you have it. At the outset Morgan told us this wouldn't be the standard acceptance speech, and indeed it wasn't. He outlined what he considers two threats to America, the effect of advertising on democracy and what he termed environmental holocaust. There was very little of the usual Democratic rhetoric, the pro-labor, pro–civil rights, pro–little-guy language we've come to expect from Democratic candidates.

"We turn now to our veteran political commentators for analysis. Let's start with you, Jeraldo."

"Jack Morgan—demagogue or honest politician? Alan, to me it's a question of, Is Jack Morgan standing up for things that he believes in, or is this something he's doing out of desperation? He's seen the polls. He knows he's got to take some big risks if he hopes to win November fourth."

"So you're suggesting it's a desperate move."

"I'd have to interview him on my show, that's at four P.M. each weekday on most of these stations, to know for sure."

"B.J., your opinion?"

"Move along folks, move along. Just another Democratic crash and burn, it's not nice to rubberneck. It was a dull speech, Al, filled with the usual disingenuous trash. Even Morgan knows the government's been paralyzed for thirty years, and shame on him if he really thinks electing him will change that. The fact is the federal government is totally irrelevant to people's lives, and you folks at home shouldn't give a hoot about what happens in the Capitol. Lord knows your elected representatives don't."

"I take it, then, that Jack Morgan has earned himself a spot on your Richard Nixon Memorial Enemies List?"

"In fact he's going straight into my hall of fame, right up there with Ted Kennedy, Jane Fonda, and anyone who believes in critical thinking without being able to define it in less than fifty words."

This is what you heard that night if you set your radio dial to the liberal late-night talk show:

"We begin our open lines with Baltimore, Maryland. Hello."

"Hi, Lare. Love your show."

"Thank you. What's your question?"

"I heard your guests talking about Morgan's speech. I was wondering what you thought about it personally."

"Thought it was terrific."

"I—"

"Thought his analysis was on the nose."

"I did—"

"Thought it will help the Democrats a great deal in November."

"My—"

"Thought it was the best speech by a politician since Cuomo. It will be interesting to see how the President responds. Thank you for the call. Can you see them jumpin' around in the White House, Chris? What do we do now, gang, the Democrats know what they're doing. We go to Toledo, Ohio. Hello."

"Good evening from Jack Morgan's backyard."

"A call from Jack Morgan's backyard. How's the lawn, sir?"

"Nothin' but weeds, I'm tellin' you. You wanna know what I think of Jack Morgan?"

"Go ahead, sir."

"If he was on fire I wouldn't cross the street to [bleep] on him."

"Right. Sleep well, sir. Kansas City, hello. . . ."

This is what you heard if you listened to the conservative late-night radio talk show:

"Williamsport, Pennsylvania—where Chinese Little Leaguers beat us at our own game every year. Welcome to the show."

"Thanks, Russ, from a devoted dittohead. Can I ask you a question? When will those Democrats quit whinin' and start respecting the intelligence of the people of this country?"

"Good question. Wish I knew the answer. You'd think by now the message would be pretty clear to them."

"You know, Morgan made me feel like I was stupid. Like I'm a dupe of all the advertisers because I watch TV or see a billboard. Only he knows how to think straight."

"Classic liberal snobbery. I mean, classic! They know more than you do. And that attack on advertising —that is the sound a Marxist makes when he claps one hand together. Let me tell you people the truth, since only *I* will tell it to you: There is *nothing* wrong with self-promotion."

"Right, Russ. There was something else I noticed. He only quoted from the Bible twice. And one of the quotes came from Ecclesiastes. I don't know if you saw that study done by the Foundation for the Lord? They found Ecclesiastes is overwhelmingly the favorite book of liberals."

"Good point, Williamsport. Thank you for the call. We go to Toledo, Ohio. Hello, you're on three hundred eighty-eight stations coast to coast."

"Dittos, Russ. Know what I think of Jack Morgan?"

"What?"

"If he was on fire I wouldn't cross the street to [bleep] on him."

"You, friend, are with me on the cutting edge of social evolution."

And if you couldn't fall asleep and watched a late-night TV news show, this is what you saw and heard after the opening fanfare and two minutes of excerpts from the speech:

"Can Jack Morgan win? We'll be asking our guests, Senator Matthew Sutchens, Democrat of Oregon, coming to us from our studio at the convention center, and, here in Washington, Warren Harding Ritter, senior fellow at the Heritage Foundation. Gentlemen, welcome."

(The two, on split screen, nod.)

"Senator Sutchens, let's start with you. Was this the kind of speech the Democrats can get behind? At times it seemed the delegates were tentative in their support."

"Well, Todd, as Morgan said himself, this wasn't meant to be the standard rouser of a speech. But to answer your question directly, as Morgan no doubt would, yes, I think it was a speech the Democrats can get behind. It was inspiring, it was powerful, and it rang true. He's backing up his words with actions, which we politicians are accused of seldom doing, with some justification. And I think his stand on the environment is something everybody can agree on."

"Even in your home state, where the logging industry employs so many people?"

"Especially in my home state, Todd. Oregonians are acutely aware of the value of a good environment. That is to say, not how many dollars each tree can bring, but how much pride of place and life enhancement forests can provide. I think—"

"Mr. Ritter, your comment, sir."

"I think Jack Morgan's done the country a huge favor with this speech. He's shown his true colors as an anti–free-enterprise, tree-hugging radical totally out of step with the American mainstream. He wants a nation of bike-riding vegetarians. And if I might add another point—"

"Quickly. We've got twenty seconds."

"This condemnation of photo opportunities and twenty-second sound bites is way off base. The fact is, twenty-second sound bites are a blessing for democracy. Instead of letting politicians drone on and on with non-committal answers, you get a yes-or-no, right-up-front response, which the politician is held to by a public that remembers. He can claim all he wants that advertising and whatever else subvert our system, but that's his fantasy."

"More right after this."

This is what you read if you picked up the national edition of *The New York Times* the next morning:

THE BULLY PULPIT

Election Process Has Been 'Reduced to War of Propaganda'

Presidential nominee Jack Morgan stunned the Democratic National Convention in his acceptance speech last night by announcing his campaign would be a 'referendum on democracy,' and that he would eschew such standard campaign methods as extensive travel, tightly structured press conferences, and television advertising.

Morgan also announced that his primary concern as president would be preservation of the environment. "If we continue to ignore the global fouling of the earth, the cataclysm that we face will make a world war look like mere annoyance by comparison," he said.

Although Morgan took several swipes at the President, at one point promising "I will not put out a feel-good image as a smokescreen while I reward the rich, deprive the disadvantaged, and ruin our environment and common heritage," and was often interrupted for applause, his speech was generally somber in tone.

He used Abraham Lincoln as an example of how advertising had distorted political discourse. According to Morgan,

who noted that the Lincoln-Douglas debates were hourslong exchanges, the unmediagenic Lincoln would have been hard-pressed to explain his stand on slavery and secession in a fifteen-second sound bite or thirty-second commercial.

Instead of advertising, Morgan will promote his candidacy through daily press conferences and videos available at no charge to interested voters. (The videos may be obtained by calling 1-800-ASK-JACK or by sending fax requests for videos to 1-800-FAX-JACK. The telephone numbers will appear in short TV commercials, the only commercials the Morgan campaign will run.) Morgan will conduct the campaign exclusively from his home in Ottawa Hills, Ohio, rather than traverse the country, a custom he dismissed as "searching out the perfect photo opportunity."

Morgan also challenged the President to a wide-ranging debate where the two would question one another directly instead of being questioned by a panel of reporters, which has been the norm in past debates.

Daniel Steinhardt, press

131

secretary to Morgan, said the Morgan camp expects to contact the President's staff and begin negotiations over terms of the debate within the next few days. "We won't budge on the one-on-one aspect of this," he said. "We want a real debate, not a dog-and-pony show."

Steinhardt also said the Democrats expect up to a million requests for videos over the next few days. "We're giving the American people a choice," he said. "Either politics as usual or a breakthrough to a higher level of discussion. We're betting that they're sick of what's been going on for the last thirty years."

In declaring environmental protection his top priority, Morgan labeled the threat to the environment a potential holocaust, "even though it's not as horrible as gas chambers or mushroom clouds." He briefly spelled out a proposal, which he called "putting the eco back in economics," to address the threat.

Under the plan, the federal government would establish tax breaks, subsidies, and other fiscal incentives to industry for preserving the environment. Press secretary Steinhardt told reporters the candidate would "speak more about this, in much greater detail" over the coming weeks.

Morgan also called for an end to the sale of federal lands as a way of paying off the national deficit. And, in a remark widely seen as an attempt to distance himself from the Democrats' reputation for free spending, he added "it's time to put a lid on the pork barrel, to end this welfare for the wealthy that costs taxpayers and the environment alike so dearly."

In regard to foreign policy, Morgan promised to make the environment and human rights prime considerations. He talked mostly of the problems of the Third World, promising to end the international sale of harmful pesticides and to promote family planning to reduce the rate of population growth.

Reaction to the speech ran along partisan lines. "I've waited forty years for a candidate I could march behind without a shred of reservation, and I've finally got one," beamed six-term House member Altenua White (D-TX), a delegate to the convention.

"At first I was surprised, but then I found myself just nodding yes, yes, yes to everything he said," said Senator Hilbert Bidings of Nebraska, also a convention delegate. "It will be a little harder getting the Democratic message across without commercials, but like Morgan said, someone's got to brake the skid [of declining political discourse], and I'm proud that he, and we as Democrats, are the ones to do it. It's the ultimate in patriotism, a great day for democracy."

On the Republican side, the Reverend Grover Mandias, chairman of the party, said, "What I want to know is, where's the money for these tax breaks and subsidies and whatnot going to come from, especially if he's cutting out the Land Rebate program? In that respect it's Democratic politics as usual, spend, spend, spend, without regard to revenue."

Mandias went on to say that Morgan's call for an advertisement-free campaign was motivated by Morgan's second-place standing in the polls, as well as the Democrats' traditional fund-raising disadvantage. "They know they can't beat us fair and square, so they figure they'll try this," he said.

(The full text of Morgan's acceptance speech may be found on page A-16.)

If you read *USA Today* instead of *The New York Times,* this is what you saw on the front page:

MORGAN: NOT A BAR OF SOAP

Jack Morgan launched his race for presidency of the USA with a speech that left many delegates to the Democratic convention in a state of shock.

Among the things he said:

Advertising is ruining elections. Candidates sell themselves like bars of soap or soft drinks.

Instead of advertising on TV and traveling across the USA, he will stay home and send issue-oriented videos to interested voters. Call 1-800-ASK-JACK for your free video, or fax Morgan at 1-800-FAX-JACK.

Morgan promised he wouldn't lie to the public over and over until the lies are accepted as the truth.

He challenged the President to a one-on-one debate with only a timekeeper between them.

You can visit Morgan at his Ohio home. See page A-2 for directions from all 50 states.

Also:

According to Morgan, neglect of the environment can bring on a holocaust if we don't start working right away to avoid it.

The world faces half a billion "environmental refugees" as the oceans rise. There will also be famine, water shortages, and disease.

Environmental regulation doesn't have to be a drag on the economy. "We can put American industry in the forefront of sustainable technology, which not only will save the environment, but will be a longterm boon to our economy," he said. For reaction from the business community, see the Money Section, page C-1.

Fixing the environment will take work. Morgan said not all of us will be happy with what he wants to do.

Morgan will help the Third World, but not with overblown projects that have backfired in the past.

He thinks Americans should be more like their forefathers and be thrifty. "Advertising tells us to consume, consume, consume. And it is the overconsumption of resources that endangers the health of our planet."

For the USA's reaction to the speech, see editorials, page A-14. Pro and con analysis from our guest columnists, page A-15.

If you happened to be in the front yard of my rented house the next morning and, like me, found the landlord staggering around with a two-foot pair of shears attempting to trim the hedge, this is what you would have heard:

"Big speech last night, eh? Guess that means you'll be stickin' 'round here till November. That's the only good thing I can say for that potlickin' bastard: He's good for local business. You do know he's a bastard, don't you? Son of a bitch's father had his cock in every pussy in Ohio. If his ass was on fire I wouldn't cross the street to piss on him."

And if you were part of the inner-circle meeting in Morgan's dining room the next night, this is what you would have heard from Erika Mitchell:

"Tracking poll results: Up fifteen percent among the baby-boomer generation. Up thirteen percent with women of all ages. Up seventeen among the college-educated. Up seven among minorities and first-time voters. Up thirteen in the Northeast, twelve in the Midwest, ten on the West Coast. Unchanged in the South, up three in the Southwest. And here's some very interesting news: nine percent defection from the other side to undecided, five percent from the other side to us.

"In plain English, you struck a nerve. You're in the lead by five percentage points."

16

THE NEXT WEEK brought good news and bad news. The good news: the surge in Morgan's favor didn't stop the night of his acceptance speech. On Monday the "secular" polls came out, and even the conservative Gallup showed Morgan with a six-point lead. Harris had him up by ten. Then *Time* and *Newsweek* added to the momentum with flattering front-page stories. By the end of the week Mitchell's daily tracking polls had Morgan out in front by as many as twelve points. It was a twenty-point swing in our direction, more than we imagined possible. Even Fallon started believing my plan could work.

The bad news was that Morgan's lead was built on image, not issues. In-depth interviews with voters indicated that they most liked Morgan's character: his toughness, proven by his willingness to stand up to his fellow Democrats; his boldness, as evidenced by his acceptance speech; his devotion to principles (although which principles the interviewees were hard-pressed to identify); and his sincerity, which had been Morgan's strong point all along. Only twenty-two percent of new Morgan voters said his environmental stand was the primary reason for their switch.

Consequently the inner circle divided anew, this time over whether to push the image or the issues. Fallon, Molineaux, and Buford lobbied hard to keep the campaign image-based. I led the fight to have Morgan hammer on the issues. But I fought alone; Mitchell, whose word would have settled the matter, and who I knew from lunch at Mahatma's was as passionate about the environment as I, maintained her usual studied silence throughout the dispute, and there was nothing I could do to flush her out. And so it was decided that until his numbers started going down, our emphasis would be on image.

For me the loss was particularly embarrassing in that I'd promised reporters Morgan would speak in depth about the issues in the coming weeks. We'd made believers of the press, as evidenced by the friendly cover stories in the major magazines. They were thrilled they wouldn't have to spend the autumn dashing hither and yon in pursuit of the candidate and their daily story. More important, they began to think they just might have a winner here and that they'd ride his coattails to the glamour jobs in Washington, D.C. And so at the daily press conferences held on Morgan's lawn they acted more like puppies than full-grown wolves, compliantly recording his remarks on paper, tape, or video and confining queries to the topics he raised.

I was sure we'd squander the goodwill if we didn't come through on our promise to provide substance. Sooner or later one of them would notice the lack of meat in Morgan's remarks and do a think-piece on it, and within a day or two the entire pack would be braying at us ominously.

Morgan, amenable as he was to relying on image ("Hey, whatever works"), was nonetheless also smart enough to realize he couldn't gloss the issues till November. He decided his Monday policy speeches indeed would be substantive, but instead of boring voters with necessarily complicated explanations of his environmental stands, he'd pick easier and more dramatic targets. He devoted his first major statement on the issues to campaign reform—and to putting a potential liability behind him.

"I was very lucky," he began. "My dad left me some bucks, and with the help of God and good advisers I built a successful enterprise. That's where I got the funds to finance my first campaign. But I wonder, would I have made it in politics if I didn't own a fortune? Would I have had the freedom to operate in the Senate as independently as I have the last ten years if I was middle-class? I think the answer is obviously no.

"Politics is just like other businesses in that when you take out a loan to get set up, you have to pay the money back. But in other businesses you pay the money back with interest, and everything is square. In politics you don't pay back the loan with interest. You pay it back by influencing legislation. Not just by how you vote in subcommittee or committee or on the Senate floor, but the little deals you cut with colleagues, or even by the things you *don't* do, like not introducing a bill, or not cosponsoring someone else's.

"So your real constituency, it turns out, isn't the voters. It's the lenders who give you the money to *persuade* the voters to vote for you. I didn't have any lenders when I ran for Senate, so I didn't have anybody to pay back. I could speak and vote straight from my conscience. I was answerable only to the people of Ohio. It was a great arrangement, the way politics is supposed to be. And now that I'm running for president, I still don't have to toady to the special interests, because the campaign's financed by the Fed, and I'm not doing stuff that requires funds above what Uncle Sam provides.

"But do you see the problem here? I got this far because I'm rich enough to spend a few million dollars on a campaign and not miss it. What about the qualified candidates out there who don't have millions to blow? This is another way we've limited democracy. If you want to be a senator or representative and vote your conscience, you *have* to be a multimillionaire. Everybody else has got to pay the piper.

"And who is the piper? The lobbyists. The influence peddlers. Anyone with lots of money and an interest in federal legislation. Bankers. Agribusiness. Oil. Autos. It's disgusting, sleazy business. I know, because my best friend is in charge of Citizens Against the Trade Deficit. He tells me all about it.

"That's why we haven't gotten any real environmental legislation through. Every time we try to clean up the air, the auto industry gets on us. Every time we try to limit pesticides, the agribusiness guys sit on our chests. It's gotten to the point where some senators introduce good environmental bills *knowing* that they'll never pass. All they want is to extort contributions. The money comes from PACs and other interests that don't like the legislation, and the senators withdraw their bills. No law—the PACs are happy. And the politician has the dough and crusader image he needs to get reelected.

"That's got to end. Steinhardt's passing around my five-page outline for campaign reform. It's designed to end the preoccupation with fund raising that overshadows every other thing that happens in the House and Senate—and the White House. It's a bipartisan approach, depriving Democrats and Republicans equally of their fund-raising advantages. Basically I want a Constitutional amendment that calls for all federal campaigns to be funded by the government. An amendment, because we need to get around Supreme Court decisions that equate campaign contributions with free speech. The challenger gets one hundred twenty percent of the incumbent's allotment. No other contributions, not even out of the candidate's own pocket, would be allowed.

"The big-lie perpetrators are gonna say, 'Why should we pay for the campaigns of the scumballs who represent us? Isn't it bad enough we pay them exorbitant salaries?' The answer is twofold: First, we wouldn't have this many scumballs if raising money was irrelevant, and two, we already *do* pay, in the form of favorable deals these guys cut in Congress for their wealthy cronies. In the long run federally financed national campaigns will save us money—and restore integrity.

"If you've got any questions, I'll be here tomorrow, same place, same time, good Lord willin' and the creek don't rise."

And then I had to clarify. I was Morgan's warm-up act and apologist, presiding at the podium before and after his appearance. The "before" part was a snap: I announced what Morgan would be speaking on and did my best to focus the pack's attention on what we wanted them to relay to the voters. The "after" part was a bear: Without the benefit of rehearsal or, oftentimes, any idea as to what he meant, I had to clarify any offhand comments Morgan made.

As Morgan undoubtedly expected, everybody wanted to know about his link to Citizens Against the Trade Deficit. Did he exercise some influence over that PAC? (No. His best friend ran it, and they talked in general terms about how PACs are run, so he learned how reprehensible the business was.) Didn't Buford use CAT-Dee to reward Morgan's friends and punish Morgan's enemies? (Morgan never had anything to do with CAT-Dee's fund disbursements.) Oh, come on, Dan, Buford is a close adviser. He couldn't have doled out the money against Morgan's interests. (I doubt he ever did, that's true. But it's not as if they stayed up nights going over whom to punish and whom to reward.) Which colleagues received the most from CAT-Dee? (I don't know. You'll have to look it up.) Why don't *you* look it up and get back to us? Or better still, why don't you set up an interview with Buford for us? (I'll try to get him for you.)

Morgan's confessed connection to a PAC became the first contretemps of the campaign. But despite Republican efforts to lock public attention on it, the matter quickly disappeared, because the next morning Buford categorically denied any Morgan involvement in CAT-Dee contributions. The few reporters who bothered to investigate further found sleaze—which Morgan had admitted—but nothing illegal.

Morgan's preemptive admission actually worked to our advantage. The daily media, satisfied that their questioning proved their "objectivity," then bent over backward stressing Morgan's innocence and gave serious attention to campaign reform, which made it look like Morgan was again boldly addressing issues that everybody else in Washington avoided.

The net result: no change in our lead.

Countering such tempests took the bulk of my work days. From one part truth, one part half-truth, and one part lies I assembled plausible, affirmative, leak-proof explanations for Morgan's remarks. I'd lose sleep at night probing my "clarifications" for weakness. I'd have dinner with Kaya and not pay her the least attention, occasionally bringing my fork to my mouth while jotting down notes and trying to anticipate reporters' takes on what I planned to say next morning. I could feel my body breaking down from stress and overwork. And we had ninety days to go.

Morgan didn't seem to appreciate the danger of loose talk. I'd warn him to speak more circumspectly to the press, explaining that the election could still turn on a single rash comment. Most politicians would never need such an admonition; no amount of coaxing could get them to speak freely in front of a notepad or microphone. But Morgan seemed to relish his new role as chatterbox, and to enjoy my discomfort as well. It made me think of Casselwaite's remark that I was first among equals. If this was what being first was like, I wondered what everybody else was going through at Morgan's hands.

Sometimes I'd sit in my office and stare at the eraser on my pencil. It was a Blackfeet Indian pencil—in Democratic campaigns every purchase must be politically correct—brand-new, the eraser edges pink and sharp. I'd erase something, just to smudge the pinkness and round away the crown. That's what's happening to me, I thought. Every time I lust after the girl he's screwing, every time I lie to make him look good to the press, I rub myself in gunk and fray away my edge. By November I'll be worn down to the metal.

At first I told myself the root cause of my discontent was Kathy Cheng. In hopes of ridding her from my brain I magnified her every little fault into a fatal defect —as in, whew, weren't you lucky you didn't wind up with *that!* I obsessed on her widow's peak, on the two thick, pointy hairs that stuck out from her left nostril like a snail's antennae, on the flaky patch of skin on her cheek she tried to mask with makeup.

I gloried in the way she looked completely overwhelmed at inner circle meetings, seldom contributing to tactical discussions. She knew she was out of her league, and many a time I was tempted to expose her during heated arguments by asking "What do you think, Kathy?" But I never did. It would have been too easy and too obvious. And besides, she was the boss's lay.

But blaming Kathy Cheng was just a dodge. My discontent was really with Jack Morgan. It wasn't only that his careless comments made my life so hard. It had also become clear that I cared more for the environment than he, and he would never take the risk of saying what I wanted him to say: that the game was over for the bullies and the time had come to punish them for all the misery and mayhem they had caused.

Yes, that's right, punish them. I hated them for not knowing. For not caring. For wanting, wanting, wanting, without ever giving. I wanted them beat up, grounded for a century without the possibility of early pardon. It was the only way to teach them. Whether they'd actually *learn* anything from their punishment except resentment was another question, but at least the world would have a chance to breathe while they were disciplined.

That's what I wanted Morgan to be—an ecological Joe Stalin. Someone who would make the oil spillers *lick* the crude up from the beach. Someone who would make the chemists *drink* the pesticides they brewed. Someone who would confiscate the hunters' guns, drive them to the outskirts of a postage-stamp-sized wilderness, and say, "You've got five minutes' head start. Then I'm coming after you with this here rifle."

But that crazy Morgan was not.

17

MOST OF THEM were gray. They came in RVs or American-made sedans and waited in the heat until the shuttle bus arrived. The women passed the time chattering. The men stared into space and grunted when the women mentioned them in conversation. Once the shuttle finally arrived they clambered aboard slowly, one step at a time, the women smiling and saying hello to the driver, the men just nodding. At least the bus was air-conditioned and they could get out of the heat.

The bus rolled onto Central Avenue and passed beneath the I-75 overpass into the lunchbox part of town. Here the houses were the same size as the ones they lived in. Nothing to get excited about. But then the bus turned onto a side street, and then another, then another, and now the lots stretched out for acres, and the houses, when they could be seen behind the verdure, were enormous, stately, and impeccably maintained. They speculated on the price of what they saw. And then the bus came to a halt and someone said, "We must be gettin' close."

The first checkpoint. A burly man in black suit and sunglasses welcomed them and explained that except for camera totes and purses they wouldn't be allowed to carry bags off the bus. Even then all bags brought off the bus were subject to inspection. Passengers themselves were subject to a search. If anyone objected to these conditions they had to leave the bus at once and return to the parking lot. Nobody objected.

The bus revved up, proceeded half a mile over gentle, rolling hills, then stopped again before a driveway gate. This must be it, they whispered. More black-suited men in sunglasses. One boarded and exchanged nods with the driver. The gate swung open, the bus passed through. As the bus turned a curve, an immense but plain white Georgian house came into view. "This must be where he lives," they said, straining for a better glimpse.

The bus parked at the foot of an expansive lawn. As they disembarked, they were patted down; the female agents, who frisked the women, looked just like the male agents in those black suits, sunglasses, and ties. When all of them were off the bus its door snapped shut and the driver pulled away, leaving blue diesel fumes curling languidly in the hot, still air. "Ladies and gentlemen, if you'll follow me," implored a gray-suited young fellow who also wore sunglasses. "He's not Secret Service," the men—more involved in what was going on and more impressed by the security than they'd admit—assured the women.

They were correct. He was one of Buford's guards. He led them to rows of folding chairs set up beneath a canvas canopy. A hostess welcomed them to the candidate's home, promised they'd meet the candidate in a few moments, and distributed consent forms allowing the campaign to use their image in videos or other election materials. Then she explained the ground rules.

They'd have ten minutes. The candidate would answer their questions for five, then shake hands with each of them as they filed from the room. A photographer would take pictures, which would be available for a nominal fee a few minutes later. "We'd like to thank every one of you for coming and sharing in a little bit of history. Now if you'll follow me I'll take you to the waiting room."

They sat in the waiting room until the group in front was finished. The men looked disapprovingly at their watches, the better to convince the women they were unaffected by the moment. "Been an hour and a half since we pulled into the parking lot," they scoffed. "Don't seem worth it for just ten minutes. We'd have been better doin' what I suggested and headin' for the Michigan peninsula. It's cooler there, and prettier, and the fishin's good."

And then the double door to what in private times would be the living room opened, and they were welcomed in. More folding chairs.

The men sat forward, potbellies cradled on their thighs, breathing audibly. They became loquacious with one another. Clean, clipped conversation; man talk. "Good campground where, you say? Full hookups?" "Yeah, got a daughter down in Cincinnati, thought we'd stop off here en route. Prob'ly take Route 68 to 42 'cause there's construction on the Interstate just north of Dayton." "Arizona? We're from Idaho. Boise. Retired two years now, love it. Spend our winters in a park outside Orlando. Grandkids fly down for the holidays. Take 'em over to the Epcot Center—want them kids to learn some science."

A door on the far side of the room cracked open. A dozen Secret Service agents took equidistant positions along the walls before the candidate himself strode in, dressed in a light blue shirt, gray slacks, and loafers. Trailing him were two more Secret Service agents and a string of campaign staffers.

For a moment the people who had come to see him were bewildered. *That's* him? Looks different than on

TV and in the papers. Thinner and smaller. Got more color in his face. And that scar—by God it's something, ain't it?"

"All right. Good to see you all. I apologize for the delay, especially on a day like today when all of us would rather lounge around a pool. I'm grateful to you all for coming. We don't have much time, so let's get right down to your questions."

"Yeah," a crew-cut, porcine fellow raised a calloused hand. "I'm from El Paso, home of Fort Bliss. They say you're gunna shut a lot of bases down. You shut down Bliss, you're gunna kill the local economy and cut the muscle from America's defense. I got your video and you don't say one way or the other."

Molineaux, camcorder focused, closed in on the questioner, who scowled. If Morgan's answer was good, starting tomorrow this exchange would be included in videos sent to the El Paso region.

"Cut the muscle? Never. Cut the fat? For sure. You know, if a three-hundred-pound man has tremendous biceps, we're impressed. No one's gonna mess with that guy, we think. But size doesn't scare a lot of people. They know it's not enough that we be strong. We've also got to have the quickness, because a little guy with lots of tricks can outmaneuver us. So there's no two ways about it, the fat is gonna have to go. Lighter, faster ground forces, simpler air and sea technology. I haven't looked directly at the role Fort Bliss is playing. The military's just too big; it would take me years to analyze the role of every base all by myself. If it's muscle, it'll stay. If it's fat, I expect to close it.

"And another thing. Looking at defense strictly in terms of firepower is outmoded. What matters is, where are we weak? There are no friends among nations, only common interests. We're weakest where we most depend on strangers. Oil, that's our number-one weak spot. Sending the fleet into the Persian Gulf doesn't cure the weakness, it admits it. I'm gonna work like heck to wean us from dependency on oil. Another question?"

A spare, bearded, balding man in his early forties rose. "I want to commend you for embracing the environmental movement. It's been a long time coming. But it seems you don't understand that capitalism can't exist without exploitation of natural resources—and people, of course. So you can't just tinker with the system, you have to go to something totally new—"

Every now and then someone with an ideological drum to bang lectured Morgan on the imperfections of his vision. The environmentalists among them called for perfect little ecotowns and villages where streams replaced the downtown streets, forests overgrew abandoned suburbs, and every couple volunteered to have a single child. Smug in the irrefutability of their vision, the ideologues argued like gentle fathers with a stubborn toddler, waiting for poor Jack to grasp the concept. If you didn't cut them off at once, they monopolized the whole ten-minute period.

"I agree and disagree," snapped Morgan. "The kind of capitalism we've been practicing the last three decades—the bottom-line mentality, where nothing gets in the way of a positive quarterly statement—yes, that's antithetical. But since I personally don't see a viable alternative to capitalism, and it works quite well at satisfying our basic needs, it seems to me we ought not toss away the baby with the bath water. I'm gonna change the rules so profit lies in preservation. I'm sure the Congress will resist. I'm sure the corporations will resist. But if people like you get behind me, your senators and representatives will get the message and support me too, and we'll turn this thing around. The woman in the red."

"Thank you. I'm from Trona, California."

"Near Death Valley, yes."

"You know it?"

"I was stationed at Camp Pendleton. Got out that way a couple times."

"I'm impressed. No one's heard of Trona. Anyway, my family makes its living off of mining claims it has inside Death Valley. They've been trying to make that land into National Park for years and cut off all the mining. Is that what you're for?"

"With all due apologies to your family, yes. I'm not going to soft-pedal it, folks. Everything's a trade-off. There's two sides to every issue, sometimes more, and as president every time you make a decision someone's got to take a hit. Will some people lose their livelihoods because I'm saving the environment? Yes. But in the long run everyone, even your family, will be winners, because we'll create at least as many new jobs in sustainable technologies as we lose in exploitation, and your kids will have a cleaner, healthier world."

"I don't see what my family does as exploitation. We're providing things that people need."

"We have other, cleaner ways to satisfy the people's needs."

Christ almighty! The man was truly skating. I warned him in my master plan to avoid discussing the economic drawbacks of a full commitment to environment. Yet there he was coming right out with it. This woman would return to her small town and, after bragging about meeting Morgan, tell her neighbors that a vote for him was suicide. If he repeated this line long enough, he'd lose.

Lucky for us no one from the press was in the crowd. They came in occasionally, especially columnists and feature writers hoping to capture the "feel" of the campaign. If just one of them took up the Trona woman's cause, Morgan would be in deep tofu.

Two more questions from the crowd, then Morgan glanced at his watch. He always knew when five minutes had elapsed. Announcing that to his great regret the time was up, he moved to the side door and shook hands with his houseguests as the Secret Service agents shepherded them by. The photographer, whose first priority was to catch Morgan between blinks, hardly waited for the visitors to pose before triggering his flash.

"You shouldn't have acknowledged there'll be dislocation if you win," I reminded him after everyone had gone and we'd retreated to the kitchen. We could hear the shiftings of the metal chairs as the next crowd filled the living room. "The press could seize on that, and you'll have everybody in the country thinking they'll lose their jobs and have to move."

"Maybe so, but don't kid yourself. This battle isn't really joined. The Republicans will raise the dislocation issue. They're sure to, given how they're doing. So somewhere down the line I'm gonna have to answer it, and when I do, I'm gonna tell the truth. I don't see any alternative. I mean, not that I'm gonna broadcast it, but when some lady from a one-horse town asks me right up front, I'm not gonna lie. I thought that would please you, Steinhardt. Well, time for another show!"

And off he went, to work the next crowd. Fifty people five times an hour for eight hours. Jack Morgan, without leaving his house, met two thousand voters every day.

But that was only one sign of his popularity. There were others. The first was the volume of requests for videos. Two weeks after the convention we were still receiving more than seventy thousand calls a day. The warehouse operation wasn't close to keeping up with the demand; Cheng estimated a ten-day backlog.

Another sign was money. Ishikawa reported contributions pouring in from individuals, mostly in amounts of one hundred dollars or less but also an occasional check for the legal maximum. We brought in about three million the first week after the convention, four million the next. We'd planned on getting that much the entire fall.

Perhaps most telling was the new trend sweeping the country: In several cities, late-night guerrillas whitewashed billboards and other advertisements. No graffiti, no ripping, just white paint. The advertising agencies and billboard owners blamed Morgan's anti-advertising broadside for the "problem." Every day nasty, even threatening messages from their PR people piled on my desk. They wanted Morgan to publicly condemn the actions of the "vandals."

Thinking the whole thing comical, Morgan wanted to say only that the whitewashers had no connection to the campaign. To make sure that wouldn't come off as too flippant, we had Mitchell do a poll. After she found little concern for the welfare of the advertisers and the billboard owners, Morgan went ahead and disassociated himself from the culprits. But he stopped well short of condemning their actions. The daily media noted this and appeased their bread-and-butter by trying to make a major issue of it, but without a groundswell from the public the matter quickly died.

Once again we'd sidestepped danger, but none of us expected that our luck would last much longer. Not with the Republican convention coming up next week.

18

It was almost nine p.m. I was sitting in the office exhausted, thinking I needed a vacation and wondering whether I could talk the man into giving me a week ("Sure, Steinhardt, and the Washington Monument has my permission to swim to Europe, too") when Kathy Cheng dropped by.

"Do you *ever* take time off?" she asked, as if she'd read my mind.

"When I sleep."

"That's not very good for you. Or your work. Don't you know the law of diminishing returns?"

"You mean the more time I put in the less effective I am? I suppose."

"You'd be more efficient if you took a play break."

"Is that what you do?"

"It's what I like to do. So far I haven't found anybody on this team to play with."

Funny, how one fetching look from the right woman can revitalize a man. "Well, it is kind of late," I pretended to notice for the first time. "The West Coast evening news reports are over. I guess I could slip out for a little while."

152

She broke into a smile. When I reached the door she placed her arm inside the crook of my elbow, and just like that, easy as pie, I was off with Morgan's mistress.

We went to a smoky bar a few blocks from the warehouse and sat in a booth. "I feel so isolated," she complained, ordering a rum and Coke. "They put me up in a yucky motel on Reynolds Road, away from everybody."

"I guess they have their reasons," I said blandly. I knew exactly why they put her out there: to minimize the chance of anyone important noticing when Morgan took a late-night drive in that direction. But I was curious whether she had realized that.

She had. "It's more discreet for Jack, I guess. You do know about us, don't you?"

I nodded—and saw my chance of going further with her disappear.

Again it seemed as if she read my mind. After a pause, she said, "It isn't serious, you know."

It isn't serious. Did you hear what she said? She isn't serious with Morgan! God, she's telling you she's available. And out of all the guys in the inner circle she could have asked out for the night—well, maybe not Molineaux, none of us are sure where he stands sexually —she chose you. This won't be hard to do. Just bide your time, make her feel comfortable, and she'll tell you when she's ready. In the meantime, listen to her talk. Listen, like an adoring puppy—while your mind turns like a wolf's.

She'd complained to Fallon about her isolation. He hired her and made all these promises about how much fun this job would be. When she told him that she wasn't having fun, he suggested she socialize with Ishikawa and his wife. You know, like, you've all got slanty eyes, you must have lots in common. Dumb fucking Texan. At first she thought she hadn't understood.

When she realized that she had, she wanted to slap the fat old slob until his head spun around. She even thought of quitting.

But Jack asked her to stay. She was doing a great job—with the computers too, he laughed. She really liked computers, they were easier to understand than people. There was a logic to them. The day she understood people half as well as she understood computers she'd feel she had accomplished something great.

That is, if it was *possible* to understand people. Like, she had friends she'd known all her life, she thought she knew them really well, but they went off and did stuff, crazy stuff, that she would never have expected. One was the valedictorian of her high school class. He OD'd on barbiturates and alcohol and became a vegetable, and no one ever saw him even smoke a cigarette before. Another guy, he was totally brilliant, the smartest guy she ever met, he wrote science papers as an undergraduate at UCLA that his professors thought were publication caliber—he committed suicide, locked himself in a room and mixed himself a lethal cocktail. And then her freshman-year roommate, she was really great, but she ran out of money so she dropped out of school and enlisted, turned into a heavy-duty alcoholic, married this guy who beat her and yelled at their kid. The kid had bruises, too—was it the father or the mother or the both of them who did it?

Story piled upon story, until I realized she was mortified by what she'd witnessed in her short time. She was too young, too sheltered to have seen so many casualties, was shocked by what life did to people, even good ones. I suddenly wanted to hold her not because I craved her body but because I craved her heart. What distinguished her (and me) from the mass of bullies was compassion; we *ached* watching others suffer. These days such a quality was so rare that it had to be protected, especially in one as young as her. So I looked upon her now with more than lust. I'd guessed wrong about her: She was beautiful, but she was also warm and good. And I wanted her for that now too.

We drove to her motel. After closing the door to her room, we embraced. We clung to one another for a long time. She smelled like the air after a rainstorm, fresh and clean and earthy. When she squeezed me tighter, I squeezed harder too. She softly whimpered, and I kissed and stroked her silky hair. Tonight we would make everything all right for each other.

We separated slowly. "So." She sighed, prepared to follow my lead.

"Kathy." I put my hands on her shoulders and brought her close so that I could whisper in her ear. "Do you know that beautiful white sundress you wear on hot days?"

"Mm-hmm."

"Could you put it on for me?"

"Why?" I think she was afraid I might want something kinky. And maybe I did.

"I love you in it. Please. Just put it on."

"Okay."

Her wardrobe hung in a doorless closet by the entrance to the room. She pulled the sundress from the rack and began to unbutton her blouse.

"No, no. Not in front of me. In the bathroom."

She frowned a little. This was definitely getting weird. But she indulged me, even closed the door behind her.

When she came out she had nothing but the sundress on.

"Unbutton the top button, please. That's right. And now, please, Kath, would you sit on the edge of the bed for me?"

Without a word she did as told. She stared up with a face a little sad, a little curious, a little bit impatient.

I slipped off my loafers, took off my tie, and stood

before her. Then I got down on my knees, opened one-by-one the remaining buttons of her dress, and buried my head deep against her breasts.

Quietly she rocked me. We stayed like that, her hands in my hair, mine around her back, until her strong and steady heartbeat became everything, and all the shit that went with being Daniel Steinhardt disappeared.

When the reverie was over, I sat back and looked up at her in gratitude.

"You would never hurt me, would you?" she asked in the most plangent tone.

"Never, Kathy, no."

She started to cry, then with a furious burst clutched my face in both her hands and kissed my cheeks, my eyes, my forehead. She pressed me close against her, released me, and sprawled out atop the bed. All I had to do was climb aboard.

But I couldn't.

"I think . . . I think," I sputtered. What I thought was that that was too violent, too quick. It wasn't what I wanted.

She pulled herself up from the bed, eyeing me solicitously. "Did I come on too strong?"

"No," I said, although she had. "I think I just need time. I . . . I need a little time to think. I'm sorry, Kath."

A lengthy silence. "I understand," she finally said, with almost enough conviction to convince me. She pecked me lightly on the cheek. "I'll see you in the office, yes?"

"You will," I promised, and then went to the red-brick house I rented. To my gray cat Nimby. To my wife of fourteen years, who slept so heavily she didn't stir when I slipped into our bed. And my wife of fourteen years was still asleep when I got up at dawn and drove off to another day of work.

19

Except for Grover Mandias's blowhard remarks after Morgan's speech, the Republicans hadn't given any hint how they'd respond to our offensive. We speculated obsessively about what our counterparts in the White House would do. Would they junk the fund-raising and public relations apparatus that had served them so well in the past and fight on our turf? Would they ignore us and conduct their usual campaign? Or would they come up with something fresh, something we couldn't anticipate, and really blow us away?

It all depended, we agreed, on how alarmed they were about their plunge in popularity. If they thought they could recover quickly, with only moderate effort, they'd stick with their traditional campaigning. But if they saw some real erosion of their coalition they might resort to a more drastic strategy—and that's what had us worried.

The worst-case scenario had them one-upping us, which would put them back on the offensive and leave us scrambling. Fallon recalled Barry Goldwater saying on the radio sometime in the 1980s that he and John Kennedy, great friends from their Senate days, informally agreed that if both were nominated in 1964 they would fly in the same plane and at every stop debate a major issue. Obviously circumstance prevented that from happening, but what if the Republicans proposed that now? It would certainly be hailed as innovative and democratic, more so maybe than our own plan. We'd look bad turning it down—and if we went along, we'd forfeit the initiative.

In the end we decided we were giving our opponents too much credit. Fallon probably had it right: The Republicans would stick with their usual tactics and at the same time pay lip service to the dissatisfaction those tactics had inspired. We envisioned commercial after commercial of the President saying "No hype, just straight talk," and then proceeding to spout the same lies his party had been spouting for the last three decades.

To Buford that scenario was almost as troublesome as their one-upping us. According to my plan our defense was to deconstruct their rhetoric. But what if people couldn't follow Morgan's logic or grew resentful of his oh-so-smart analyses? As Buford never tired of repeating, this was a nation of bullies, and the biggest target of the bully was the smart kid, who made him feel the most inadequate. What if all we did was make the nation feel inadequate?

We had Mitchell conduct polls. Polls to find out what both pro- and anti-Morgan voters disliked most about him. Polls to find out what would cause new Morgan voters to switch to the incumbent. Polls to find out whether a show of raw intelligence would drive voters away.

The only thing that came through clearly was that people didn't like being lectured to by a politician. But Morgan wasn't perceived as having a didactic manner, thanks to his sincerity, his frequent invocation of the deity, and his hokey midwesternisms (my favorite being "can't dance, too wet to plow," which I think meant there was nothing better to do). The only NABR districts in which Morgan struck the public as too smart were hard-core Republican strongholds that Mitchell labeled Yahoo Country. As long as he continued in a likable vein, we concluded, he could proceed with sharp critiques of Republican rhetoric.

At inner circle meetings Kathy Cheng sat next to me. Formerly she placed herself outside the conversation, her sense of nonbelonging creasing up her face. Now, in my shadow, she sat with her back erect like a dancer and regarded the other members of the group with cheeky condescension. Everybody noticed, yet no one said a word, which made me nervous. I didn't want anyone, especially Morgan, thinking Kathy liked me for some reason other than my primacy within the organization. Yet I couldn't just blurt out a preemptive denial; not only would it be a lie, it would reinforce whatever suspicions the other inner circle members had. I figured I would wait. If Morgan was displeased, Buford would be sure to tip me off. And as far as everyone else—hey, I didn't pass judgment on what *they* did when their spouses weren't watching.

During the day I tried to avoid Kathy, but with the video operation running smoothly she had time to wander and occasionally stopped into my office for a chat. I tried to cut our conversations short by eyeing papers on my desk—hey, Kath, I'd talk if I weren't so hellishly busy—but it took her an eternity to catch on. One afternoon, having gotten the signal for what must have been the tenth time, she said, "Don't you think we need a chunk of time, just you and me?"

She had me there.

"Why don't you take me out to Mexican for lunch, like you promised, so we can have a chance to talk?"

She pronounced that last word in the standard southern California way—*tock*—which, on this warm, sunny day, jarred loose memories of beaches and blue sky. I had cousins in L.A., and when I was in high school I'd visit them in summer. We hung out at Venice Beach, not because of the kinky scene but because that's where the best-looking girls were. The combination of hormones and sun and bare skin produced the rawest sense of wanting I have ever felt. When my cousin Wayne and I weren't too turned on to stand up without embarrassing ourselves, we'd take the chance of hitting up a pair of local beauties. I always had an in because I was from San Francisco—it was a great icebreaker, something to get us *tocking*.

But just because I had an in didn't mean I wasn't nervous the whole time. When Kathy asked me to lunch, that same stomach-twisting anxiety came back, and it wouldn't go away—not for the rest of the morning, not for the ride to the restaurant, not for the duration of the afternoon. I was thirty-six years old, going on sixteen.

I'd had days to think things through, but I couldn't move beyond the basic questions. What was it I really wanted from her? Why did I stop where I did that night? And—this one I could ask but hardly bear to dwell upon—why did I bring my wife east for four months and then seek what I needed from another woman? Lust, love, guilt, habit, need, need, need—jumbled all together in a great, big, knotty mass.

All right, Steinhardt, time to unravel that knot. Start with this: You *do* like Kathy Cheng. Maybe you even love her. She excites you more than Kaya. Simple as that.

But now: Besides better looks, what does Kathy have that Kaya doesn't? Will Kathy look as good as Kaya when she's Kaya's age? And that heart of hers you fell in love with; isn't Kaya's every bit as good? You just don't see Kaya's pain so readily, because you've lived with her for fourteen years and she's learned to cope over that time.

Ah, now you're making progress. There's a paternal thing for Kathy here, a *protect* imperative, which you don't feel for your wife. Kaya's grown up. Kaya's independent. She doesn't need you for a daddy. But little Kathy needs a daddy. How else do you explain her flings with older men?

All right, there can be a million explanations. Maybe it's not so much that Kathy needs a daddy but that Daniel needs a daughter. Eh? Consider that, old man! Maybe that's why you can't sort out how you feel: Something incestuous is going on! And let's not even mention that she's Morgan's girl, okay? Why drag Grandpa into this when we don't have Daddy and his daughter figured out yet?

Hold it. Hold it right there. How can this be incestuous when you don't even *have* a daughter—or even a sister?

Man, you *do* need a vacation like nobody's business.

Rio Lindo has long been touted by the locals as the best Mexican restaurant in Lucas County. "That's where your Puerto Rican Mud Hens go for their home-cooked meals," my landlord stated matter-of-factly when we first moved to Toledo. I guess he figured that since Mexicans and Puerto Ricans spoke the same language, they ate the same food too. For the record I never saw a Hispanic player there, and for good reason: Even by California Anglo standards Rio Lindo is abominable. They make cheese enchiladas with *Velveeta,* for Christ's sake. But as its few competitors are even worse, it had to do for lunch.

We got a lot of looks as we were seated, not for being Morgan staffers but for being interracial. "Don't see many Orientals who don't stick with their kind," one heavy matron drenched in Youth Dew perfume *sotto voce*'d to another.

Kathy reveled in the stares. When I pulled out her chair she seated herself regally, smoothing her skirt beneath her.

She resisted the bowl of nachos set before us, and out of deference I only picked.

"This make you homesick?" I asked.

"And how," she nodded. She looked down at the nachos and fingered the corner of one absently. "I feel like you're my only friend here, and I don't even know you very well."

My discretion failed me. "What about Jack Morgan?"

"Him too, I guess." She suddenly became aware that she was playing with the nacho. "Let's not talk about him, okay? Let's talk about us." She stared down at the table, then at me. "So?" she asked, more insistently than she had that night in her room.

I was silent for a long time, squirming in my chair. "I still need time, Kathy. I'm major-league confused."

"Why don't you try to sort things out aloud?"

"Okay." I wasn't any clearer approaching the subject verbally than mentally, but plunged ahead anyway. "I like you," I confessed. "And I think I fell in love with you a little bit that night."

"But?"

"But—I'm married."

"You hadn't told me that."

"I know. It's not the first thing a man says when he meets someone he likes."

"Or the second either."

"Or the third," I agreed.

"Is your wife back home?"

"No. As a matter of fact she's here."

"Oh." Her posture suddenly straightened, and her manner cooled. "Then she matters to you."

I shrugged. "I'm not sure. I'm not sure you'd call what we have a marriage. We've been apart so much the last ten years. She hates the East. Normally she lives in San Francisco."

"What does she do there?"

"She's a veterinary assistant at the Lindsay Museum in Walnut Creek."

Kathy hadn't heard of it.

"They rescue wounded wild animals and nurse them back to health. If the animals recover fully, they're released. Otherwise they become part of a zoo for kids."

"And how long have the two of you been married?"

"Fourteen years," I sighed.

"You have kids, then?"

"No. But we do have a cat."

She was not amused. "Are you sorry you're apart so much?"

"Yeah, kinda, I guess."

"Then why do you spend so much time at work?"

"May I plead the fifth on that, Your Honor?"

She looked to the sky, choked back emotion.

"What's the matter?" I asked.

"There was a guy just like you in the Weldon camp. He even *admitted* he thought women were the game and politics was real. Like that was something to be proud of. You're sweet, Dan. You seem better than the others. But I'm looking for a guy who's interested in *me*. Who's interested in *us*."

"Jack isn't."

"No, he's not, which is why we aren't serious. But at least when Jack's with me, *all* of him's with me," she said with an involuntary smile, adding, a bit too moralistically considering the context, *"He* has no use for his wife. He calls her Boo-Boo, because that's what she is."

"I see."

Lunch arrived—none too soon. Shredded iceberg

lettuce with a slice of pink tomato, drenched in Eye-talian dressing. Lavalike refried beans, crusted on the top, oozing toward the low spots on the plate. An oily, soggy heap of Uncle Ben's Rice washed in thin tomato sauce. With a knife and fork Kathy tentatively sliced into the doughy end of her burrito and tasted. "This *is* terrible," she cringed.

I chewed joylessly on my Velveeta enchilada, the corn tortilla stale and crunchy, and pushed my plate toward the center of the table. "Give me a little bit more time, Kath," I implored.

"For what?"

"To figure out which way I'm going."

She stared at me with a combination of disgust and mild interest, as if I were an unexpected error message blinking on her screen. "Okay. But I'm looking for Prince Charming, not Prince Hamlet," she warned, scarfing down the rest of her burrito.

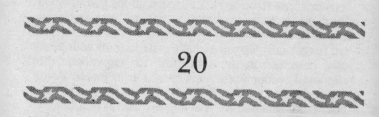

20

THEY CAME AT US with everything they had. It was a smart move, and a courageous one given the risks. They knew they had to win back voters quickly, before the Morgan worldview penetrated public consciousness too deeply to be uprooted. By creating doubts about Morgan they could pull defectors back into the undecided ranks and bring a lot of undecideds into their own camp. So they punched everywhere, hoping one thorough beating would put Morgan down for good.

But in hitting with their best shot now they took a risk. If Morgan was still standing after the barrage, they'd have nothing in reserve to hurt him further. Morgan would go back on the offensive with the edge of knowing that the worst was over, and the remainder of the fight would be for him to shape.

They had decided our weak spot was assuming people cared about environmental issues. In his keynote speech the Reverend Grover Mandias, wearing his trademark string tie with the Elvis Presley portrait on the bolo, sneered, "Environment? I thought that went out twenty years ago! Next thing you know they'll be promising a hula hoop in every garage and a pet rock in every living room." And it got worse from there.

Clinging stubbornly to the false dichotomy between business and preservation, they challenged Morgan's claim that environmentalism could rebuild a strong economy. They accused him of using environmentalism as a pretense to bring back the regulations that hobbled business in the past. And they harped unceasingly on the dislocation issue. Smithson Butcher, the senior senator from Utah who was actually quite friendly with Morgan, described in terms befitting TV melodrama the supposed economic consequences of environmentalism. "Morganvilles in every little town dependent on earth's bounty for subsistence. And in every canvas tent hungry children, with no school to go to, forced to watch the humiliation of their moms and dads, whose sole offense was to labor honestly as farmers, ranchers, lumberjacks, and miners."

"Oh, spare us, Smithson, please!" Buford groaned as we watched in Morgan's rec room. Privately I was grateful to Butcher, and Mandias, and the string of governors and senators and cabinet officials who took turns hacking at the straw Jack Morgan they'd created. By playing down anxiety about the environment they dared us to prove our case, which meant arguing the issues. Once we did that, I was fairly sure, the election would be in the bag; they could no more refute the harmful effects of ozone loss than cigarette companies could refute tobacco's link to cancer.

But then, people were still smoking. Average Americans had to decide the time had come to change their attitude about the land and air and water, and then be willing to break some nasty habits. If they were more concerned with image or transient issues, the Republicans would slaughter us.

After the Republicans finished chiding Morgan's stand on the environment, they smeared him as a demagogue and cynic. The message was that Morgan, not the Republican machine, debased the electoral process.

"How dare he set himself up as the nation's judge and declare that our republic is in danger? Only God can be our judge!" thundered Missouri governor Harley Howe. Ranted Vice President Engel, "I've seen my share of red herrings, but this business of democracy in danger has got to be the most outrageous, the one most closely tippy-toeing on the borderline of treason."

We took heart in the knowledge that we had them running scared, but the unremitting assault on Morgan's policies and character still put us into dour moods. You take it as a personal affront when someone blasts the candidate you've worked so long and hard for; at one point I asked myself whether I'd be as angry if my wife or Kathy Cheng had been the object of such vitriol, and I really wasn't sure. Nor was I the only one to take it personally. Molineaux and Buford took turns talking back at the TV, speculating on the size of speakers' genitals and whether said parts met with any use, and if so what kind.

Morgan watched passively, occasionally smiling as if recalling an old joke he still found amusing after countless tellings. Talking among ourselves and at the TV, we all but forgot he was in the room. That is, until he climbed out of his worn reclining chair and slipped a tape into the VCR. He set the controls for audio only, and seconds later the GOP convention played to the sound track of an old Godzilla movie.

We switched back to regular sound when the Chief Liar Himself took center stage. In his acceptance speech the President gave the conclusive sign that the Republicans were running scared. "I'm not afraid to meet the people on their own terms, in their own towns," he declared. We had flushed him out! Most incumbent presidents sit in the White House during reelection campaigns, coming out only for tightly controlled pep rallies at carefully selected sites. It was a strategy virtually guaranteed to keep a campaign error-free and in the lead. But this incumbent didn't feel he had that option. Morgan would be the presidential one, holding court at home, while the President exposed himself to the hazards of the road.

Hoping to defuse one of our counterstrategies, the President also addressed Morgan's reference to the Big Lie. "He won't be a fascist with a smiling face, he said," the President intoned, "implying someone else is. Who might that be, Jack Morgan? Did you have me in mind? I'm not the one who claims democracy's in danger and only I can save it. Although, given the panic-mongering tone of your campaign, it's a claim that I can make legitimately."

The rest of his speech was predictably upbeat: America was on the rise, but he needed four more years to make it paradise. Evidently he meant for his vassals to do the negative campaigning while he remained the optimistic good guy, the wrong target for Morgan's peevish attacks. And in the most dramatic gesture of the speech, he said sure, he wasn't afraid of any one-on-one debate; he'd duke it out with Morgan in October.

That came as news to us. Fallon had been dickering with his opposite number in the Republican camp for weeks, to no avail. We wanted six debates, each side to name the subject of three. The length of the debates would be two hours, with the candidates questioning each other directly and having the right to ask two follow-ups. Initial answers would be limited to five minutes, with two minutes for each follow-up response, and after the follow-ups the questioner would have two minutes for rebuttal. There would be no closing statements.

The counteroffer was for two debates, with a panel of mutually acceptable journalists asking the questions. Answers would be limited to three minutes, with ninety seconds for rebuttal and a five-minute statement by each candidate at the end. In other words, the standard sham. After several intermittent and acrimonious negotiating sessions, there had been no progress toward agreement. Now the President was unilaterally announcing one debate, essentially on Morgan's terms.

Fallon was so steamed he phoned reporters from the *Times*, the *Post*, the *Wall Street Journal*, *Time*, *Newsweek*, and the major networks and denied that any such agreement had been struck, explaining in minute detail how far apart the two sides were. It was dirty pool—negotiations between rival factions are by custom held in strictest confidence—but he felt the other guys were first to break the rules, so he was free to tell all.

He shot his wad too soon. The daily media naturally gave the bulk of space and time the next day to the President's renomination. Comments from the opposition were relegated to the inside pages or to five-second asides in TV newscasts. Had Fallon waited just another day or two he might have grabbed the headlines, and we might have been on the attack again. Instead we had to counterpunch with something else.

We were really bollixed as to what. If we repeated Fallon's allegations, going so far as to produce memoranda and meeting notes as evidence, we might be seen as harping on a minor point and avoiding the more serious charges of demagoguery, cynicism, and irrelevance. Yet we didn't have much else, except clever words, which the Republicans would label further demagoguery. The campaign was in danger of turning into a pissing match—You're the demagogue/No you're the demagogue—and, as an only marginally repentant Fallon reminded us, Republicans always win pissing matches. "You ever seen one who *don't* look like he's holding back, just waiting for a Democrat to pass?"

Directly following the President's acceptance speech Mitchell tracked and TRACEd and NABRed frantically to find a sure-win counter, but her results were too mixed to be of any use. If we hammered on point X, we'd alienate one vital constituency; if we hammered on point Y, we'd alienate another. The only fact emerging clearly was that Morgan's lead was vanishing. He went from ten points up before the Republican convention to a virtual dead heat the day after the President's acceptance speech. We expected them to make a dent, but nothing this precipitous. The first real crisis of the campaign was upon us.

And as if that weren't enough, Joe Perez embarrassed us two days after the convention ended.

A condition of Perez's taking the number-two spot on the ticket was that he be free to travel. His motive was simple: Unless he made appearances he couldn't gather the political IOUs that would aid him in a future "Perez for Prez" bid. We concentrated him in California, Texas, Florida, and New York, states with big blocs of electoral votes and Hispanic voters. Many of his speeches were in Spanish, which irked the English-only crowd but proved a big hit otherwise.

Sometimes, knowing his Spanish remarks would not be quoted by the mainstream press, he spoke a bit too freely. After a particularly well-received address in San Antonio, he bantered recklessly, in English, with reporters—having temporarily forgotten that the rules changed with his choice of language.

A reporter asked what he thought Jack Morgan missed by staying home. "He don't hear what people are concerned about. They concerned about environment, but also they concerned about a lot of other things he don't talk about. Like, a lot of people want to know what we'll do for the working homeless. I wish I could tell them something, but the man don't give me no instructions, know what I'm saying? There's nothing I can say unless the man approves, and he don't give me no direction."

PEREZ: MORGAN SKIRTING ISSUES, blared the headlines. And so, instead of firing back at the Republicans, we had to spend the next days mitigating damage we'd inflicted on ourselves. The danger was that while we cleared up the Perez furor, the doubts about Morgan sown by the other side would grow. It was imperative we put this thing to rest as soon as possible.

But Fallon was noticeably slow doing his part. He answered at length reporters' questions about relations between Morgan and Perez and their respective staffs, precisely what we didn't want. Indeed, so forthcoming was he that it seemed he *wanted* to keep the matter on the front page. Although I didn't voice this to anyone, I thought I knew the reason: The focus on Perez's error made everyone forget his own. Fallon had been hurt politically and professionally by spilling the beans about the debate negotiations, and he wanted to get back into someone's graces, even if that someone was the press.

It also seemed (although this might be my paranoia talking) that he was hitting back at me. For one thing, he obviously agreed with Perez's remarks, which were an implicit criticism of my front-porch campaign and environmental emphasis. For another, he resented that in many eyes, including perhaps Morgan's, I had become his equal, even though he had the bigger job. By cozying up to the press he partially usurped *my* role as official spokesperson—turnabout was fair play.

Morgan forthrightly tackled Perez's charges. Here is what you heard him say: "I think it's obvious from my videos I know what's going on in every corner of the country. And of course I'm concerned about these other issues, and mean to solve them while in office. But I think issues like the working homeless should be one step lower on the national agenda than the environment. None of our current social crises, no matter how pressing or tragic, compare with the immediate necessity of cleaning up the air, cleaning up the water, and purifying our food.

"Being as he's voiced concern about these issues, I will assign Vice President Perez a primary role in developing efficient, long-term, environmentally sound policies to solve them. Or, to answer your real question, no, I'm not mad at him at all. I welcome dissent; it's the lifeblood of democracy. I selected Joe in part *because* his views are different. In my White House Joe will not just be a stand-in at functions I'm too busy to attend. He'll be on the inside, involved in policy decisions from the git-go."

Here is what you didn't hear him say: "That jackass better hope I lose, because if I win I'm gonna bury him so deep they'll have to dig to Shanghai to uncover him."

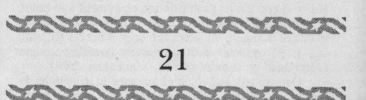

21

MEDIUM SHOT OF the Reverend Grover Mandias addressing the Republican Convention.

AUDIO: "Environment? I thought that went out fifteen years ago! Next thing you know they'll be promising a hula hoop in every garage and a pet rock in every
living room." (Laughter and applause)

During AUDIO jump cuts to: (a) pile of dead, oil-
soaked seabirds (Olympic Peninsula oil spill, 2006); (b)
townspeople fleeing toxic-waste disaster (Perth Amboy,
New Jersey, 2006); (c) long shot of smog-layered skyline
(Denver, 2008); (d) pull-away shot of bulldozers atop
Fresh Kills landfill (Staten Island, New York, 1998); (e)
close-up of ulcerated, deformed fish (Lake Erie, 2007);
(f) brown water running out of kitchen faucet (Boston,
2005).

MEDIUM SHOT of Scott Engel addressing Republican
National Convention.

AUDIO: "I've seen my share of red herrings, but this
business of democracy in danger has got to be the most
outrageous, the one most closely tippy-toeing on the
borderline of treason." (Applause)

During AUDIO jump cuts to: (a) backhoes uncovering mass grave of civilians after United States invasion (El Salvador, 2005); (b) police and National Guardsmen beating anti-invasion demonstrators (Washington, 2005); (c) President toasting General Cho of mainland China (Hong Kong, 2006); (d) FBI raid on *Anderson Valley Times,* hauling out printing equipment and boxes of documents (Humboldt County, California, 2006); (e) midnight roundup of innocent drug suspects (Miami, 2007); (f) medium shot of elderly homeless couple found dead on subway grating (Manhattan, 2008).

Cut to red and blue, horizontally striped background. No AUDIO. In bold white letters: TIME TO CLEAN UP THE MESS. One-second delay, then: VOTE DEMOCRAT. (Last, in small disclaimer lettering, bottom of screen: This message paid for by the Democratic National Committee, Kevin Fitch, Treasurer.)

"So, what do you think?" Molineaux asked, yanking the video from the VCR.

No response.

Morgan was in one of his moods again—despairing for his lost lead. Like the rest of us, his unstated fear was that the moment he fell behind the bloom would come off and he'd plummet into what Fallon labeled Mondaleland. Molineaux's eyes darted furtively from face to face, looking for encouragement—or at least some indication that he wasn't in the room alone with Morgan.

"It's certainly high-impact," Ishikawa ventured.

"Visceral. Nice and visceral." Buford smacked his lips.

"So, we run it?" Molineaux queried.

"I don't know," Morgan replied. "What do you think, Steinhardt?"

I had hoped he wouldn't ask me; his deference at moments such as this cemented my image as Rasputin and alienated me from the other members of the inner circle. I could see the mix of horror and disgust come over Fallon, the pall of resentment color Molineaux's features. Even Buford looked askance; whereas during the primaries and immediately after he treated me like a younger brother, now he stared at me with narrowed eyes that said I'd overreached.

It's not as if I wanted them to look at me that way. I wasn't seeking Morgan's favor. Nor was I competing with my comrades. It was just that these days, whenever the funk came on him, Morgan called on me. It was a smart move, deflecting resentment away from himself. And if he wanted to unnerve *me,* he couldn't have found a better way.

"It's the sort of thing that could boomerang," I cautioned. "We pledged no commercials. We pledged no quick hits. If we run it, they'll be all over us."

"You don't get it, Dan-o," Molineaux shot back. "It isn't our commercial. It's the Committee's."

"You could make that a little clearer. I could barely read the paid-for blurb."

"And you were looking for it."

"Damn right I was."

"There's something I don't understand," Kathy Cheng interjected. Now that she'd become accustomed to the give-and-take of inner circle meetings she contributed more often. The others still considered her a lightweight, though, and Molineaux was unable to conceal a condescending smirk as he waited for her question.

"If it's the Committee's commercial, why do you need our approval?" she asked.

Molineaux's smirk transmogrified into a hostile grin. I could see the thought turn over in his mind: *Maybe she got lucky there.* "I don't understand what you're getting at," he tested.

"I'm just saying that you wouldn't run it by us if you didn't think it was dangerous."

"Ah-hah. Go on."

She sensed that he was playing with her, which made her mad. "You're covering your ass. The Committee asked you for permission to run it. You were afraid to tell them yes all by yourself. Because, like Danny said, this thing could boomerang, and if it does you don't want to be the one responsible."

"I thought this was a major decision and all of us should be aware before we went ahead," he dissembled.

"Then don't bust on Danny for saying what you're thinking," she hissed, eyes locked remorselessly on Molineaux.

"All right, enough of this," Morgan barked irritably, although I would have preferred to hear more of Kathy Cheng defending me. "The question is, do the potential benefits outweigh the risks?"

"It's a gamble. This could be our fatal misstep," I said darkly.

"Oh, don't be such a coward, Dan," retorted Buford. "Remember the Republican trick you talk about? Make the cheap hit, then, when the other guys complain, act like *you're* the one who's wronged? Why the hell not turn the tables? Run the damn commercial and let them whine *their* asses off for a change. That's the problem with Democrats. They're afraid of sucker punching."

"I agree," Fallon said. "Time for us to piss on them."

"Any other objections besides Steinhardt's?" Morgan asked. "Erika?"

"I'll do a TRACE, find out how it registers."

"No, Erika. No polls. I want your opinion."

She looked around the room hoping someone would come to her rescue, but no one did. Everyone, not just me, wanted to flush her out, make her risk the boss's wrath as we did every day.

"Oh, hell, run it," she said with a nervous laugh.

"All I'd suggest is that we have them make the paid-for blurb more prominent, like Dan suggested, so that we have more obvious deniability if it backfires. And if it's successful and it leads to more commercials, they should be even more outrageous."

"Why's that?"

"Because then it becomes a drama in itself. People will be looking forward to the next one, then the next one, to see how far out they can get."

"Yes, yes, it'll keep us fresh," Molineaux seconded excitedly. "And the subliminal message will take root: The Republicans are weenies."

Morgan rested his chin on a fist and pondered. "Ah, fuck their asses, run the thing," he finally ordered, rubbing his face with his hands. "But I want deniability. Bold up the paid-for blurb. And absolutely no one in this room, except for Molly, got a preview of this ad, and Molly didn't think about it, figuring it wasn't up to him to yea or nay it. Understood? Not even the Committee people are to know I saw it. Molly."

"Boss?"

"That tape in the dictaputer. Destroy it."

"Yes, boss."

"Put in a new one. There'll be no more mention of this ad. All right. Let's get on to other business. Erika, you got the state-by-state results?"

"I do," she nodded, thumbing through a sheaf of papers neatly stacked before her. This was safer territory. "If the election was tomorrow, we'd win seventeen states plus the District of Columbia. Connecticut, Georgia, Hawaii, Iowa, Maine, Maryland, Massachusetts, Minnesota, New Jersey, New York, Ohio, Oregon, Rhode Island, Vermont, Washington, West Virginia, and Wisconsin. That's one hundred eighty-seven electoral votes. We've got five major toss-ups: California, Florida, Illinois, Michigan, and Pennsylvania. That's one hundred forty-five votes. Everything else, I'm sorry to say, is in the other camp."

"They have any weak spots?"

"None significant. If everything goes our way, we could pick off New Mexico and Kansas. Maybe Nebraska. But that's only seventeen more votes."

"And where are we vulnerable?"

"Everywhere. The key is that we *have* pulled in suburban voters. That's what puts New Jersey, Maryland, and a couple others on our side. And that's what's giving us a chance in California, Illinois, and Pennsylvania. They're big on toxic cleanup and pollution, and they like the sustainable economy idea. But we have to keep them with us when the White House puts out rosy economic numbers in October."

"So keeping the suburbanites is first priority," Morgan reiterated.

"At this point, yes," Mitchell acknowledged.

"Give me those numbers one more time. We have?"

"One eighty-seven. Them, two hundred six. A hundred forty-five votes up for grabs."

"And all of them in five big states?"

"That's right."

"God, it really is a horse race. So if we win California, that brings us to—"

"Two forty-four. We have to win two more of the five."

"And without California?"

"Then we've got to win the other four. There is no other way."

It was scary news, but it gave Morgan a sense of mission and lifted him out of his low. "Fallon, Molineaux, I want a doubled effort out in la-la land," he ordered. The two men scribbled on their legal pads. "Get Perez out there. I want our Hollywood celebrities making speeches every day, up and down the state, not just in L.A. I got three Californians on my staff. Any bright ideas?"

Ishikawa, Cheng, and I shrugged. "Hit hard on environment," I finally volunteered.

"Johnny One-Note," Fallon muttered.

"Hey, it's a major issue out there. Maybe number one," I snapped. It was late, I was tired, and I couldn't stop myself from taking the attack: "Too bad it's not in Texas. Otherwise we'd have this thing sewn up."

"Son," Fallon explained slowly, "if not for oil, Texas would be nothing but a quarter million miles worth of dirt. We could give it back to the Mexicans, for all anybody cared."

He said it without rancor. In addition to his usual responsibilities, Fallon had been wrangling yet again with the Republicans over the debates and was haggard from exhaustion. I reminded myself that as campaign manager he had more duties than the rest of us, worked longer hours, and made more difficult decisions. Wonder was that lumbering old body didn't give out from the pace and pressure. Also, I'm sure it hurt him that he couldn't deliver his home state for Morgan. I gave him a conciliatory nod, which he acknowledged with a weary wink.

"Cheng, how many videos have gone to California?" Morgan asked.

She reached into the backpack below her chair for a hand-held computer, plugged it into the nearest phone jack, and punched furiously at the keyboard. While she worked, a contagious yawn-and-stretch swept the room, causing Molineaux to quip, "There's never a cot around when you need one."

"Almost two hundred eighty thousand," Cheng answered. "About thirteen percent of the total."

"Fourteen million voters in that state, and less than three hundred thousand videos. Damn, that's barely more than two percent," fretted Morgan. "Ishikawa, you have those membership lists from the Sierra Club?"

"All six hundred thousand names."

"Pull up the Californians. Get the Greenpeace, Nature Conservancy, NRDC, and Earth Island rosters and do the same. I want a list of every Californian who's given money to environmental causes and hasn't ordered a video. And while you're at it, do the same for those other states Mitchell mentioned. What are they again?"

"Florida, Illinois, Michigan, and Pennsylvania."

"Florida? Goddamn it, Perez should have his state in hand. Fallon, get in touch with Estevez tonight. I want to know what's going on down there."

"Right, chief." He scribbled a reminder on his legal pad.

"You're planning on sending out videos unsolicited?" I asked.

"We need more impact in those states. Especially California."

"Don't you think it's early? It isn't even Labor Day."

"You think the press will say I'm panicking?"

"At the very least they'll see it as a sign the video campaign's not working. And that's the sort of thing that could sink us, even more than any commercial we might run."

"You weren't supposed to say that, Steinhardt."

"Say what?"

"You said commercial *we* might run. We're not running any commercials, except to advertise our order numbers. The National Committee runs commercials. Don't make that mistake again, eh? Don't anybody make it. Molly, erase the last half-minute of that tape."

We waited until Molineaux was finished. "Now, what were you saying, Steinhardt?" Morgan asked.

"If the public perceives that our campaign's not working, it will translate into mass defections."

"I agree," said Buford. "We're a trend, not a cause. The minute we look like yesterday's excitement we're as good as gone."

"I'm thinking, too, that if we send unsolicited videos, we should hold up on Michigan," Mitchell cautioned. "Did you read the *Times* headline today? OIL, AUTO COMPANIES LINE UP AGAINST MORGAN."

"All right," Morgan conceded. "Put a hold on sending out the videos. Steinhardt, line up local interviews in those states. Maybe I'll take a weekend vacation in Traverse City or someplace, bring the press along, pick up a couple points in Michigan. Is there any other news?"

Downward glances.

"All right. You're tired, I can see it. We'll see how this commercial does and get the response to tomorrow's talk. If everything goes well, I'll give you Labor Day off."

"We'll see how this *what* does?" I needled.

"Oh, shit. Molly."

"It's already out of the dictaputer, boss."

"What *are* you going to say tomorrow?" Ishikawa asked.

"I'm not exactly sure yet. All I know is that we're going back on the offensive."

22

"GOOD MORNING. I'M not answering any questions about the supposed differences between me and my running mate. As far as I'm concerned, that incident is history. Instead I want to talk about a few things said at the Republican Convention. I want to talk about the tack they took, how they responded to my challenge. It's important because it proves everything I said in my acceptance speech. That is, there are a lot of big lies being perpetrated in this country, and my opponents are the perpetrators.

"What their message boils down to is that their lies are true, and *I'm* the cynic for casting doubt on them. It's a clever ruse. Any time I call them on their lies, they'll label *me* the cynical manipulator, and like all their other lies, if they say it long and loud enough, maybe the people will believe them.

"Morgan the cynical manipulator. I love that. Did you see the headline in *The New York Times* yesterday? The one about the oil and auto industries lining up against me? You know, in a couple weeks both sides will have to disclose their campaign contributions. You check their list against mine. I'm sure you'll find more than just big oil and big auto filling up their coffers. You'll find big everything, to the tune of probably a billion dollars. On my side you'll find some environmental groups, some small contributors, and that's it.

"What does that tell you? If I were a cynic, if I were just talking this environmental stuff to get elected, do you think I'd have big oil and big auto worried? No way. Or if I weren't cynical, merely buyable, do you think I'd have big oil and big auto worried? No way. They'd be sending me a fortune so that when I got elected I'd go easy on them. But they're lining up against me.

"There are two reasons it's important for the Republicans to make people think I'm doing the standard political con job. The first is it perpetuates their most cherished lie: that you can't expect good things from politicians or the government. It's become an article of faith that the system's all screwed up, Washington's a cesspool, and so on. The Republicans are purveyors of hopelessness. The second reason is that my new approach to national campaigning is a threat to *their* campaign machine. They've got the best media handlers, the best PR flacks, the best makeup people, the best speechwriters. If I make Madison Avenue campaigning obsolete, they're in major trouble, not just this year but down the line. So they want to nip the new campaigning in the bud.

"This week I want to talk primarily about the role of government. A couple nights ago I couldn't sleep, and sometimes when I can't sleep I watch a video. The one I watched a couple nights ago was *Grapes of Wrath,* with Henry Fonda. Do you remember it? About the Okie migration during the Great Depression? The family's forced off its farm and heads for California because they see these fliers advertising high-paid work. When they arrive, they go through hell. The pay stinks, the work is grueling, and the natives persecute them because they're outsiders and poor. The family gets shunted from one camp to another, and at each stop they're ripped off, degraded, and dehumanized.

"But then, toward the end of the picture, they find a clean and safe and happy place where they're not cheated, not picked on by the local yahoos. They're so relieved, they think they've gone to heaven. And do you remember what the older man who runs the camp so proudly tells Tom Joad? 'This, son, is a government camp.'

"Well, I jumped with such a start I woke my wife. 'Do you believe that, honey?' I said. 'Government as a force for good! Government as rescuer, protector!' The concept seemed inconceivable in this day and age, like Santa Claus or the tooth fairy. And that's because the way it's run today, government *isn't* the people's guardian. The main job of the government, according to the folks who run it now, is to stand aside and let the so-called free market operate without constraint.

"That's code for 'let the big guys run all over the little guys.' I'll tell you something that isn't a big lie. In the beginning, when a market is new, free enterprise is great. You've got lots of competitors, and the system really does work as described in all the economics textbooks: Overpriced and inferior products are weeded out.

"But what no one talks about is the inevitable result of competition. There are just a few winners, sometimes only one, and they take all. Without meaningful competition the winners are beyond the checks and balances of the free market. You do business on their terms, and if you don't like their terms, too bad.

"There's no way you can fight them by yourself. If they're doing something wrong, like pouring toxic waste into the local stream, the ordinary citizen alone can't stop them. They're just too big, too powerful. But there is one agency the people can call on to protect themselves against giants.

"That's the government. In the name of the people the government can set the rules by which the giants operate, and stop them from abusing their advantage. Theoretically that's the purpose of a democratic government: to look out for the interests of the people. To protect their rights.

"The giants know that. Nothing threatens their pre-eminence like government. And so they do everything they can to keep the government at bay. Through advertising and other means they legitimize their agenda. And when their propaganda alone won't do the trick, they buy the politicians.

"And that's why government is no longer the people's guardian. It's been co-opted by the very giants it's supposed to keep in check. That's why eighty percent of the American people are concerned about the environment, yet government does nothing to address the problem.

"My message isn't cynical at all. A cynical message is precisely what my opponents say: Give up on government, distrust the government. Give up the only weapon that might protect you from the selfish interests of the moneyed giants. That's not even close to what I'm saying. In fact, I'm one hundred eighty degrees the opposite. My message is one of hope. We *can* address the problems that are plaguing us. We *can* get government to move decisively. All we have to do is take it out of the hands of the people who are crippling it.

"The perpetrators of the big lie warn us not to trust big government. Big Brother's watching you! But you know what? Big Brother's already here. The monster corporations dictate our standards of success and happiness and normality. They tell us what to wear and what to eat. You think I'm kidding? Ask high school kids sometime how they feel about not having the things the national advertisers tell them they're supposed to have.

"You know, the very image of Big Brother is revealing. We're obsessed with avoiding the drab oppression that afflicted Eastern Europe all those years. But no one ever talks about another vision: Aldous Huxley's *Brave New World.* Ever read that book? You can finish it in a night. The society envisioned there is every bit as awful as the one in *1984,* except people are enslaved by mindless pleasure rather than fear. Their every material whim is catered to, until they become docile, thoughtless, and conformist.

"The time has come for us to ask whether we're not creating our own brave new world, brought to us by the forces that *really* shape our lives: the giant, global monopolies and cartels. And whether that's what we genuinely want for ourselves.

"If it's what you want, don't vote for me, because I intend to fight it. My America will not go gently into thoughtlessness. My America will not sit back and demand to be entertained while everything around it falls apart. My America will be lean and clean and smart, not slovenly. You know, when I worked closely with the Eastern Europeans, their image of the typical American was a fat, middle-aged man sitting by the television set. I think the time has come to put an end to that bad image.

"But to do that, we've got to get tough with the forces that encourage us to waste our time, our energy, our resources, and ultimately our lives. Using the positive power of the government, I'll protect us from the forces that are lulling us to sleep. I'll make the government the people's guardian again.

"At this point you may be wondering if this is even possible. Maybe it's too late. The cartels and monopolies I'm talking about have transcended the United States and gone transnational. They've made the whole world their arena. Their shareholders are from Japan and Western Europe, not just from Grand Rapids. Their employees are from Taiwan, Mexico, and Spain, not just from Pittsburgh. And their market is the whole world, from the socialist democracies of Scandinavia to the dictatorships of Africa and South America. How much impact can America alone have on these global giants?

"The answer is a lot. Because for all the economic problems we've been having, America is still the world's top market. If we force changes here, we'll change standards everywhere. And another thing. For almost thirty years *we're* the ones who've been the laggards when it comes to global issues. We're the ones resisting international agreements about acid rain, carbon dioxide emissions, CFCs. If we become the major force for change, the difference will be sweeping.

"But all of it depends upon our attitude toward government. We've got to take it from the predators and give it back to people who will guard the interests of the flock. If I could vote forty-five million times, the whole thing would be taken care of. But I can only vote one time. And my wife can only vote one time. Which leaves us about forty-four million, nine hundred and some-odd thousand short. That's where the people of this nation come in. The choice is theirs.

"One aside I'd like to make before I step down from my soapbox: There's something paradoxical about my depending on you people of the press to get my anti-monopolistic message across. Steinhardt tells me only fourteen corporations control over sixty percent of the media outlets in the country, and decisions about what gets on the news are often made with an eye to the bottom line. News is now big business. And from what I've said today, it's obvious that I'm a threat to the unhindered profiteering of the Big Fourteen.

"My question is: Do you, as reporters and Americans, have the integrity to pass on my message undistorted to the voters of this country? And are you willing to make sure your editors and anchorpeople don't distort my message further down the line? Because if you're not, there is no greater proof this country has become a corporate oligarchy. You will have proven you're more powerful than me, that your sway over the minds of voters exceeds that of a presidential candidate.

"Think about that as you put your stories together. Think about the role you play as repeaters of the big lies. Is that something you can justify? If you can, let Steinhardt know. I want to talk about it with you personally. Because—speaking off the record now—I just can't fathom how anyone would let themselves be willing agents of a system that's endangering the human race's long-term health, not to mention democracy and all the freedoms we hold dear.

"Well, that's it for today. Thank you once again. See you tomorrow, same time, same channel, good Lord willin' and the creek don't rise."

23

First they tried to label him a socialist, but that didn't work. "How can anyone call me a socialist? I've been an entrepreneur my whole life! The system's been good to me, I'm not gonna turn around and trash it. I believe in capitalism as the best way to produce and distribute the things people need. Someone find me a volume of Milton Friedman to swear on."

Then, through a whisper campaign, they tried to label him a puppet: Ishikawa was the conduit for covert contributions of billions of yen, and if Morgan won, the Emperor would run the country. It took two hours better spent on other things to convince Ishikawa to let Morgan and me handle the situation. "My grandfather fought at Anzio!" he said repeatedly, square jaws clenched so tightly I thought his teeth would shatter. We denounced the rumor as unfounded (which it was; the big Japanese money didn't want Morgan any more than the big American money did) as well as racist, and it ran its course without harm.

Finally they tried to label him a latter-day Jesse Jackson, and that one stuck: a two-point swoon in the polls. But the erosion came in states we didn't count on winning—the solid South mostly—and didn't affect our standing in the electoral college, so rather than get embroiled in a dangerous flank skirmish we let the slander pass. "I'm his son," Morgan quipped when asked for a response.

Video orders fell off, but not so much that we had to send out cassettes unsolicited. The Democratic National Committee ad was well received—meaning only the Republicans complained about it—and so, following Erika's suggestion, the party produced even spicier commercials.

Gradually Morgan regained a slight lead. By the middle of September he was two points up on the incumbent. More important, four of the five swing states —California, Florida, Illinois, and Pennsylvania— leaned in his direction, and it looked possible to snatch away Nebraska and New Mexico as well.

In politics, as in so many endeavors, one good thing leads to another when you're on a roll. The analysts and commentators made the trend to Morgan the story of the campaign, presenting theories as to why the electorate had turned on the incumbent. Their ruminations transformed into reality the impression we'd been trying so assiduously to create: The Democratic jinx had ended and Morgan had a genuine chance of winning.

The media explanations for Morgan's popularity ranged from the facile ("It's the scar, which evokes sympathy from women and admiration in men") to the semicredible ("He's tapped into anxieties that have too long been ignored") to the far-out ("The Democrats were blocked for thirty years by a Uranus opposition in their tenth house, but now that's passing and Jupiter is ascendant, meaning they can start anew"). I had my staff clip the more amusing columns and send them to the members of the inner circle; at night we'd recount the blatherings of the op-ed poobahs and gale with laughter.

The actual reason for Morgan's success was simple: He appealed to people's hopes. This appeal manifested itself two ways. First, in any national election people vote their wallets. After twenty-eight years of debt-driven Republican economics it had become obvious even to the dimmest voter that the rich were getting richer and the vast majority was getting poorer. Morgan, with his promise of a revitalized economy based on sustainable technology, offered a way to hold on for a middle class sliding into penury. Or, as Buford put it, quoting his beloved Horace, *"Omni tulit punctum, quae miscuit utile dulci"*—those who mix the pleasant with the profitable gain all votes.

Second was what George Bush once referred to as "the vision thing." Morgan offered more than just specific policies; he offered an entire worldview. And whereas the Republican worldview was white-lipped and scoffing, Morgan held aloft the possibility of greatness, played on America's old perception of itself as lean, resourceful, and innovative. It was a strong vision, a step beyond Republican flag waving, and evoked a warm response from everybody to the left of the VFW.

By the end of September the Republicans realized they would have to engage Jack Morgan on his own terms if they hoped to win. After a month and a half of dickering they agreed to three debates over the last five weeks of the campaign. The first two would be one-on-one, as Morgan had proposed. The last would be the standard meaningless exchange, with a panel of journalists asking the questions and the candidates prevented from directly quizzing each other.

Buford argued adamantly against holding the debates, especially the last one. "You can only lose," he argued. "You can't improve on your current standing, but if he should nail you, even on the dumbest thing, the polls will shift his way."

"But we made such a foofaraw about holding these

debates," Fallon drawled. "It would look real bad to back off now. Might give those charges that we're cynical fresh impetus."

"Yeah. Remember how we're for real democracy?" Molineaux asked. "It's true we have a chance of losing ground in the debates. But we will definitely lose ground if we pull out."

"No, we won't," Buford snorted. "Just say they blew their chance a month ago. We negotiated in good faith, they pissed around, and we couldn't wait for them. Case closed."

Molineaux: "People won't buy that. They'll know we're ducking the debates because we have the lead."

"I agree with Buford," I said. "We're cresting early. The key to holding the lead is *minimizing* our exposure. The debates leave us wide open."

Buford, glad to have me for an ally, pressed his attack. "Look, on this democracy thing we can talk about how they stonewalled us until the polls showed their asses were in trouble, and only then did their tune change. It's too late, guys. You can't adequately prepare for three debates in five weeks. When's the first one set to go, next week?"

Fallon nodded.

"That doesn't give us time," Buford fretted. "Just say it's a ploy on their part. We can document their stalling."

"Yeah, but Mel, the first debate is on environment," Fallon said. "They can counter that we shouldn't need time to prepare, it's their man who needs the time to get acquainted with the issues."

Sitting in on this meeting, Elena Morgan stared grumpily at each speaker. We'd taken her husband away for the last fifteen months, and thanks to our efforts it looked as if we might take him away the next four years as well. She hadn't expected that. She figured she'd indulge her husband's imperial ambitions, then, after his certain defeat, reclaim him once and for all.

Periodically I studied how Kathy Cheng reacted to Elena. Although Kathy was subdued, nothing in her manner indicated she was troubled. For her part I don't think Elena even knew that Kathy had supplanted Lucy Casselwaite in Morgan's eye. She probably figured that with Lucy fired and the nation's spotlight fixed so brightly on him, Morgan didn't dare engage in hanky-panky.

If only she knew. The campaign rented three adjoining rooms at that motel on Reynolds Road. Kathy lived in the right room. Visiting field people or public officials would be put up in the left room. Late at night Buford would drive Morgan to the motel on the pretense they were meeting with the visitor. They'd go in the center room, which had a common door with Kathy's. Buford would watch for photographers or other snoops until Morgan finished. Then, before dawn, the two of them would drive back to the house.

"What do *you* think, Jack?" Elena asked, tired of our jabbering. She had no feel for inner circle give-and-take.

"I ain't scared," he said. "Tell them I accept."

"They're going to sling the yellowest shit they can find at you," Buford warned.

"You forget, Mel, I can sling shit too."

Morgan was in splendid fettle these days, primarily because he had regained the lead, but also because his schedule had considerably eased. After Labor Day the crowds thinned out, and visiting hours at his home were reduced to noon to four. That gave him late afternoons off, which he used to rest, knock around the house, and spend time with Elena and his kids.

One evening, before dinner, he took Wes into the backyard and played catch. Just turned seventeen, Wesley was as moody and uncommunicative as you would expect the son of such parents to be. The two hurled rockets at each other, as if trying to break each other's hands. Nonetheless I couldn't resist. While guiding Alexandra Whitt, the Reuters photographer, on a tour of the premises, I brought her around the side of the house to a protective hedge and let her fire to her heart's content. The picture of father and son flinging a softball made front pages across the country—and since it was so natural, so homey, no one brought up the subject of manipulative photo opportunities—or the spirit in which the ball was thrown.

A couple of evenings later I was working at the warehouse when I got a call from Morgan. "Get over here at once," he said gruffly, hanging up before I could respond. I shot across town, wondering what he would chew me out for. Probably the picture of them playing catch. He didn't like his privacy violated. He didn't want his kid dragged into the campaign. I should have asked permission before I made a move like that.

I rushed past Buford's guards at the front door and punched the intercom. "I'm here, sir, where are you?"

"Upstairs. In the master bedroom."

Oh, great. He'll be there with Elena, and she'll stare daggers at me. Steinhardt, you offended my wife when you let that woman take those pictures. We told you everything upstairs and in the backyard is off-limits. Now apologize. Oh, yes, I do beg your forgiveness, Miss Elena. I don't know what got hold of me. I just thought it would be sweet to let the public see Jack playing with his son.

"Where's your wife?" Morgan asked amiably as I knocked on the open door and stepped into the bedroom. Elena wasn't there.

"At home, I guess."

"Call her. Tell her to be here in fifteen minutes. We're going to a ball game."

"Sir?"

"Did you ever think you'd see the day the Mud Hens got into the Minor League World Series? I swear, the way things are going for this town God must be alive and living in a house on Dorr Street. Anyway, I'm gonna use the season tickets I paid a fortune for and haven't used all year. You, me, the ladies, Wes, and Ellie."

"Don't you think the Secret Service guys will have a cow?"

"We'll bring a few of them along. Although I don't know where they'll sit. I've only got six tickets."

"We should call the Rec Center. The police. Make proper arrangements."

He shook his head. "Steinhardt, I never thought I'd see the day you sounded as stupid as a Secret Service agent. Think about it. No one knows I'm coming, so who's going to bring a gun? The biggest danger is a player will throw his bat and it'll conk me on the head. Now, let's go."

After his romp through Manhattan the Secret Service was alert for Morgan's spontaneous peregrinations; as soon as Kaya arrived and we pulled away in Morgan's dark-windowed minivan we were flanked by government vehicles. An agent tried to persuade Morgan to let someone else take the wheel, but Morgan refused. "I've almost forgotten how to drive, the way you people chauffeur me around," he fumed.

The Secret Service having radioed ahead, a pair of squad cars met us at the entrance to the parking lot and guided us to a spot by the stadium wall—the player's lot. It all came back to me now: those long, hot evenings, the moths flitting in the lights, the calls of the vendors as they labored up the rows, and me sitting with a box of season ticket holders, hamhandedly attempting to make them feel a part of something wonderful as another batter took strike three right down the middle.

Surrounded by burly agents and policemen, we were hustled through a dank concrete tunnel, where the roaches grew two inches long and flew, to the home-team dugout. A little door into the stands was opened, and we walked up to our seats two rows behind the dugout. Nearby fans, noticing the escort, craned their heads to see who'd come. When they found out, they broke into applause, which caught the attention of neighboring sections. As word spread, so did the cheers, and within half a minute the entire ballpark rang. "I think we'll carry Toledo," Morgan said, beaming as he acknowledged the applause.

He spent the game signing scorecards, baseballs, napkins—anything the Secret Service relayed from the crowd. He did it absently, attention focused on the game. The Mud Hens weren't doing well, flailing help-lessly against the Albuquerque pitcher, an erstwhile ma-jor leaguer who'd found his level down in Triple-A. By the seventh inning they were trailing five to one, and the fans were nearly silent.

"What's the answer to the trivia question?" Wesley asked, pointing to the scoreboard. He and his father had a truce when it came to watching baseball. They talked throughout the game, speculating on what the next pitch would be, anticipating stolen-base attempts and hit-and-runs. Elena and Kaya talked about what kind of dog would make the best First Pet. I sat by myself, drifting off.

"Name the four brother combinations playing in the major leagues," Morgan read. "Let's see. The Darcys, Ken and Mike. The Lewises, Steve and Lee. You know the other two?"

"One. The Merrifields."

"Gary Merrifield's still playing?"

"With the Yankees."

"Steinhardt, you know the fourth? Ladies?"

"I know. The Alous," Kaya volunteered.

"Who?" Wesley sneered.

"Don't you remember? Felipe, Matty, Jesus, and Boog."

"Boog Alou?"

It took a while for the kid to get the joke. "Jeez, were you alive when they played? I bet you got your food out of an icebox too."

I saw the glint in her eye, which meant she'd decided to play with his adolescent mind. "How about the Boggses, Wade and Peat?" she persisted sweetly.

"Wade Boggs isn't playing anymore either." He waved a hand in disdain. "You're old. Dad, who's the fourth pair?"

Morgan put his arm around the kid's shoulder. "The fourth pair," he said, "are the Griffeys, Ken and Autobiog."

The Mud Hens stormed back from their deficit and won the game in extra innings.

24

Moderator : Mr. President, you won the toss backstage, therefore you may ask tonight's first question.

President: Thank you, Phil. All right, Jack, let's cut to the heart of it. What do you think are the causes of our so-called environmental problems?

Morgan: More than so-called, Mr. President. If you're still denying it at this stage of the game, you're proving not only that you don't hear the American people's concern, but that you're dangerously out of touch with reality.

So let me outline for you the eight basic environmental problems that we face, along with their immediate causes. Then I'll discuss the two underlying causes, which we must address if we're to make this world a healthy place for our children.

The first problem is water pollution. Only one percent of the water on this planet is drinkable, and we're pumping it full of inadequately treated sewage, industrial wastes, pesticides, and other harmful chemicals.

The second problem is solid-waste disposal. We have so much garbage we've almost run out of places to put it. Burning it is no solution, because that contributes to air pollution.

The third problem, related to the second, is hazardous-waste disposal. There is no safe place to put the powerful chemical and nuclear wastes our technology produces. So we have disasters like the Perth Amboy spill a couple of years ago.

The fourth problem is the loss of pristine land and wild habitat. Every time we fill in a wetland or put a road through wilderness, we cut down on the places wildlife can live. That leads to extinction and severely reduced animal and plant populations.

The fifth problem is air pollution. Its immediate causes are automobile exhaust and factory smoke.

The sixth problem is acid rain, which destroys our northern lakes and forests. It's caused when we pollute the air with sulfur and nitrogen oxides.

The seventh problem is ozone depletion in our upper atmosphere. We're still using chemicals that destroy the ozone layer, which is our protection from the sun's deadly ultraviolet rays.

The eighth major problem is global warming. Scientists disagree over how fast the atmosphere is heating up, but all agree that it's a problem. The causes of global warming are the release of carbon dioxide from burning fossil fuels and a reduction of the plant life that consumes carbon dioxide and turns it back into oxygen.

There are two underlying factors behind each of these environmental problems. The first is overpopulation; the second, wastefulness. The planet earth was never meant to support billions of people. It developed over millions of years with either no humans at all or just a few million scattered across the globe. Now, with every new person we make more demands on limited supplies of water, food, land, and shelter, until the demands exceed what earth can readily provide.

Overpopulation by itself might not be so terrible. But people don't want just to live, they want the good things too: a big house, a fancy car, good-tasting food and drink, higher education, entertainment. And they want convenience. Providing these things takes resources and creates waste. The more people who attain the good life, the more resources we use up and the more waste we create.

The reason the environmental movement never really caught on until now is that it offered us a stern solution. It told us that we shouldn't want the good life, that we should deprive ourselves of everything we've yearned for. I don't turn my back on that entirely. I think we do need conservation, and we do need to adjust our lifestyle to the realities of a crowded planet. But I also think we can create a good life for ourselves by developing sustainable technologies.

Sustainable technologies are technologies that don't use up resources. For instance, instead of gasoline-powered automobiles, which use up a nonrenewable resource like oil and cause a tremendous amount of pollution, we should commit ourselves to hydrogen- or solar-powered cars. The cost of combustion-engine cars is already getting out of reach for many Americans. If we commit ourselves to the new cars now, in a few years they'll be cheaper than existing cars, and produce much less pollution to boot.

As for the overpopulation problem, this gets us into the realm of foreign policy, because most of the problem lies in the Third World. It is vital we do everything in our power to persuade the people of the less-developed world that the fewer of them there are, the more resources there will be to go around. We must make life more secure for Third World peoples so that they don't feel the need to have so many children. We must also encourage family planning, make it a cornerstone of our foreign policy. One columnist has labeled me the condom candidate. I accept that label.

In short, the situation's grim, but we have solutions. All we need is the resolve to do them. In the last four years—in the last twenty-eight years—we've done almost nothing as our problems grew and grew. We've conducted enough studies. We've appointed enough blue-ribbon panels. The time has come to act. And I will act, with your support.

Moderator: Mr. President, your response.

President: Jack, I won't question your intentions. I think you have the country's good at heart. But I do question your judgment. I think you've been duped, like so many other well-meaning Americans, by the environmental movement.

Let's look at some of the problems you brought up and their causes. Overpopulation. Jack, scientists have been warning that the world is overpopulated since the time of Rome. It's the basis for pogroms and genocide, abortion, and countless other crimes against humanity. Thomas Robert Malthus went around warning Britain that the world was overpopulated, and that was two centuries ago. Since that time world population has increased from less than one billion to more than six billion.

And look at us. We're still here. And we live a whole lot better than our ancestors did two hundred years ago. A professor at Humboldt University in California said the earth could support eight times as many people as it does now at the present standard of living, using the same technology—and half the earth would still be wildlife and conservation areas.

So overpopulation is a myth, Jack, promulgated by socialists who would restrict the growth of markets. I'm not saying you're a socialist. You've convinced me that you're not. But I'm not so sure the advice you're getting isn't tainted.

Let me raise a couple of other points before my time is up. Acid rain? You say it's caused by chemical emissions from our factories and cars. But did you know that most of those chemicals are produced by natural causes? Every time a volcano erupts it spews acid chemicals into the air, and Lord knows we have our share of volcanoes in this world. How long has our own Kilauea in Hawaii been erupting? Thirty years now?

Another source is ants. They make formic acid, which they release when they communicate or fight or die. Scientists estimate that ants release six hundred thousand metric tons of formic acid in the air each year, equal to the contribution made by cars, plant life, and decomposition.

Don't even get me started on climatic change. A myth.

Moderator: Time, Mr. President.

President: Termites, ladies and gentlemen. They put out twice the methane in a year than all our cars combined.

Moderator: Senator Morgan, your rebuttal.

Morgan: I'm just flabbergasted, Mr. President. I mean, my staff prepared me for a lot of way-out answers from you, but I never expected you would blame global warming on termites.

President: It's scientifically proven, Jack.

Moderator: Mr. President, this time is Senator Morgan's. I must ask you to refrain from interrupting.

Morgan: No, Phil, if you don't mind, I'd like to yield a portion of my time to him, because I think it will demonstrate just how out of touch our chief executive is.

Moderator: A minute? Mr. President, Senator Morgan has yielded you a minute of his time.

President: First of all, I'd like to ask which is more dangerous: to be out of touch, presuming that I am, which I'm not, or to be a dupe of liberals and socialists?

But let me get back to the matter at hand. As long ago as 1982 *Science* magazine reported that the gross amount of carbon dioxide created from termites is more than twice that of fossil-fuel combustion. You can look it up.

Also, I want to talk about solutions. We could reverse climatic change just by seeding the middle of the oceans with iron filings. That would increase the amount of plankton out there, and the little critters would use up the carbon dioxide in the atmosphere. End of crisis. We don't need to stop the country in its tracks, send people packing hither and yon because of plant closures and other drastic disruptions in the economy, and wreak havoc on a country and a world left better undisturbed by government.

Moderator: Senator Morgan, you have one minute left.

Morgan: Mr. President, I guess you and your strategists must have decided that when the big lies stop working, the thing to do is tell even bigger ones. Because you've become the Joe McCarthy of environmental politics. You make outrageous charges, support them with vague references to obscure, outdated magazine articles, and expect us to believe it. How can you stand here with a straight face and tell the American people that the cause of global warming is flatulent termites? That isn't even worthy of a response.

Moderator: Senator Morgan, your question for the President.

Morgan: Mr. President, you wanted to cut to the heart of the matter, so let's do that. Eighty percent of the American people are concerned about the environment. Seventy percent call themselves environmentalists. The polls consistently show overwhelming support for preservation and anti-pollution legislation. So the question is, whose interests are you representing when you veto the Omnibus Clean Air Act, the Endangered Species Preservation Act of 2006, and recommend do-nothing policies at international symposiums like the one on ozone depletion in Sydney last year?

President: Well, you may not want to believe this, Jack, but the interests I'm representing are the American people's. As you've so often said yourself, and it's one of the few things I can agree with you on, it's not a president's job to do the popular thing, it's his job to do the right thing. And I refuse to let this country be stampeded into sweeping legislation whose main impact would be to cripple our economy.

You've talked a lot about sustainable technology. It sounds exciting even to me. But I think we have to take a long, hard look at drastic new proposals before we willy-nilly rush into them. The fact is, Jack, everything in life's a trade-off. There are no perfect answers. We've built up a pretty good thing here in America. A great standard of living, a well-fed, comfortable, free people. And if the down side is a small amount of pollution, I think we can live with that. It's a more than worthwhile trade-off.

I think it's illuminating to analyze the origins of this environmental hysteria. It's no coincidence that the movement started in the nineteen-sixties, when subversives tried to tear apart the nation's moral fabric. For a while they succeeded, helped by the media. And to some extent those times still haunt us, in drug abuse, sexual promiscuity and disease, and an overall lack of respect for our institutions.

But starting with the Reagan years we turned a lot of that around. We put this country right, Jack, and it really threw the crazies for a loop. When we defeated communism, it should have been the final repudiation. The leftists should have realized, like the Eastern European communists, that they lost, and it was no use clinging to their silly ideology.

But they didn't. It frustrated them so much to be

stripped of all their issues, and to see the causes of freedom and free enterprise triumphant, that they decided to fight on in a new guise. I call them watermelons: green on the outside and red on the inside. They mask their socialist agenda behind mom-and-pop issues like concern for animals and kids. Very clever.

But they don't fool the American people for a minute. Environmentalism isn't just some innocent and hopeful way to make a million flowers bloom. It's an ideology diametrically opposed to everything this country's stood for up till now. It makes war on individual initiative. It puts restrictions on our freedoms. It shackles down free enterprise.

You give us the choice between our current levels of pollution and our current levels of free enterprise and freedom, and we'll take the pollution. Because it's tolerable. Restrictions on our freedom, on the other hand, are not. Oh, we should be careful no more Perth Amboys happen. I'm certainly not in favor of toxic waste spills. But in the main, Americans are not affected by pollution. It's a threat blown out of proportion by radicals who are totally out of step with the people. And I still don't see how you can call yourself a good American and fall for that agenda.

Moderator: Senator Morgan, your response.

Morgan: First let me correct your history, Mr. President, because like almost everything else you've said tonight it's so self-serving that it constitutes a lie. The environmental movement started way before the nineteen-sixties. In fact a hundred years before. It started with the preservation of the land that later became Yosemite National Park, and that was the idea of Republicans.

It was a response to the rapaciousness of earlier tycoons blinded by greed to our long-term good. And environmental consciousness was really made a national priority by yet another Republican, none other than the old Bull Moose himself, Teddy Roosevelt. That was in the early nineteen-hundreds, sixty years before your history begins. It's shameful, Mr. President, but not surprising, that you've so thoroughly forgotten your party's roots. I mean, it was Richard Nixon, of all people, who started the EPA.

As for links between the commies and environmentalists, again you're telling big lies. The Eastern European communists were among the world's worst polluters. And they suppressed environmental movements in their countries with the same zeal they suppressed religion. It's no coincidence that once the communist regimes were toppled, environmental organizations sprang up throughout Eastern Europe. I know that for a fact; I did business with those people. The real link, I'd say, is between oppressive governments and the denial of environmental problems.

You know, Mr. President, I'm getting real annoyed at all your story telling. Why don't you come down to earth and level with us, instead of pandering to fear and relying on old myths?

President: On the contrary, Jack, you're the one who's pandering to fear.

Moderator: Mr. President, you're speaking out of turn.

Morgan: Almost everything you've said tonight flies in the face of mainstream science and accepted history. It shows unparalleled contempt for your constituents.

President: You don't understand, there's two sides to these issues, Jack. You act as if there can't be any argument with what you say. Is that the kind of president we want? A Mister Smug? Self-righteous Jack?

Moderator: Gentlemen!

President: Butt out of this, Phil, it's our debate. Come on, Jack. You said you wanted to go one-on-one. Well, here I am. Call me a liar one more time.

Morgan: One-on-one, yes, but my purpose is to elevate discussion to an intelligent level, not trade—
President: Call me a liar one more time, Jack.
Moderator: (Banging on his podium) Gentlemen!
President: Call me a liar, Jack! Call me a liar!

25

You do what you can to limit the damage.

Chiefly you insist that you've won. One of them went out there with a grasp of the problems and comprehensive, workable solutions, the other went out there with the sole purpose of exploiting people's cynicism and anxiety about change. Guess which one we are? From the opening bell we had the President against the ropes. That's why he counterpunched so desperately.

When the press tells you that Roper, Gallup, and even Harris show voters thought the other guy had won, you laugh as if the numbers lack significance. What you don't mention is that your tracking polls reveal the same bad news: Overnight, Nebraska and New Mexico fell back into the other camp; Michigan's almost gone; of the other four big undecideds only California has you in front by more than the margin of error. In the states you've counted in your camp from the beginning, questions are being raised that sound like preludes to defection.

When "Call me a liar, Jack" buttons, bumper stickers, and T-shirts spring up overnight, and by the weekend the phrase becomes the riposte of smart-alecks everywhere, you accuse the other side of manufacturing the goods in advance and planning to use those words at the most loaded moment. The entire thing's been orchestrated, you insist, a typical display of style over substance. What you don't mention is that that very morning you called your notions people and ordered a slew of products with the logo of a termite inside a red-slashed circle. Nor do you mention, a few days later, that the termite logo isn't catching on.

You don't mention that the inner circle is in chaos, bickering and blaming while attempting to devise a strategy to stem the bleeding. "I told you this would kill you," Buford tells the candidate repeatedly. "It's not so much that you were outdebated. You weren't. He was full of shit, and people knew it. But you got bullied. He broke the format and went after you *ad hominem,* and you didn't hit back. That's what lost you the debate. You played by the rules, and it killed you."

And, most importantly, you don't mention that the candidate's spirits have sunk deeper than the Marianas Trench. You hold your breath each time he goes before the press and pray the next question about the debate isn't the one that pushes him beyond the breaking point. You can tell he's getting closer. "Look, I said this is more than just a choice between two men," he snaps at one reporter. "It's a referendum on democracy. I didn't go into the debate intending to win style points. Style counts, I make no bones about that. But it's secondary. Substance is what's most important. And on substance I blew the other guy away."

You don't mention that his wife confided that she thinks he needs prescription sedatives. That he upbraids her at night until he blows out of the house with Buford and drives off to God-knows-where, she hasn't had the courage to send someone after them. That one night when he did stay home he had a flashback to his time in Lebanon and woke up screaming, which hadn't happened in years. That the kids sneak through the house on tiptoe, fearful of provoking him. That last night he spent an hour in the bathroom, and when he came out he'd shaved a pentagram on his chest and made her put on red nail polish and trace the pattern with her fingers while the polish was still wet.

You do what you can to turn his mood around, but nothing works. You buy an ant farm and a can of Raid and suggest he do his bit to end acid rain. He glares at you. You strike up a conversation about what the Tigers have to do to be contenders next year. He isn't interested. You suggest a visit to the craft show at Crosby Gardens. He says craft shows are a waste of time. You bring up Dingo Hutson, who has his own campaign in hand, for a visit. He isn't cheered.

It's getting cold now in Ohio. The first chill winds come off Lake Erie, the first frost settles on the trees and fields. School buses stop at corners, red lights flashing, and halt traffic while disgorging coated, hatted children who skip in groups of two and three toward afternoons of computer games and homemade tollhouse cookies. You see one boy walking by himself and think, that was Jack Morgan once. Alone. Already troubled.

And you realize that as much as you wish he'd shut up, Buford's absolutely right, it's a nation full of bullies, and the reason Morgan dropped in the polls is that he let himself get pushed around. He has to hit back in the next debate. Not just call the President bad names, but wrest control from him. Interrupt. Monopolize the time. Ignore the moderator.

Can he do it? you ask before that evening's inner circle meeting. Naw, he's too much the polite midwesterner, Buford answers disgustedly. Too much do-pretty in him. And you agree. Morgan can be bold, he can be forthright, but it isn't in his character to be obnoxious, at least in public. And since the next debate's on foreign policy, where the President's on sure ground, it doesn't look real good for us. You sigh, and Buford nods.

And as you look into the faces of your fellow staffers you realize that although no one will say it, everybody's thinking the same thing: We peaked too early, now we'll lose.

You leave work each night determined that this election *must* be turned around, but one sleepless night after the next the solution eludes you. Those bastards, playing on the lowest instincts and emotions! They've got nothing to offer except greed and smugness—yet people buy it!

Your wife, wakened by your restless turning, suggests you sleep on the couch. You grumblingly comply. As dawn nears, you finally fade into unconsciousness—and ten minutes later your cat jumps on your chest, purrs loudly enough to wake the dead, and starts you on the next day of frustration.

After a week you decide it can't go on like this. Rather than wake your wife again, you go down to the kitchen and dial your closest friend in the campaign. A suspicious male answers—one of the thugs—but, once assured the voice on the other end belongs to you, discloses that the man you called for isn't home. Playing a hunch (and curious as hell) you head for the trio of motel rooms out on Reynolds Road.

Before you can knock at the middle-room door, Buford opens it. "What the hell you doing here?" he hisses as you walk in.

"We have to turn this thing around."

"At one o'clock in the morning?"

He mixes you a drink, dumping what seems like an entire fifth of vodka into a plastic, eight-ounce cup and reaching into a tiny, square refrigerator on the floor for a splash of orange juice. You thank him and sip cautiously at first, then more thirstily.

He begins to sermonize. We should have listened

when he warned us that we'd only get into trouble by debating now. Yes, yes, you nod, while through the wall you hear a noise. It's her. She's lying with him, he's taking pleasure in her, and she's moaning.

Buford sees that you're distracted. "Vodka hits you quick, eh?" he says, as if he doesn't know what's really on your mind. "I forgot you shy away from the hard stuff."

"I'm really tired, Mel."

"We all are. But one way or another we'll be done with it in four more weeks."

"At times I almost hope we lose, because there'll only be more madness if we win."

"Yes, but what sweet madness."

Now you want to go home and crawl back in your bed, but it's too late. Buford's lecturing continues. "This whole thing is about perception. We didn't lose because the people disagree with what Jack's saying. We lost because he didn't stand up to the President. If he can't handle the President, how'll he handle the Japanese? The Germans? The Arabs? Remember, it's a nation full of bullies. The man has got to prove that he can hold his own in the arena."

"So how does he do that?"

"Not by calling in his foreign-policy advisers and cramming for the next debate like a high school exam. No one's tuning in to see if he knows more than the President. What they're tuning in for are the fireworks. They want to see how Jack will make up for what happened last time. If he doesn't hit back, hard, then he's as good as gone. Nothing else will save his candidacy. Are you with me on this?"

"Absolutely."

"Then you've got to help me figure out how to hit them."

"But we've already discussed it. Morgan's too much the polite midwesterner to hit that hard."

"He has no choice. He has to snap in public," Buford says.

"You mean, go off during the debate?"

"Precisely. He can't do what the President did—interrupt and go into a 'Call me a liar' routine. Everyone would see that he was copycatting."

"But if he goes bonkers on the air—"

Buford presses a finger to his lips. "The walls are thin," he warns.

Now the vodka gets hold of you. "He's depressive," you recite, trying to recall why that was significant a moment ago. "Very inner-oriented." Ah, you remember now. "He doesn't lash out publicly, he gets moody."

"But the potential's there."

"What makes you say that?"

"Because he's angry. Why is he running in the first place? Because twenty-five years ago a bunch of assholes in the White House sent him off to Lebanon to die. Because everyone in government's been bought off, and Washington is paralyzed, and the country isn't a democracy so much as a corporate dictatorship. We have to prod that anger. Tell him this is his last chance. *America's* last chance. That the moron at the other podium stands for everything he hates. Stoke him to a fever pitch and send him out there with the veins popping out his neck."

"And you think that'll do it?"

"I don't know. But it's our only chance."

Maybe it's the alcohol, but after you go home you sleep better than you have in days. When Nimby tries to wake you up, you successfully resist, and your wife gets up to feed him.

You go to work a little late. Even the sight of Kathy Cheng can't complicate your pleasant, hopeful mood. Buford has a plan. Maybe it'll work.

And then Fallon rushes into your office. "Have you seen this yet?" he questions angrily.

When you scan his copy of *The New York Times,* your heart stops. It makes perfect sense—the Republicans did exactly as they should have, hit while you were down—but still you don't believe it. The blood races through you like a siren, and all you want to do is run for cover.

SECRET MORGAN CAMPAIGN DOCUMENT REVEALS PLAN FOR NEW CAR TAX, the headline blares, followed by the subhead WOULD RUIN U.S. AUTO INDUSTRY, GM CHAIRMAN CLAIMS.

You skim through the story so fast you barely comprehend it, until you arrive at your own words: *This warning, though: I wouldn't make this public until after you're elected. It'll kill your chances in Michigan and could cost Ohio also. All those Toledo Jeep workers voting against the favorite son would embarrass us no end. What will voters elsewhere think when they see you can't carry your home state?*

"Where the hell did they get this?" you demand, knowing copies of the plan were restricted to the inner circle. You go back to the byline and notice that the reporter who broke the story covers the Republican campaign.

"I've got bad news," Fallon announces.

"I'll say," you agree, throwing the paper aside. "There's a mole inside the inner circle. Someone has defected."

"That's right. And until we know for sure just who it is, Jack Morgan has suspended you."

26

I TRIED CALLING Morgan at home, but there was no answer. They'd probably activated that gizmo that displays the caller's number and left instructions not to answer if the number was mine. Well, I'd circumvent that lame strategy. I ran to Buford's office.

"I need to use your phone," I said.

"What for?" he pounced on the receiver before I could reach it.

"I have to speak to Morgan."

"He doesn't want to talk to you."

"He can't just up and do this to me, Buford!" I shouted, not caring who heard. "I've stood by that fucker every day for the last ten years. He can stand by me this once."

Except for a frosty stare, no response.

"At the very least he should hear me out," I pleaded.

"Look, Dan, he may be even more upset by this than you."

"I find that hard to believe."

"Believe it. You may have lost your job, but he may have lost his chance to be the president."

I sat in a wooden chair in front of Buford's desk. So many questions! But I couldn't get myself together enough to ask them. Every attempt at thinking logically was dashed by rushes of humiliation and anger.

"Buford, what the fuck is going on?"

"Somebody in the inner circle, or very close to it, is working for the other side."

His face was taut and ashy white. But it wasn't for me, that pallor, nor for Morgan's worsening prospects. It was for himself. Mel Buford, Security Incarnate, had been caught looking the other way. He knew the fault for this was his, not mine or the informer's.

"So why the hell am I being suspended?" I asked resentfully. "I'm not the one who fed the *Times* that story."

"Oh, no?"

"My God, you think I did?"

"Everyone's a suspect."

"I totally deny it! Strap me to a lie detector. Search my office. Search my house. I swear to you I didn't do it. What in hell could be my motive?"

"You can't think of any?"

From the way he said it I began to think I ought to get a lawyer, or at the least not say anything that might incriminate me. "No," I answered hesitantly.

"You're playing stupid."

"Look, Mel, the two of us have waded through a lot of shit together. Don't start giving me the third degree, like I'm some sort of goddamn traitor."

"All right, then, I'll be plain. Kathy Cheng."

"Mel," I stammered, but I didn't have a thing to follow.

"Now it's your turn to be plain," he pressed, in a voice turned hard with menace. "Admit it. You want her."

"No. I like her. That's all. I just like her."

216

"You're the beta male, Dan. Morgan is the alpha. You can't stand it that he has her. Don't deny it."

"I do. Besides, how would my leaking a self-incriminating document help me win her?"

"It wouldn't. But you know how jealous minds work. If you can't have her, no one can. If you're going to fall, you'll take the big guy down with you."

"For the love of God, Mel! Somebody set me up."

"Hey, don't take too much offense," Buford consoled with a hollow laugh. "Like I said, everyone's a suspect. What about your wife? She's not happy in Ohio. She likes D.C. even less. It would suit her fine if Morgan lost. And if you lost your job to boot, that would just be gravy. The two of you could go home to California and fix that sagging marriage."

"I keep all documents in my office. The whole time we've been here she's dropped by once to visit. I'm the only one besides you who has a key. So she may have a motive, but she doesn't have the means. I can name at least eight people with a motive *and* the means."

"Go ahead."

"Lucy Casselwaite."

"I've got a team en route to check on her. If she's the one, they'll find out. Continue."

"Molineaux."

"Why?"

"He and I have barely talked since we went with my plan. I must have cost him millions in commissions. You want a motive? There's one, about as basic it gets. And no one has more access to our tapes, transcripts, and documents. He could duplicate stuff secretly and send it off, and I doubt you would ever know."

"You're failing to make an important distinction here. Morgan is the target, not you. You've given Molineaux a motive for burying you, not Morgan."

"Hey, you know how jealous minds work."

Buford was not amused. "Who else?" he prodded.

"Fallon. He's been out to get me since the primaries. He didn't like the campaign plan either. I took away a lot of his authority and forced him to operate in a different style. I always get the feeling he thinks I'm an upstart and resents that Morgan listens to me as much as him."

"Morgan listens to you more," Buford conceded. "He knows Fallon is an asshole. But same objection: You've given him a motive for getting you, not Jack."

"If Morgan wins, this style of campaigning becomes the standard, and Fallon's out on his ass," I offered.

Buford shook his head emphatically. "On the contrary. He managed this campaign. He gets a lot of credit and becomes a power in the party for the rest of his life."

"So you don't consider Fallon a suspect?"

"Everyone's a suspect. I just haven't thought up a good motive for him, and neither have you."

"Then there's Cheng," I suggested, getting a little more desperate. It didn't matter whether I could figure out the motive, I was willing to bet the turncoat was either Molineaux or Fallon! "Ever wonder what she thinks of the man now that she's been with him awhile? Maybe she's not as serious about him as you or Morgan think. Maybe she's decided to do to him figuratively what he's been doing to her literally."

"She wasn't here when we decided on that plan. I don't think she even has a copy. Don't get me wrong, we're checking her out just the same. But she's hardly on the A-list."

"All right, then, how about this? Morgan himself."

"I've thought of that."

"He's down, way down. No telling what he might do in that state. Maybe he's given up and figures the best way out is to sabotage his own campaign."

"I wouldn't put it past him. Only thing is, he

wouldn't make himself look bad. He gets depressed, but he doesn't self-destruct."

"He hasn't yet. These are extraordinary circumstances."

"I suppose. Any others? You told me you had eight."

"Maybe I exaggerated just a bit. I only have one more."

"Who's that?"

"You."

Buford's lips curled into a pasty smile. "Ah-hah? Go on."

"Your best friend is in trouble. You're smart enough to realize that for his own sake maybe he shouldn't be president. You spare him the ultimate disillusionment, maybe prevent his suicide. And none of us could ever prove that you're the one who gave the *Times* the goods."

"I like the motive you attribute to me. I do it purely out of love for Jack. Such an altruistic fellow, that Mel Buford." He sighed, placing a hand over his heart.

"All right, then. Maybe someone in the other camp bribed you. Maybe in December you'll be head of Secret Service, or get some plush appointment in intelligence, some job where you could get back at the jerks who forced you out of NSA."

"Now that's a good one, Steinhardt. I would consider doing it for that."

"So then why the hell didn't Jack suspend you? After all, you're the one in charge of security."

That registered. But before I could take pleasure in my hit, Buford raised his eyes and looked beyond me. I swung around to see Ishikawa just within the office door.

The comptroller frowned. "There're reporters waiting to see Steinhardt."

"Send someone to tell them he's not here, and even

if he was, he wouldn't answer questions," Buford ordered.

Without so much as a nod at me Ishikawa ran to do as told.

I was already an outsider, a nonentity. I deserved better from the inner circle. For all our differences, in the past year-and-some we'd built a close-knit camaraderie. The least Ishikawa could have done was acknowledge that I'd been the victim of a tough break. And Buford—assuming the worst and treating me like an ax murderer! Finally there was Morgan, whose reaction was way out of line. Why, we didn't even know yet if this harmed us in the polls!

But then, maybe we'd never built a bond among ourselves. We weren't friends, merely strangers brought together for a common purpose. Shared circumstance and prolonged proximity made for a skin-deep solidarity that fooled me into thinking we were more than petty subchiefs vying for the boss's favor. When the shit went splat against the fan, as now, the illusion disappeared.

The coldest feeling in the world is a sudden sense of isolation where you thought yourself most comfortable. At that moment I felt more isolated than I had since encountering the hunters in the wilderness.

"No statements, Dan. Don't make this situation worse than it already is."

"That's another question. What makes you think it's so bad?"

"The image has been tarnished. We built a lot of credibility with voters. They believed in Morgan as a straight shooter. Now it turns out that under the influence of his conniving press secretary he hasn't leveled with the public."

"So I'm the fall guy."

"Until we figure a better way out of this, that's right."

"I assume you'll have Erika find out how much damage has been done, and in what regions?"

"Naturally. If it's a tempest in a teapot, you'll be back in no time. If it's worse, I don't know."

"Are you speaking for the man here?"

"I told you, he isn't happy about this. He knows how much you've done for him. He knows that Avery's incompetent, and it's the worst time to switch spokespeople. If we can find a way to bring you back, I'm sure we'll do it."

"I'd like to hear that from him personally."

"Not right now. Maybe tonight. At the motel."

"That isn't good enough. I want to hear it from him right now, up front, and if I have to parachute my way into his house, so be it. And when I get there, Mel, I'm walking in the front door."

"This is no time for theatrics," he said reprovingly. "Don't you understand that there is more at stake here than your pride? Confidential campaign material has been stolen. We don't know how much. Lord knows what they'll throw at us tomorrow, or the next day, or the day before the election. We've got to inventory everybody's files, see if anything is missing. We've got to go through reams of documents and formulate defenses to every word that might embarrass us. We've got to line up public figures who'll denounce the theft."

"I should be helping with that."

"No, you shouldn't. Not under the circumstances."

"I take my orders from Jack Morgan. Unless he personally tells me not to, I'm talking to the press."

Over the years I'd gotten to know Buford well enough so that even when he masked his emotions, as now, I could reliably intuit what he thought, and it seemed that he was pleased by my insistence on an upfront confrontation. It didn't convince him of my innocence—nothing short of finding the real culprit would accomplish that—but it proved that if I was indeed a traitor, I was a bold one. He respected that.

"I'll have Avery pack up your personal possessions and send them to your house," he said. "Then we'll wait for the reporters to give up. They can't stay too much longer, Morgan's scheduled for a press conference in forty minutes. We'll move you to a neutral location, and this afternoon we'll sneak you into Morgan's house. Is that too furtive for you?"

"Yes. But fool that I am, I have too much respect for you and Jack to drive a harder bargain."

"Ah, you're a good man, Daniel Steinhardt," Buford said laudatorily. "I think."

He paid prolonged attention to the papers on his desk. It was a message I understood. Slowly I rose out of my chair.

"So, Professor Buford," I asked, appealing to him as a friend, "have you any words of wisdom for a man down on his luck? Some ancient truth that might sustain him in his time of woe?"

He eased back in his chair, rested the back of his head in his hands, and pondered for a moment. *"Nil desperandum,"* he said finally, and then laughed, a harsh, prolonged laugh I'll remember with a shiver for the rest of my life.

27

HE WAS SITTING in the rec room, feet propped on the couch, playing Virtual Reality. Although the helmet covered his eyes, he knew it was me.

"Ah, Steinhardt, check this out. Programmer from your neck of the woods sent it to me. Isn't out commercially yet. They're hoping I'll give 'em a prerelease endorsement. It's called Battle for the White House."

With his left hand he punched buttons on the TV remote control. On the screen a lifelike image of the President ducked and dodged behind a podium, holding a soft brown substance in his right hand. "This is level one," Morgan explained. "The object is to hit him in the face with your mud before he hits you in the face with his. Here, look what happens."

He stopped maneuvering his VR controller. The President's hand came slinging forward, and a split-second later the entire screen dripped brown. "See that?" he laughed. "Just like the damn debate."

"Are you sure that's only mud, sir?" I inquired.

"No, I'm not," he said, chuckling. "Now, here's level two." The President stood much closer, without a podium to hide behind. His zipper was wide open, and from it protruded a tiny penis.

"This is the pissing contest. See the bladder in the top right corner? That's how much ammo you've got left. The bladder on the bottom tells you how much he has left. The idea is to get more on him than he gets on you. So far all I've managed to do is get his pants wet."

"I wonder if there's a Republican version, where you're the target?"

"Probably. But I'm so much easier to hit, it mustn't even be a challenge."

"Sir, if you could spare me a few moments."

"There! I got the bastard on the shirt. See the wet spot on his tie?"

"After all these years, sir, I think at the very least I'm entitled to an explanation."

"All right," he said, reluctantly removing the helmet and swinging his feet to the floor. "What the hell would you have done, Steinhardt?"

If he was hoping to catch me off guard he made a big mistake; I'd pondered that very question at Mahatma's for the last three hours.

"The first thing I'd have done was stall for time," I said. "Tell the press an investigation was under way to determine the authenticity of the documents. You don't remember all the details. It could be a dirty trick, like that innuendo about Ishikawa working for the Japanese. Then, with the time you bought, you could figure out a better plan."

"Like what?"

"You admit the document's authentic, but then you prove the car tax won't destroy the domestic auto industry."

"Except it will, certainly in the short term and probably in the long run. Ishikawa's people did a study on it."

"How come I never saw it?"

"Must have been one of the zillion things that circulate and everyone signs off on without reading."

"Even so, if we'd been more issue oriented instead of pushing image, image, image, we might have talked about the cost of an environmental agenda earlier, got it behind us in the beginning. Then the leak wouldn't have damaged us so badly."

"Damn it, Steinhardt, don't be so young!" he said in rebuke, shaking his head angrily. "After all this time you still don't understand how politicians get elected. What kind of chance would Gorbachev have had if he told the Politburo"—and here he broke into a Russian accent—" 'within five years, comrades, I will put end to Warsaw Pact, dismantle KGB and military, stop censorship of press, give republics more autonomy, and whisper love words into ears of Western capitalists'? They'd have shot him then and there.

"I'm in the same boat. I can't go out and tell people that if I'm made president, in four years everything will change. That's frightening, even when the people know deep down things *need* to change. You have to make them think you're strong, capable of guiding them through the rough waters. Then, *after* you've got their faith, you can start to lead, like Gorbachev.

"I've said it a hundred times, Steinhardt, and I'll say it for the hundred and first: The power of the presidency isn't in its Constitutional authority. Not in an era where transnational commercial interests control most everything that matters. The power is in shaping the zeitgeist, the zeitgeist from which mass behavior flows. To accomplish that, you have to capture people's minds and then hold on. Most politicians capture minds through fear or hate or cynicism. But the really great ones capture minds through hope.

"The scandal here, if that's the word for it, is not that changing profit sources will cost jobs. The scandal is I didn't level. That turns me into just another politician, a scumbag like the rest. And that will cause some voters not to vote and others to turn against me.

"I need those voters, Steinhardt, and that's why you're the fall guy. It's not because you didn't do your job. You submitted a good plan, anticipated weaknesses, and suggested a solution. That's exactly what I wanted. But the public doesn't understand it that way. They think you told me to deceive them and I blindly obeyed. So I haven't got a choice. I have to send the message that I'm in charge of my own campaign and that I'm all up front."

It was final, then: I was on suspension. The time had come to ask the question I was most afraid of asking. "What's my chance of coming back?"

He walked across the room, stopping by the intercom. "Can I get you something? Coffee?"

"No, sir."

He pressed the glowing button on the panel. "Scotch neat to the rec room," he barked, then sat back down.

"How much older than you am I, Steinhardt?"

"Nine years."

"Not much, eh? Yet you call me sir, and I address you by your last name. Not very collegial, is it?"

"Everybody calls you sir. Even Fallon, and he's fifteen years older than you. You're the boss."

"I think there's more to it than that, though, at least between the two of us." He regarded me pensively. "Do you know the difference between an innocent man and a naive one?"

"There is a difference?"

"Oh, yes, an enormous one. Are they synonyms to you, *innocent* and *naive*?"

"I guess so."

"Let me explain the difference to you, then, because, among other things, it explains why I admire you."

He was manipulating me, but I couldn't help responding to his flattery. For a couple of seconds, anyway, I suppressed a smile by diverting my gaze floorward.

"A naive man is unaware that evil resides within himself, and so routinely and unwittingly commits evil acts. An innocent man *does* recognize evil in himself, but then does everything he can to avoid evil. In other words, he recognizes temptation—*is* tempted—but successfully resists.

"There are three types of people in this world, Steinhardt. The naive, the innocent, and the experienced. Most are naive. They think they know all about evil because some preacher told them about Satan. Then there are a handful of innocents, like yourself. And then there are the experienced, like me—the ones who recognize the evil in themselves and have succumbed to it.

"That's why there's a gulf between us, why I call you Steinhardt and you call me sir. Nine years shouldn't make that much of a difference. But I have crossed the line into experience, and once across, you can't come back. You still haven't crossed, and that makes you an innocent."

"I'm not as innocent as you might think, sir."

He smiled sardonically. "You're faithful to your wife, right?"

He had me in a bind. If I said yes, I conceded that I was an innocent; if I said no, I gave substance to Buford's allegation that jealousy for Kathy motivated me to leak those documents. "More or less," I murmured.

"And you love her, don't you?" Morgan went on, seemingly oblivious to my evasion.

I hesitated. "Most of the time."

"And you love your work?"

"Until this morning, yes."

"I mean, you have no moral qualms about it? You can sleep at night?"

"That's where I'm not as innocent as you might think. I knowingly lie for you every day. Kind of mitigates that innocence."

"I don't think so. You're lying out of love for life. I mean, at bottom, isn't that what being an environmentalist is all about? Fighting for the living planet?"

I granted that was so.

"You lie because, as helpless as you are when it comes to practical politics, you realize it's impossible to get elected telling the hard truth. In fact you may even understand that truth is different for each person, and therefore everything you say will be regarded as a lie by someone. And maybe after all your talks with Buford you even understand that all of us lie to *ourselves*. We have to, otherwise we'd go insane from shame and weakness." He pointed to himself. "You see what happens when the inner lies are unpersuasive.

"Fact is, Steinhardt, the naive—the mass of people —must be led. And the experienced must lead them. But the experienced have blurry judgment. They're compromised. That's where the innocents come in. They serve as examples. And so the question isn't whether or not you lie, because as long as you are human, you will lie. The question is, to what end."

"Maybe, sir, but no matter how well they're intended, the lies have clouded my judgment too."

"But they haven't killed your innocence. The fact you worry about lying is evidence enough that you're still innocent. Believe me, once you're really in the habit, you aren't troubled by it anymore."

Elena appeared with his drink. Upon seeing me she scurried off. To her, too, I'd become a nonentity.

"Anyway, I don't mean to hoe this row forever," he said apologetically. "Here's what I'm driving at: In this organization no one fills the role of innocent like you, except perhaps Mitchell, but she couldn't talk less if you sewed her mouth shut. So I want to bring you back as soon as possible. To guide me, if you will. But you have to understand that this is politics—I can't make any promises."

"I understand, sir, sort of."

"Consider it a favor—Daniel." That last word clunked out like a wrong note at the opera, the first time I'd ever heard him sound so obviously insincere. He seemed to notice it as well, but was too much the performer to stop at a mistake. "Politics is no place for the innocent. No place else is, either, but at least now you have a chance to decompress and get your head clear of the lies."

I didn't bother to hide my bitterness. "You sound as if you want me to say thank you."

He forced a smile. "The suspension's with full pay. Given the financial shape we're in, you could at least say thanks for that."

I looked at him hard. I wasn't sure I liked him anymore.

"My regards to the wife and cat." He waved. And then he swung his feet onto the sofa, snapped the helmet back on, and returned to pissing on the President.

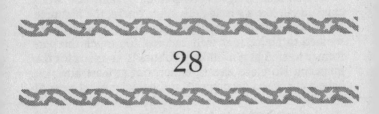

28

I UNDERSTAND NOW why the two of you don't count me in your league: It takes me a day to invent smart comebacks to your bullshit.

I'm not mad at you, Mel. In your own way you've been good to me. Besides, I don't think I could beat you in a verbal joust even with the advantage of an extra day. But you, Jack Morgan, I have a couple bones to pick with you.

It isn't what you think. Despite the fact that a more enlightened boss would have given me the benefit of the doubt and not so swiftly sacrificed me on the altar of public opinion, I'm not taking you to task for suspending me.

The first thing is this business of my innocence. Nice try there. You did the best you could to make me feel upbeat about myself, even as you kicked my butt off the campaign. But I must say, I'm insulted by the shallowness of such a ploy. Back in Washington I used to laugh when you went into back-patting routines with stupid colleagues you were screwing. How great it was to feel like an insider! But now that I'm the screwed, I find it hard to laugh.

In that respect, then, yes, I was an innocent. I felt secure, figured I had my job until I fucked up royally or quit. I knew you had problems, but I never thought I'd be one of your victims.

Other than that, though, you're dead wrong about this innocence malarkey. Beneath my California-friendly surface there's a power junkie every bit as rabid as the jackals running the country. Alone I lacked the strength to fight the ruiners, the bullies, the annihilators. Behind you and Buford, though, I saw the chance to prevail. So I gave you one-hundred-ten percent. I invested all my dreams and hopes in you.

For some reason you couldn't see that. You saw how hard I worked, realized no one like yourself would labor so for such a piddling reward, and concluded that I had to be a different kind of fool. And so you invented the term *innocent* for me—smarter than the average chump, but just as manipulable. And you marveled at your good fortune at having found one.

I must have provided you and Buford with hours of amusement.

But enough of that. I want to talk about another thing, something more personal. To prove I was an innocent, you asked me whether I loved my wife, and my answer was "most of the time." For once I was being honest—no microphones in front of me, I guess—and the more I think about it, the more I realize those words pained me more than any others.

Work is the reason why I don't love Kaya all the time. Not Kathy Cheng—who, by the way, in three months understood me better than you did in ten years —nor any of the several other women I could have taken tumbles with in my political career. It's my work, Jack. My work for you.

Those first few years Kaya and I lived apart, whenever I went back to San Francisco we were together every minute. I don't mind telling you we made love like seventeen-year-olds—all urgency, without a shred of art. But despite the nightly phone calls, in time our worlds diverged. She would be good friends with someone for six months before I met them for the first time. Same at this end. There'd be surprises, like the new furniture in our San Francisco place or the roommate I took in at my Georgetown flat. The last couple years I'd fly home during a recess, and instead of making love we'd go to sleep.

We both knew what was happening, but we also knew that jobs like mine didn't come around too often. I'm a good American, Jack. I had an opportunity, and I seized it in spite of the huge cost. And when I realized you were running for president, well, I just had to stick around. The lure of working in the White House, being an *in* after feeling so much like an out my whole life, beckoned like an opiate.

I admit, I felt guilty. Now Kaya and I wouldn't even have congressional recesses to ourselves, and our estrangement would accelerate. For all those years she more than held up her end. She did the shitwork, from the million details that go into keeping up two households to the sympathetic listening. Not once did she demand emotional support from me. Not once did she trouble me with household business. The worst she did was go on and on with Nimby stories. And I took her for granted.

None of this impresses you, I see. You've ignored Elena—or should I say Boo-Boo?—almost from the day the two of you got hitched. But there's a major difference here: Kaya deserves better. She isn't vain or grasping or resentful. Although I've acted like a weasel she's never betrayed me, and it seems to me that when someone holds up their end, plus a lot of yours as well, you have an obligation. Which is why it troubles me so much that I only love her most of the time.

It looks to me as if you still don't understand. I can

see you shrugging quizzically. "Just because you've thrown yourself into your work doesn't mean you can't love her all the time," you say. But that isn't true. When there's a conflict between work and Kaya, guess who wins? I've said "Got to run now, talk to you later" a million times to her, never once to you.

Which brings to mind the end of yesterday's discussion. "Consider it a favor, Daniel," you said of the suspension. That's when you became too obvious: when my name fell out of your mouth like glass and tumbled to the floor, where it broke into a thousand bits. I keep hearing it, and it makes me cringe each time. You never thought about how much I sacrificed for you until that moment, when it became useful to remind me that my dedication almost killed my marriage.

But now, I suppose you'll be happy to know, I *do* consider it a favor. Because I will use this time to make amends to Kaya. To love her all the time.

I'm going back to someone who'll return my loyalty. That is, if it hasn't grown too late.

29

ONE OF MY favorite things to do on nights I'm camping is to pull in distant signals on my radio. My radio is ancient, with lots of metal parts and a yard-long antenna to increase reception. The reception is further enhanced if I camp by a mountain lake, which, for reasons a more scientific-minded person could explain, acts like a giant reception dish. My family went to Yellowstone and Grand Teton National parks when I was in high school, and we took a campsite overlooking Jackson Lake. That night I pulled in baseball games from Los Angeles, Seattle, Minneapolis, Detroit, Cincinnati, and Houston. I felt like I was hearing the whole country.

Partly to indulge this silly pleasure we camped at the Tenaya Lake walk-in campground in Yosemite. The campground closes after Labor Day, but by one entrance there's just enough room to squeeze a compact car around the locked gate. So long as the shallow ditch around the entrance isn't wet from rain or snow, you don't leave tire marks, and if you park in a spot hidden from the main road no one knows you're there. Nor will anybody check, because the few rangers assigned to the park in winter patrol mostly in the valley, which remains wall-to-wall with visitors.

To further elude detection we chose a site on the far side of the lake, a quarter mile from the road, and pitched the tent in a tree-shrouded hollow. There was no running water, so we brought our trusty Swiss-made filter and drew our supply directly from the lake. Using a gardening spade we dug a foot-deep latrine. Garbage we deposited in grocery bags and periodically hauled to the car. We locked our food in a metal bear-proof box, even though it was so cold the bears were either at the lower elevations or beginning hibernation.

The scheme worked perfectly. We didn't see another soul for days.

Kaya doesn't mind my nightly fiddling with the radio. As the sun sets and the temperature dips below freezing she burrows into her thick sleeping bag, dons a woolen cap to keep her head warm, and by flashlight writes the journal she keeps during camping trips. When she's through she clicks the flashlight off, rolls over, and goes to sleep. The radio works like a lullaby, especially baseball games, the news, or talk shows—which is convenient, because that's mostly what I like to hear.

When we first arrived I considered not playing with the radio at all, the idea being this would be complete escape from the campaign. But it wouldn't be a camping trip without a signal search. Nor could I kid myself: I just had to know how Morgan and the gang were doing.

Mostly I pulled in the old reliables: KGO from San Francisco, KSL from Salt Lake City, KOA from Denver. I could also get KNX and KABC from Los Angeles and KNBR and KCBS from home. KFBK, the Sacramento station at the high end of the dial, also came through loud and clear. Occasionally I picked up Albuquerque, Phoenix, Portland, and Seattle. One night I got Great Falls, Montana. The news reports were pretty much the same, since all the stations subscribe to network services.

The big story was that Morgan went back on the

offensive, introducing a tax-simplification plan so stunning the car-tax scandal was forgotten. The proposal was straightforward enough that reporters could explain it in a ninety-second spot. The first $30,000 of a person's income—$60,000 for a married couple—would be exempt from taxes. Everything beyond that would be taxed a flat thirty-eight percent. There would be but three deductions: charitable contributions made in cash; interest on home mortgages; and contributions made to Individual Retirement Accounts. Social Security would be lumped in with the income tax. No more corporate tax, either, except for Social Security and a stiff assessment on environment-degrading products and processes.

It was the most crowd-pleasing statement he'd ever made, giving millions of low- and middle-income voters bottom-line incentive to support him. The sound bites featured Morgan boasting his plan would lead to tax reductions for almost half the public, stimulate business, raise more money for the government, and "be so simple you'll finish your return in seven minutes."

Unmentioned was how the tax plan dovetailed with an environmental agenda. Under the guise of simplification Morgan eliminated deductions for dependents, meaning the federal government would no longer subsidize large families. I detected Buford's deft touch here, deflecting criticism from what may well have been the proposal's biggest weakness. Had Morgan talked about deductions for dependents, limiting them to, say, two, he'd have been attacked as anti-family.

On the surface the abolition of corporate taxes looked like a bone tossed to the private sector, something to reassure it after the car tax. But Ishikawa had been arguing for months that the standard liberal call for higher corporate taxes would only cause inflation, since the companies would pass the increase on to consumers. The idea, he said, was not to tax the corporations but the people running them, which could be accomplished by eliminating shelters. That would raise more money from the rich without hobbling industry or sparking inflation. And by simultaneously introducing a special tax on products that pollute, polluting corporations would be put at a competitive disadvantage, prompting them either to take their products off the market or to clean up their acts.

Morgan's announcement also blunted the latest attack from the other side, the release of a study by the Institute for Business Freedom (one of those corporate-funded, right-wing propaganda tanks) that claimed turning to sustainable technologies would lead to economic downturn. "It's a prescription for negative growth," warned Bill Plager, head of the IBF and a member of the board of directors of two oil companies, a weapons manufacturer, and a car maker. What colors Plager's face must have turned when Morgan called for ending corporate taxes, something the IBF flacks couldn't even sell to the Republicans!

Morgan's tax plan virtually overnight put him back in the race. The pollsters once again were saying the election was too close to call.

Games three, four, and five of the World Series were played in the Pacific time zone, and despite the piss-poor quality of the announcers (why does it seem there are only six guys in the country who can call a game and not grate on your nerves?) I listened to the ball games in entirety. The most disturbing thing about the Series was the noise the bats made as they hit the ball. The major leagues had switched to aluminum bats, so instead of the authoritative *thwack* of wood you heard that dinky metal *tink.*

On Friday night, as the two teams headed for the East Coast and the last weekend of baseball for the year, Morgan and the President debated for the second time. I wish I could report in detail what transpired, but

I stopped paying attention about fifteen minutes in. When you're not on the inside, these confrontations don't pack the same drama. The candidates sound like actors shoved onstage before they've fully memorized their lines. I waited for Morgan to snap the way Buford wanted, but when it didn't materialize early I turned the radio off, burrowed into my sleeping bag, pulled up my knees, and tried to sleep.

But I couldn't, quite. For one thing, it was incredibly cold; whose idea was it to camp in the high country this time of year? For another, there were just too many thoughts. Morgan. Buford. Kathy. Kaya. I was suddenly afraid we'd be discovered and arrested by the park police, even though in all my years of watching campground vandals run amuck I'd never seen a soul so much as cited. I imagined the story in the *San Francisco Chronicle:* FORMER MORGAN AIDE ARRESTED IN YOSEMITE. Dateline Yosemite Village. The suspended aide to presidential candidate Jack Morgan plunged further into national disgrace today when he and his wife were booked for squatting in a closed campground in the Sierra. . . .

It was probably past midnight when I heard the first coyote howl. I chuckled softly, hoping that if Kaya was awake she'd hear me and we'd talk. But she was out completely. A second coyote called. Then a third, closer to the tent—perhaps in the meadow at the other end of the lake? I was in a sleeping bag, with an air mattress and a tent floor between me and the ground. Those poor animals had but their scraggly, matted fur to keep them warm. Back in the days when people could be trusted, coyotes were condemned as thieves and tricksters. Now they were the tricked and robbed, by man, until the only places they could howl away the cold were island wildernesses such as this.

I often fantasized about running the Department of Interior. I'd get the Indians out from under the thumb of the BIA and their Vichy tribal councils. I'd quintuple national park entrance fees for RVs—that is, if I allowed RVs at all. I'd be in the President's face until he switched responsibility for national forest land from the Agriculture Department—where it never belonged, since you can't eat trees—to Interior, and then, just to spite those troglodyte senators from the West, I'd turn every forest in Idaho, Montana, and Wyoming into wilderness area. And I'd populate those forests with the predators and scavengers whose continent this used to be: the grizzly bears, the black bears, the wolves, and the coyotes.

The howling ended as abruptly as it started. I'd warmed up in my sleeping bag but, try as I might, was still unable to doze off—I had women on the brain.

Sex is a messy proposition in the woods, where you go for days without a shower. Condoms reduce the mess, but don't eliminate it. Then, too, in conditions where you need three layers to keep warm in the middle of the day it's too damned cold to make love. I suppose if we were more determined we would do it—cold doesn't stop the Inuit—but for some reason we weren't that determined. My penalty was sleeplessness.

I didn't think of any woman in particular. Even when I tried I couldn't summon Kathy Cheng. Something about being in the wild made that infatuation seem ludicrous, like a subplot in a sleazy novel. Hard to believe it ever happened, or that Mel Buford considered it the motive for my leaking documents.

But happen it did, and here in the realm without lies I had to admit that Buford was justified. If I was to repair the breach in my relationship with Kaya, I had to come clean. And there was no more fitting place to do that than the wilderness.

So at breakfast the next morning, having barely slept, I proposed a hike up to the Sunrise Lakes.

I walked behind Kaya as we followed a long, level stretch of trail that took us through white pine and hemlock forest. Within an hour we reached a steep, steady ascent that stole our breath. Although a chill wind blew in hearty gusts, our foreheads, necks, and backs grew slippery with perspiration.

At the crest of the ridge we hit our junction, but rather than go on toward Sunrise Lakes we took a little detour that my father had shown me years before. Judging by the informal trail beaten into the ground, the detour was no secret, as I'd imagined when my father, finger pressed against his mouth, first guided me this way. We zigged past boulders and steep drops until at last we came to a spot with an unobstructed view to the southwest.

Miles away, past the sloping, pine-dotted, granitic canyon of Tenaya Creek, the profile of Half Dome rose up from beyond the flank of Clouds Rest like a watchful eye. Across from it, the gray-brown face of North Dome plunged more than a thousand feet. Between them we could see the flat, evergreen valley floor, and beyond it the furrowed, sheer walls leading up to Glacier Point.

"My God," gasped Kaya, sitting beside me.

For a solid fifteen minutes we said nothing, marveling at the view while letting the wind cool down our bodies. So many times I almost started saying what I had to say, but stopped. I was scared to death of her reaction. I wouldn't mind if she got mad—I deserved that—but what if she was really hurt? What if she began to cry? Up here there was no place to escape. Yet I had resolved to come down from that promontory as pure and open as the vista it afforded. The alternative was to let my marriage sink into the same abyss as Morgan's and Elena's.

Kaya slung her daypack over her shoulders and prepared to move. "I have something I've been meaning to say," I finally sputtered.

Instantly she wrapped her hands around her drawn-up knees and looked away. From the tone of my voice she knew this wasn't going to be pleasant. In fact, she may have known exactly what was coming.

I drew a long breath of the frigid air. Then I drew another. And another. Damn. I never would be ready. "During the campaign I fell for someone else," I blurted, feeling so weak and shivery my body seemed to lose its substance.

She said nothing, resting her chin on her knees and rocking herself back and forth.

"Nothing really happened," I elaborated. "We came close, but we never did it. And it's over now."

I looked down, afraid to meet her stare. I picked up a couple of pebbles and tossed them down the hill.

"I'm really sorry, Kaya. I just . . . forgot about you. That was a mistake. Maybe the biggest one I've ever made. It's just that, you know, there's a whole subculture to politics. You get caught up in it."

"I understand," she said in a consoling but troubled voice. "I have something to tell you too."

Uh-oh.

After a halt to let her lips stop trembling, she spoke the next words in a rush. "I met someone too. And we did go all the way." Another halt. "I didn't know how to tell you. You were never home, and when you called the only thing we talked about was the campaign. I was going to tell you when we went to Caribou, but then that deer got shot in front of you, and I just didn't have the heart.

"I needed someone, Dan. That's all. I needed someone to be there for me."

And here I thought I wasn't such an innocent.

30

She squeezed my hand. "I'll be back at the campsite, okay?"

Okay. I didn't watch her go.

I'm not into religion, but from time to time I fancy myself a spiritual man. When we were in college, Kaya and I went for a hike in the East Bay hills. From the ridgeline at the trail's end we beheld the golden hills of Contra Costa County to the east and San Francisco Bay, spanned by the Golden Gate Bridge, to the west. I gazed back and forth, from hills to bay, trying to reduce the vista to something I could embrace.

And then I noticed an ant dragging a morsel through the grass below me. It, too, was at the top of the ridge, but unless ants possess intelligence undreamed of by the entomologists, it had no way of comprehending the scene below. Poor ant, incapable of even *suspecting* the wonders at its feet!

But then, what about poor me? What magnificence, plain as open sky and sea below, escaped *my* ken? Was it not a possibility, a probability, that as the ant was oblivious to all I saw, I was oblivious to something greater? It is easy to accept that an ant has limitations. It is something else again to accept that our windows to the world give but a partial view of all that's really there.

I could dismiss the questions that arose when Kaya confessed her infidelity as mere morsels to haul through the grass. I didn't care to know his name—if indeed it was a him—or how they met, or how often they did it. The real question was whether I could see the larger picture and respond to it; whether I could gain perspective not just on my marriage but on my entire life, a life that had spectacularly unwound the past few days.

The one religious text I've ever liked is Lao-tzu's *Tao-te-Ching*. The best translation, my professors at Berkeley said, was that of the renowned Far Eastern scholar Arthur Waley. Waley tried to understand the *Tao-te-Ching* in the context of its own time and society, and thus his version is blessedly free of hippie-dippy nature worship or New Age mysticism:

The practice of Tao consists in subtracting day by day,
Subtracting and yet again subtracting
Till one has reached inactivity.
But by this inactivity
Everything can be activated.
Those who of old won the adherence of all who live
   under heaven
All did so by not interfering.

You can see how this would appeal to a budding environmentalist. Don't interfere; minimize your needs and actions, and let all things thrive according to their nature. So long as we do nothing, the earth will be restored and the future will be well.

But there was also a political agenda behind that call for inactivity. Lao-tzu lived in interesting times. Tyrants and warlords divided the country into seven warring kingdoms, brutalizing the populace. His book was a plea to those rulers to loosen their grip before they destroyed the world they were fighting to control.

Today Lao-tzu would be pleading for the same desistance from the landowners and manufacturers. But what do you do, Lao-tzu, when the powerful ignore you? When they cut and burn the forests, fill the wetlands, mine the mountains, poison the air and sea and land? Do you sit around and mind your navel?

Well, now that I thought about it, maybe. Because so long as none of us does anything the two main problems facing humankind—overpopulation and overconsumption—*will* inevitably be resolved. Resolved by famine, drought, disease, and warfare over what remains. So Lao-tzu had the idea after all. There is no need to panic, to *do* something for the environment. The environment will save itself, without a shred of action on our part.

So maybe I should forget this thing I have about environment. Move on—take some courses and become an accountant or something.

But I can't help wondering which humans would survive an environmental holocaust. Obviously, those rich enough to buy the air, water, food, shelter, and weapons necessary for survival. And who are they? The exploiters who caused the problems in the first place! They'll pass on their aggressive genes and meddling mores to a streamlined generation, and the rest of us, who know the wonder of a landscape bigger than ourselves, will leave only blood and tears upon the cracked earth as our legacy.

That didn't seem what Lao-tzu had in mind. Inaction—at least on the part of his adherents—wouldn't lead to tolerance or justice or those other things he wanted, but to a world in which such qualities grew increasingly uncommon. To enlighten a society you had to fight. And though the struggle would most likely end in failure, you had to take that risk. Because doing nothing guaranteed disaster.

All right, then, the thing to do was fight. But how? The best way, I still believed, was through a Morgan presidency. Here in Yosemite my head had emptied of the panic that had obstructed my thinking after the suspension. I realized that Morgan easily could have sidestepped the car-tax embarrassment by claiming it was something he'd considered for a moment but then dropped. But that would have meant no car tax. Was he more committed to the car tax than he was to me? That would be tremendously encouraging, proof he really was sincere about environmentalism. Under those circumstances I'd work for him even harder than before, if he'd have me back.

But if he wouldn't have me back, I'd find another way to fight for nature. Maybe take a PR job in the local office of the NRDC or Sierra Club. That way I could live in San Francisco, and if Kaya wanted, we could give ourselves another shot.

Which was another question. Did we *want* to give ourselves another shot?

The only things keeping us together these last few years were Nimby and inertia. Obviously we needed more than that. But the passion of our youth was spent, and we finished meshing life-styles years ago. We had to decide which we preferred: the boring security of a partnership grown cold, or the excitement and anxiety of active singledom.

I had to look at this realistically. I was no Jack Morgan. I didn't have his drive. Nor did I have much in the way of status: no gobs of money, no mansions and big cars, no entrée to the elite. I was an average-looking schmo with a hairline receding in inverse proportion to his waistline. Cold-eyed D.C. women wouldn't deign to look me over twice.

As for the San Francisco singles, it seemed that every personal in the *Bay Guardian* demanded a financially secure, professional, and family-minded, not to mention good-looking and health-conscious, respondent. I envisioned an unending string of introductory chitchats in caffeine bars as woman after woman judged me—jobless, aging, nerdy me—a loser.

And what of those who didn't see me as a loser? What would I attract? The hard-core singles, probably: the drinkers, the nail-biting neurotics, the serial divorcees more loyal to their kids than they could ever be to me. Or I'd pick up someone on the rebound who would vent on me her anger at her former mate. The fact is that at this age you don't run across too many single people without heavy baggage.

Which got me thinking about all I took for granted about Kaya. She was everything I wanted in a woman: smart, and unafraid to show her smarts to other people, even men; honest and forthright, not a game player who made me jump through hoops; unpretentious and nonmaterialistic, oblivious to social hierarchies and clothing labels. In short, she eschewed the standard nonsense that has come to be confused with femininity. I not only loved that, I admired it. I wished that I could cast away my standard masculine behavior so completely. And, on top of everything else, she was still a pleasure to look upon.

So what would really happen if I broke it off with her? A lot of mornings waking up alone, picking out the least-wrinkled shirt in the hamper to wear to work. Then coming home at night and heating up canned beans to wash down with a beer while watching ball games until bedtime. The same thing, day after day, interrupted by the occasional, joyless one-night stand. And that would be my life until I died. Now and then I'd hear from Kaya, who'd no doubt find a wonderful guy and have a much steadier relationship with him than she'd ever had with me.

I knew a good deal when I saw one. As long as she would have me, I would hold on to my wife. We would fan the embers of our relationship and fight the warlords of pollution as a team.

It was getting very chilly; the sun was sinking toward the canyon walls. I got up—man, did my ass ache —and thanked the vista for its long and clear perspective.

The trail wound down the east side of a ridge, so I had to scoot along to beat the darkness. In tree-shrouded stretches at the bottom of the ridge I often had to stop and reorient myself to make sure I didn't lose the trail. As the last hues of orange faded from the high clouds I got back to our camp.

Knowing I'd return by dark, Kaya was readying dinner—our favorite, imported angel hair pasta and tomato-basil sauce made by some Mafia firm in Hoboken. She wouldn't look me in the eye until I stood a foot in front of her.

"Hey, babe," I said, "how about a dance?"

She cried and giggled at the same time, burying her head inside my coat. We stayed that way a minute, rocking slowly, then retreated to the tent.

We kept each other warm for hours.

Around midnight, lying on my back and snug in my sleeping bag, I reached over and flipped on the radio. I had the dial tuned to KCBS. "CBS News, I'm Jeff Dooley in New York." Ah, the three-minute headline service that passes for the news! "That tanker that ran aground and broke in two near Alcatraz this afternoon continues to spill oil into San Francisco Bay. Officials fear the *Prince William Sound* will ultimately pour eight million gallons into California's largest estuary. Already reports are coming in of birds and harbor seals smothered in Alaskan crude—"

Kaya shot bolt upright. We looked at each other as if stricken. "We must go back," she said.

31

To RESCUE ONE bird from an oil spill, here is what you have to do.

First, you have to walk in teams of two along the black, reeking beach to find a bird who's struggled to the shore alive. The birds who live along the water's edge—gulls, sandpipers, willets, godwits, dunlins—are your most likely find. They're in the best shape, less thickly oiled and not so badly battered by the surf. You approach them slowly but confidently and pick them up by slipping a hand under each wing, your thumbs over the top and your other fingers supporting their bellies. You don't press. It's a good sign· if they struggle—it means they may be strong enough to survive what lies ahead.

The birds who live out on the bay—ducks mostly—won't be happy when you grab them, but after struggling for hours to stay afloat and reach the shore, they won't have the strength to resist. On some the oil is a half inch thick, feathers so completely matted the quills stick out like toothpicks. Oftentimes you come upon a seabird that is dead. You pick it up anyway, because you don't want predators to get hold of it and pass the oil up the food chain.

The initial threat to a bird that's lost the insulation of its feathers is hypothermia, so once you've scooped it up you place it in a thick, brown paper bag and fold the top as gingerly as possible around its neck. This is very tricky if the bird decides to flap its wings or otherwise protest; you may receive an oil shower or a nasty peck. (You wear two rubber gloves on each hand to protect yourself from jabbing beaks.)

Once you bag it, you have to carry the bird to the intake center, which may be a mile away. There your bird's species and condition are recorded, and it's placed in a rag-cushioned cardboard box for transport to a treatment center.

At the treatment center, usually a high school gym or other public space commandeered for the occasion, you have to inspect the bird carefully for injuries. If it's okay except for the crude, you clap a tiny metal ring around a leg so that it can be identified, then shove it in the same sort of plastic cage you use to carry your cat to the vet. If the bird is showing signs of hypothermia, you put a heat lamp by the cage door, turned on high.

Now that you've done what you can to remove the threat of hypothermia, you have to preempt the next most likely troubles: dehydration and starvation. To stay afloat, struggle ashore, and stay warm, this bird has probably metabolized its fat and perhaps a portion of its muscle too. Food will give it strength for the recovery, as well as calm it down. While you grab the bird by the wings and sides, your partner pries open its beak and shoves a long tube full of warm electrolyte solution down its throat. Pressing a syringe deposits a few ounces of the goo directly into the bird's stomach. Later on you feed the bird again, this time a stew of fish chow, vegetable oil, vitamins, and more electrolytes.

Assuming your bird perks up, you have to transfer it to a dirty-bird pen, a ten-foot-square plywood enclosure filled with wadded newspaper. The paper absorbs waste and oil and is soft enough for the bird to hunker down in, relieving the stress on its legs. (Remember, you're dealing mostly with aquatic birds who swim more than they stand up and are unaccustomed to such pressure on their feet and knees.) There are other birds in the enclosure, usually of the same species, but they're too weak and scared to socialize.

At last the time has come to clean the bird. It's taken forever to set up the bathing pens—the process demands thousands and thousands of gallons of warm water, which few public places are equipped to supply readily. It also demands an Astroturf floor, utility tubs, hoses topped with plastic shower heads, fisherman's waders for the cleaners, detergent, toothbrushes, cotton balls and swabs, and countless other odds and ends. You don your waders, poke holes for your head and arms in a plastic trash bag to protect your upper body, and fill your tub with a one-percent solution of detergent in warm water. Then you fetch your bird and dunk it in.

It doesn't like the bath, but this is the only way to get the oil off. And you must get every single molecule of oil off if the bird is to survive. One of you holds it down, clamping its beak, while the other does the cleaning. At first you wash a ton of crude away—all the caked-on stuff—but then the process slows to a crawl as you go feather by feather from the bird's face to its tail. You use the cotton swabs and toothbrush for the fine work, like a sculptor finishing the details on an ornate statue. Only this statue writhes and splashes as you work, slowing down your progress. Before too long the floor beneath you is a couple of inches under water; good thing the Astroturf mat is there to give you traction.

An hour passes, then another. You're still working on this one bird. If you're the holder, your arms and hands are getting tired from maintaining a firm yet delicate grasp. If you're the washer, your eyes are crossing from the close work. You begin to wonder aloud whether saving birds is worth it; if they all die in this spill, the cleanup for the next one won't require so much work.

When the oil's finally off you have to give the bird a rinse. Now it's vital that you get the detergent off, because the wetting agents in the soap will destroy the feathers' waterproofing. So once again you go the length of the bird's body feather by feather, this time with the shower head. For the tight spaces you use a dentist's water sprayer. The job is finished when, ironically, the bird looks dry, because that means the waterproofing is restored. You sit the bird up on a metal table and inspect it for injuries incurred while bathing, daub a drop of saline solution in its eyes for lubrication, and put ointment on its legs and feet to prevent chapping.

Now your bird goes to a clean pen, about the same size as a dirty pen but with a nylon-mesh floor, below which are waste-catching newspapers. The clean pens for newly washed birds have heat lamps and blow dryers, and are topped with fabric to keep the birds from trying to fly out. About a dozen birds of the same species are put inside each pen. The feistier ones occasionally squawk. The rest just sit and wait for their next torment.

For many of the avians the worst is over. They become strong enough to take food by hand and begin flapping their wings vigorously. Assuming your bird is deemed restored to health, you move it to an outdoor pen. There it's tested in a kiddie pool for buoyancy. For ducks the pool is lined with treats along the bottom, to entice them to immerse their bodies. If your bird stays dry, it's ready to return to the wild.

If, however, water soaks through to the skin, back it goes for another bath. Usually at this stage the problem isn't overlooked oil so much as leftover detergent, so you spend extra time rinsing. Then it's back for another buoyancy test.

Some birds make it through all these stages only to turn suddenly for the worse. Probably they swallowed oil in the beginning, and only now is the poison affecting their internal organs. Kidneys and livers degenerate. Anemia sets in, cutting the bird's oxygen capacity by as much as one fifth, leading to general weakness and, in ducks, an inability to hold breath while diving after food. Gulls are particularly susceptible to oil poisoning, being scavengers who pick at the remains of carcasses in the initial stages of the spill.

But let's say your bird makes it. First of all, congratulations; only forty percent of the birds brought in for treatment survive long enough to be released back to the wild. Second, consider for a moment what it took to keep that bird alive. The process took anywhere from one week to a month or more, requiring dozens of hours of labor and hundreds of dollars in resources. Multiply that by the thousands of birds brought to the rescue stations and you realize that to save this one tiny part of the local ecosystem, you and your neighbors had to mount an effort equivalent to a moonshot minus all the fancy hardware.

Once your bird is healthy, where do you release it? You can't just let it back into the Bay. There's still oil everywhere, from the marshlands of Milpitas to the headlands of Marin, and cleanup efforts won't be finished for another several weeks. (Even then, will all the oil have been picked up from the water? Hardly.) So, working with officials from the U.S. Fish and Wildlife Service, you try to find another place in which your bird can thrive.

I could give you more details, but this is the essence of what you have to do to rescue a bird from the sort of disaster that struck San Francisco Bay. I didn't know the task was so complicated when I started out, and wouldn't have if I hadn't done it all myself. Most volunteers concentrate on just one facet of the rescue. They either pick the birds up from the beach or transport the birds to rescue centers or feed the birds or clean the birds or wad up newspaper hour after dreary hour. But because of Kaya's connection to the Lindsay Museum, cleanup officials allowed us to follow one bird through the process. And when our bird finally passed the buoyancy test, I called a press conference.

Since I had purposely omitted any reference to the subject of my talk, reporters showed up assuming I would discuss my suspension. They crowded around the makeshift podium set up on the Marina Green, the camerapeople jostling for good angles like basketball players going for a rebound. Also appearing at the conference, but standing more to the periphery, was a stocky, sunglassed fellow I couldn't quite place at first, until I realized he was one of Buford's guards. Surprise, surprise, I was being watched by my own people. In retrospect the real surprise was that Buford's thugs hadn't followed us into Yosemite—so far as we knew.

Kaya and I each carried a shrouded kennel cage to the podium, causing the reporters to whisper apprehensively among themselves. No doubt Buford's spy was every bit as delighted as the reporters were disappointed when I issued my disclaimer. "I want to mention right up front that I'll be speaking as a private citizen and not as an official of the Morgan campaign. Nor will I have any comment in connection with my suspension."

I expected some reporters to leave right then, but perhaps figuring they could prod me into talking about Morgan later, they all remained. "This is Via," I introduced, pulling a bird from Kaya's cage and holding him up to the cameras precisely the way I picked him up from the beach a week before. "Via is a greater scaup, a kind of duck. We call him Via after the Marx Brothers routine. He has a wing span of two and a half feet and weighs about two pounds. As you can see, Via has a greenish head and neck, a black breast, grayish-white flanks, and brownish wings with a big white stripe along the back. One week ago, though, Via was all black."

Via squawked and flapped his wings. I almost lost control of him.

"We're putting Via back into his cage. In you go, boy, come on! My wife and I personally nursed him back to health this week. We found him on the beach barely able to stand up. We brought him to the rescue station at the Marine Mammal Center. We warmed him, fed him, fretted over him, and when he seemed strong enough for the ordeal, we washed him up.

"I never knew how much it takes to keep one bird alive in a disaster like this. Just cleaning off his wings took more than an hour. You have to wash the oil off of every single strand of every single feather. The primaries, the secondaries, the scapulars, the axillaries, the coverts. If you miss so much as one drop he may preen it off, and if he swallows it he'll suffer serious internal damage. Then if you don't rinse off every molecule of the detergent used to clean the oil, he can lose his insulation, his waterproofing, even his ability to fly.

"Via is a lucky one. He survived. So far nearly thirteen thousand birds have been brought to rescue centers here in the Bay Area. Only sixty-three hundred of those birds are still alive. That's actually a pretty good percentage compared with previous rescue operations, but as you can see, even if a bird survives the oil spill, its chances of returning to the wild are less than fifty-fifty. And that's only counting the birds who washed up on shore alive.

"For every bird that came ashore alive, officials estimate another seven or eight died either at sea or in the Bay. So we're talking around one hundred thousand birds killed by this spill. Maybe that doesn't sound like much to you, but you must remember San Francisco Bay is a central link in the Pacific Flyway, and this is the migration season. Many of the birds killed here come from Alaska, or are on their way to Central America. That means ecosystems throughout the Americas will be affected. And they will continue to be affected for the next twenty years, which is how long biologists estimate it will take this estuary to return to normal.

"I'd like to introduce you now to one of those migrating birds. We call him C. Turnbull, after the chairman of the board of the company that owns the *Prince William Sound.*" Out of the second cage I pulled an enormous dead bird, which I also held up for the cameras. "C. Turnbull, as you can see, is a mature bald eagle. The national symbol. We found him yesterday at a site that I've been asked not to disclose because there's evidence of other endangered birds inhabiting it. We don't get too many baldies this far south. Usually they only come as far as Oregon and northern California, so his being here is—was—very special. Bald eagles are scavengers, especially of fish. Experts at the Golden Gate Raptor Observatory speculate that C. Turnbull ate one too many fish or dead ducks contaminated by the oil and was poisoned.

"The reason I've called you here today is to make more tangible the tremendous ecological destruction that's been caused by the *Prince William Sound.* Here it is, folks, your national symbol: a bald eagle choked to death on fossil fuel."

"Dan," interrupted a reporter, "you say you're not here as a member of Morgan's staff, but doesn't your message coincide all too neatly with his environmental theme?"

"I'd like to go a whole lot further than Jack Morgan. Morgan is constrained from saying what we really need to hear. And what we really need to hear is this: The company that owns the tanker is not responsible.

The company is just playing by the rules, fulfilling a demand. The blame—the reason why C. Turnbull here is dead—belongs to each and every one of us who drives a car. When we stop demanding so much oil, then less of it will come in these big tankers, and less of it will spill into our estuaries. It's that simple. Reduce demand, reduce pollution."

In a highly irritated tone: "Dan, didn't that rhetoric go out of fashion twenty years ago?"

"You know, one thing I'm sick of, maybe sicker of than anything else, is this presumption that environmentalists are dreamers and industrialists are practical. It's quite the opposite. The ones who argue for the status quo are the dreamers. They want life to go on uninterrupted in the face of imminent—and, in the case of the San Francisco oil spill, immediate—disaster. *That's* impractical, you guys. By contrast, environmentalists are the ultimate hardheaded realists. They're looking at the basic issue, survival, and trying to do what's necessary to ensure it.

"And while I'm at it," I said, unable to control myself, "I want to add that smug remarks like that indicate you guys have unexamined biases on the environmental issue that distort your ability to report about it objectively. Remember? You're supposed to be objective. But you can't be objective if you swallow whole the myth that environmentalists are dreamers and exploiters are realists. All you can be is an apologist for the corporate and political establishment."

"Dan, you sure you're not flacking for Jack Morgan here? Being his hatchet man or something?"

"No. Laugh all you want, guys, but this is literally true: Everything I'm saying's for the birds."

32

AFTER THE PRESS conference Reed Gordin came over to shoot the breeze. Although it had been a year since he'd landed that job at NBC, the change in his appearance still startled me. His sandy hair, which flew every which way when he worked the campaign beat for *The New York Times,* was now razor-cut, blow-dried, and so sprayed that even the Bay breeze couldn't muss it. In place of the usual wrinkled Oxford shirt and jeans he wore a custom-tailored charcoal suit.

Gordin had shot to the top of the reportage biz with a meticulously researched series of articles that destroyed Elbert Nelson, the Tennessee governor who won the Democratic nomination in 2000. The usual saga of booze, broads, and bribes, it had a particularly devastating effect because Nelson cultivated a clean image and was considered the strongest candidate by party insiders. Gordin's hit came after Nelson had garnered enough delegates to win the nomination, and touched off a fracas over whether to release convention delegates from their first-ballot obligation to vote for their pledged candidate.

Even after receiving word that Gordin had more

dirt and intended to print it, Nelson denied the revelations and rejected pleas to release his delegates. In August Gordin published stories that demolished what remained of Nelson's credibility; three months later Nelson became the first major party candidate to lose the popular vote by two-to-one since they started keeping records in the nineteenth century.

That landed Gordin a job with the *Times*, where he became the new R. W. Apple: a wunderkind who single-handedly held down the national political desk and during campaigns got his byline on the front page three times a week. Although Gordin didn't expose any killer skeletons in 2004, he wrote with an erudition that distinguished him from every other daily scribe. The candidates knew an interview with him was as crucial as a debate or hot TV ad, and consequently treated him with a deference usually reserved for financial patrons.

Like most other writers, though, Gordin discovered that his earnings weren't commensurate with his acclaim. The *Times* could only pay him so much, so when NBC News, a dismal last among the major networks, offered him big bucks to do a thrice-weekly, five-minute segment on the 2008 campaign, he jumped. During the primaries he did a favorable segment on Jack Morgan. Then he did that profile between the primaries and the Convention. During the presidential drive he did stories on tourists visiting the Morgan house in Ottawa Hills, the economics of sustainable technology, and a survey of the garbage coming out of Morgan's home and Senate office to see whether the environmental candidate recycled. (He did—started years ago, at my insistence.) Any other correspondent would have looked ridiculous poring through a dumpster full of garbage—literally muckraking—but Gordin managed to pull it off with a measure of panache.

His stories about Morgan were warm if not effusive, in contrast to his pieces on the President, which occasionally crossed the line from coldly neutral into disapproving. My favorite was the interview he did with Marian Lundquist, the entomologist, about the impact of ants and termites on atmospheric change. "Remember when Ronald Reagan said that trees cause most pollution?" the amiable, elderly scientist asked. "That was perceptive by comparison." The story helped mitigate the President's advantage after the first debate.

"What brings you to San Francisco?" I asked as he followed Kaya and me to Marina Boulevard and an awaiting cab.

"President was in L.A. last night, and when I heard you'd called this conference I decided to fly up. Where you headed?"

"Off the record?"

Gordin nodded.

"Monterey. Fish and Wildlife found a flock of greater scaups down there. They've already released a few San Francisco birds into it. We're going to release Via."

"Mind if me and my guys come along?" he asked, indicating his cameraman and soundwoman.

"Don't you have to file?" I asked.

"Not till tomorrow. I was thinking I might do a story on you."

Reed Gordin! Damn! I *wanted* him to do a story on me. There was still a lot I had to say. But I didn't want to show my eagerness. "Five days from the election, and you want to do a story on me?"

"You're the guy who focused this campaign on the environment. You're the brains behind the new campaigning. I think that merits coverage."

"It's a three-hour ride each way. We're going down by bus. Don't want to go by car and waste a lot of gas—wouldn't look good for the movement."

"Understood." By now Kaya and I were in our cab. "You leaving from the station at Seventh and Mission?"

he asked. "Give us a couple minutes. We'll be right behind."

"Well," I said to Kaya as we drove off, "I figured
we would get attention, but this is a PR wet dream."

"Congratulations, pumpkin."

We gave each other a great big hug, and Via
squawked.

The bus was fairly empty. A couple of young men
who looked like soldiers sat in back and smoked on the
sly. A Hispanic woman shepherded three little kids
aboard and settled near the bathroom. An older couple
sat directly behind the driver and chatted with him. A
fortyish man with slick, carefully combed blond hair and
tattoos showing under his rolled-up sleeves chose a
space in the middle of the bus, near us. If anyone
aboard was Buford's spy, he was probably the one.

Gordin's technical people sat in front of me, leaning over the backs of their chairs to point their equipment at me. I sat by the window, with Gordin next to
me. Kaya and Via sat behind. We did a number of takes
on each question, until I thought I got it right. He asked
mostly about why I thought the environment was so important, and then we got to talking about the election.
"The Democrats had two ways to go," I said. "Either try
to out-Republican the Republicans, which would effectively give the nation one party with rival wings, or do
something to provide genuine opposition and preserve a
real two-party system—and hence democracy. To become a genuine opposition you need a strong base of
popular support, and the only way I saw us doing that
was through environmentalism."

"So you think democracy's in danger?" Gordin
asked.

"Oh, come on, Reed, even Morgan's said as much."

"I know, but the point can't be made strongly
enough. I can't say it on the air. You can. Give it another take. So you think democracy's in danger?"

"What real choice do we have when both parties are backed by the same interests and, with only minor variations, stand for the same thing?"

The bus wheeled into Salinas, and the smokers in back disembarked. It wouldn't be long until we got to Monterey. I hoped there'd be enough daylight for us to spot the flock of scaups. Otherwise Kaya and I would have to stay in a hotel. We'd brought along some just-in-case stuff: food and bedding for Via, a change of clothing for ourselves.

Finally crescent-shaped Monterey Bay spread before us. The bus lurched along congested Del Monte Avenue, prompting me to suggest we get off at the next corner. I was afraid that Via, already agitated by the long ride, would hurt himself on one of the driver's abrupt stops. But just as my patience was about to snap we swung into the bus station.

Once down at the Municipal Wharf, Kaya pulled out her binoculars and scanned the water. "Well?" I asked as Gordin's crew trained their equipment on us.

"I see a bunch of pelicans in the marina. Oh, and there's an otter. Don't see any scaups, though. Maybe farther south, below the Coast Guard pier. I think that's where the ranger said they were, near Mussel Point."

We hiked along the train tracks by the shoreline, tracks that once connected Cannery Row to civilization but had since become a walker's shortcut from the wharf to the Aquarium. "This is off the record, totally," I said to Gordin as we passed the Coast Guard pier; seals at the far end raised their heads and barked at one another. "Maybe after this we should head back to Salinas and check John Steinbeck's grave, see if he turned over after Morgan told that story about *Grapes of Wrath.*"

"Did that embarrass you?"

"Hell, yes. But did it surprise me? No. There's no such thing as excess sentimentality for a politician."

We traipsed through Cannery Row, past the restaurants and schlock shops to the Aquarium. It was getting on toward dinnertime; the place was emptying out. After the Aquarium we hit the less touristy part of town, and I pulled out my map. "We're getting close to Mussel Point," I said, but there wasn't any beach, just crumbly yellow cliff. We walked along Ocean View Boulevard, looking for an access ramp, without success.

And then "Scaups!" Kaya cried triumphantly, holding the binoculars with one hand and pointing with the other.

They were hard to make out with the naked eye. All we could tell was that a flock of ducklike birds was wading by a tiny beach. We doubled our pace until we were there, then approached cautiously so as not to alarm the birds.

"Yep, they look like greater scaups. Guess this is it, my friend," I said to Via as the camera rolled. I set the cage down by the water's edge. "After all we went through to clean him up, his future's still uncertain," I explained. "He probably had a mate in San Francisco. There's not much chance she made it here, so the odds are he will have to find a new mate, not to mention be accepted by the other males. And though he hasn't shown the symptoms, what if he ingested oil? He may turn sick and die within a couple weeks. So this," I opened up the cage, "is an act of faith in one small bird and Mother Nature. Godspeed, Via."

With that Via ventured from his cage. He hung back at first, expecting to be picked up, but when it didn't happen, he flapped his wings and in a blur flew off to join his fellow scaups. None of them seemed to notice his arrival. Within a minute, unless you kept your eyes on him the whole time, you wouldn't have been able to distinguish him from all the others.

"I have to do some wrap-up," Gordin said. "That'll

take awhile. Why don't you go to dinner, and we'll meet you at the station at, say, seven-thirty?"

"Got yourself a deal," I said.

Heading back toward the Aquarium, we found a restaurant a cut above the usual. "So," I said, clasping Kaya's hand, "today turned out real well, didn't it?"

"I'm worried about Via," she grumped.

"His fate's no longer intertwined with ours." I pulled her hand toward me and kissed it. "Did you listen to the interview on the ride down?"

"No. I was trying to keep Via calm. Don't you wonder how he's getting on with all the other scaups? Is he happy or confused?" She sighed. "He's so vulnerable."

"I can't believe that you, who said that Via would make a great meal for Nimby, are being so sentimental."

Oops. Wrong thing to say. She bit her lip to hold back tears. "Hey, he'll do fine," I said consolingly. "He had to be tenacious to survive our ineptitude."

"That's true." She smiled. "I'm surprised we didn't kill him ourselves. I still laugh when I think how you held his beak shut when we washed him and had your thumb over his nostrils."

"I wondered why he was getting so upset."

"Oh, well. I guess we did everything we could. Still, I wish there was a way to know what happens to him."

"Maybe he'll fly back to the cleaning pens to spawn."

"Har-har. Tell me about your interview."

"It came off great. I said everything I wanted to say and said it well for a change. Smart guy, Gordin. The other reporters probably figured they wasted their time, since I didn't talk about the suspension. But Gordin, he goes to the press conference and sees the perfect way to tie together everything he's covered. And now, because he followed up, he gets the scoop: what happened to Via."

"No, he gets the scaup."

"Ouch."

"But didn't you tell me that anything you say can be turned against you by a slick reporter? Reed Gordin is a slick reporter."

"Yeah, but you know, in this instance I think that works to our advantage. He's one of the few who really understands the power of the media. He knows how he can influence elections—he's done it. And I think he's on our side. That report he did on whether Jack recycled—just about every other reporter, after finding that we *did* recycle, would have said there was no story there. But Gordin went ahead and did a positive report. He wouldn't have bothered if he wasn't pulling for us."

Kaya suddenly tensed and frowned.

"What's the matter?"

"That's the first time since Yosemite I've heard you sound like Morgan's press secretary."

33

"DID YOU SEE the headline in *USA Today*?" Gordin asked me as the bus home turned inland toward Salinas.

"Can't say I did."

"AIDES SAY HIT THE ROAD, JACK," Gordin quoted. "Apparently some of your buddies are trying to talk Jack into barnstorming instead of prepping for the last debate. What do you think?"

A *very* slick reporter, this Reed Gordin. He knew how to be patient. He didn't ply me with Morgan questions at the press conference, didn't push me during the ride to Monterey or the release of Via. Only now, after I'd had hours to be grateful for his attention and we were isolated on this bus, did he finally press.

I was tempted to open up. Gordin understood what politics was about. He was trustworthy, in that he wouldn't make a mountain of a molehill for a story's sake. Nonetheless, I hadn't grown so rusty that I could be seduced by a reporter. "Anything I say about the man is deepest background," I insisted. "Not for attribution under any circumstances. Understood?"

Gordin nodded.

"I can just about predict who's on which side. Not

that I've had any contact with the staff since leaving. Erika Mitchell left a wish-you-were-here message on my phone machine one night, but that's been it.

"Anyway, I'm sure it's Buford who wants him to go out. Mel never wanted the debates. This last one must be scaring him shitless. I mean, they're holding it the Sunday before the election, and it's the President's format. Jack could really stink it up, and if he does, there goes the election. So Buford's thinking, 'Let's play down its importance and make Jack's emergence from Toledo the story. That way if he fucks up the debate he can say it's because he thought it more important to meet the people.' You risk turning off some voters by breaking the promise to stay home, but Buford knows we have to make some kind of move, and the debate is *their* guy's opportunity, not ours.

"On the other side you've got Molineaux and Fallon. Principally Fallon. He's looking at this from a logistics angle. In two days or less he's got to create an itinerary, coordinate the advance people, arrange for security with the local police—a million nightmares even for a staff that's used to travel. Botch-ups are inevitable, maybe massive ones that'll embarrass the campaign. Like, he schedules a huge rally but there's no publicity and sixteen people show up. One mistake like that could mean we lose.

"Molineaux is thinking along the same lines, except more from a PR view. There won't be time to make things look good. No fancy podium to speak from at press conferences, no red-white-and-blue bunting in the background at rallies. Mismatched plates at the fundraising dinners. No glossy press kits to send the local broadcast people. Again, one mistake, disaster."

"What would you advise Morgan, if you were still with the campaign?" Gordin asked.

"I don't know. Probably to go out. That's how the

battle lines formed up the past few months, me and Buford versus Fallon and Molineaux."

"And whose advice do you think he'll follow?"

I shrugged. "Hard to say. He's unpredictable."

"Hmm. Interesting you put it that way. I heard from a very reliable source that Morgan experiences fits of depression that seriously impair his judgment. Care to confirm?"

Never in a career when I've often been lost for words have I ever been caught so off guard. The very worst possible thing that could happen, the public revelation of Morgan's madness, was one step from becoming a reality—less than a week before the election. No matter how completely Morgan captured the public's imagination with his personality and politics, if a reporter of Gordin's stature broke that story, the election was over. And I was being asked to play the role of Judas.

I knew better than to answer right away, even though my silence let Gordin know he'd hit on something. Floundering in an ocean of adrenaline, my brain wasn't up to thinking through this gambit. Only one cogent thought connected: Gordin was in contact with the inner circle mole! From whom else could he have obtained such closely guarded information?

"Who's your source?" I asked, trying to sound casual and achieving predictable results.

"Now now, Dan," Gordin tutted, "you know the rules. I'd no more reveal my source than you'd endorse the President. Do you confirm?"

"I need to know your source. How do I know you even have one? Maybe you're taking a payoff from the other side to do a hit piece the weekend before the election. You pick up on a vicious rumor and go to a disaffected member of Morgan's staff for confirmation. How do I know that's not what's going on?"

"I give you my word that's not the case here."

"Oh, that's right, I forgot. Journalists never lie to get a scoop."

Gordin wrung his hands. "Listen, Dan. Two things. First of all, I like Jack Morgan. In fact I'll tell you right up front I'm voting for him, even if it's true he's off his rocker. But number two, my duty as a journalist comes first. The people have a right to know whether the man they're voting for loses his hold periodically. If I or some other correspondent doesn't tell them, you sure as hell won't, and that's not fair."

"I'm surprised to hear you sound so sanctimonious, Reed. I thought you understood the process better."

"I'm a reporter, Dan, not an amplifier. I thought *you* understood *that.*"

I exhaled loudly, closed my eyes, and pressed my head against my seat. I didn't want to be there. I looked out the window, hoping to glimpse a sign that we were close to home, but from what I could tell we were still well south of San Jose.

"Think about it, Dan. Who are you protecting? A man who cut you loose for no good reason. What he did to you is by itself enough to make me think he isn't rowing with all oars."

"He had his reasons, Reed."

"Oh yeah? Name one."

"The leak to the *Times.*"

"You telling me you *are* the one who leaked those documents?"

"Of course not. But I'm the fall guy."

"Fall guy?" he shook his head incredulously. "For what?"

"Oh, come on, Reed, didn't you follow the story? Morgan saw the car tax as a credibility problem. He was scared the voters would turn away because he hadn't leveled with them. Since I was the one who recommended keeping the car tax secret, my head had to roll."

"Of course I followed the story. And you know damn well that doesn't jive with anything Jack said."

"You're kidding. What did he say?"

"Are you toying with me, Dan, or do you really not know?"

"I went camping for a week. I didn't hear what happened after I left."

"He said he didn't disclose the car tax because it was one of the million ideas that come up in a campaign that don't get adopted. He said, unequivocally, that he had no plans to impose one. And that was that."

"Well, knock me over with a feather." No wonder I hadn't heard a thing about the car tax on the radio! That bastard! "And what was his official reason for my going?"

"He didn't give a reason, just figured we'd infer from the timing it was because of the leak. But we knew you didn't leak. My old contacts at the *Times* confirmed that. So I had our beat guy ask specifically why you were suspended. Morgan said he couldn't answer. We thought maybe there were legal goings-on that prevented his talking." Gordin shrugged. "So we're still wondering why you're off the campaign."

"I don't know, if the car tax isn't the reason. There aren't any legal problems, far as I know. Maybe he still thinks I'm responsible for the leak. Either that, or—"

"Or what?"

"Or there's something else that I don't know about," I said as visions of Kathy danced across my brain. No way I'd tell Reed Gordin about *that*.

"You didn't have a disagreement over policy or anything?"

"No."

"Then it was a highly irrational move, wouldn't you say, to dismiss for no good reason, in the middle of a neck-and-neck campaign, the adviser who gave him political life?"

I couldn't answer; my mind didn't reel this much when I was drunk.

"Look, Dan, you said you were disappointed that I didn't understand the process better. Well, try this on for size. I took great footage of you today. I can make you look real good. The heavy hitters tune in to watch me, smart people, executives, professionals. They'll see you as the conscience of the country, a man of integrity who fought for the environment and truth in campaigning. That'll give you all the credibility you'll ever need. You can become the spokesperson for the entire movement if you want. *But I will not run that story if you don't tell me about Morgan.*"

"You do understand the process," I granted wanly.

"Shall I turn on my dictaputer?"

"Not yet."

My first impulse when the screws are put to me is to say the hell with it and refuse to cooperate. Don't run that piece tomorrow for your oh-so-influential audience. So what if I fade into obscurity? I can handle going back to work for bush-league baseball teams. Got plenty of 'em here in California. I could latch on with the Stockton Ports or the Modesto A's. Spend my nights in the dry heat of the central valley, entertaining the ham-fisted, shirt-sleeved local agribusinessmen. At least we'd only be a couple of hours from home—and a couple of hours from the mountains. Kaya ought to like that.

But wait a minute. Day after day of old-line Republican farmers asking whether I'm the one who was the spokesman for Jack Morgan and giving me a smirk when I acknowledge that I am. Snickers of "Long way down to here, eh?" from people satisfied that being stuck with them is my comeuppance. It's not that bad, I'll tell myself, just for the summer. But after the season's over, how will I afford that flat in San Francisco? Doing free-lance work back home? Hah. Nothing like the daily hand-to-mouth to remind me that I pissed away a lifetime opportunity.

Gordin sensed my wavering. "Think of the movement," he pressed. "Planet earth. Maybe Morgan's not the savior. He's too fresh to the cause—never was that outspoken in the Senate. He saw a way to win November fourth and gambled. You don't know that he'll follow through once he gets in."

"He really did back off the car tax?"

"Do you want me to show you the video when we arrive in San Francisco? I can get it from the network in five minutes."

"No, that's okay. I believe you."

And I'm so damned pissed off that you have a deal, I almost added. But I hesitated. Even if Morgan had betrayed the car tax—and me—it didn't necessarily follow that he'd betray the whole environmental agenda. There was still a chance he'd do a lot of what he pledged, whereas with the other guy there was no chance for the environment at all. So my interests were still best served by protecting Morgan. Besides, it would be too self-negating to undo, five days from election day, the many years of effort I put into bringing Morgan so close to the White House.

Then I pictured Morgan saying "Thank you, Steinhardt," and turning to Buford and sniggering "What a chump! We let him loose two weeks ago and here he is, still lying for us! Not that, in our overweening smugness, we didn't expect it, but sometimes it's just staggering to see how people willingly make patsies of themselves!"

Ah, Steinhardt, they know what you are. You're like Jack Morgan's bimbos—how many of them are there now, almost a hundred? But every single one holds in her disappointment. Not one has told on him, not even now, when it would bring her notoriety and wealth!

I'm not the innocent you think I am, Jack Morgan.

You hear? I'm not the innocent you think! You think it doesn't grind me that I covered for you all those years? Or that you've sold out your commitment to the planet? You think I wouldn't step on someone's face to get ahead? Well, fuck you, buddy! Get a load of this!

"He's off," I blurted to Reed Gordin. "The man's as crazy as a loon."

Home at last, exhausted, I sat by the telephone table and petted Nimby while replaying our messages. I was hoping there'd be follow-ups from the reporters at the press conference, but instead heard only this:

Beep! "Steinhardt, this is Morgan. I'm coming out to Frisco Friday morning. Meet me at the airport, gate sixteen, nine-thirty sharp."

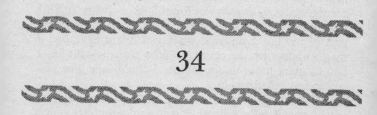

34

FOR IMMEDIATE RELEASE   CONTACT: TIM AVERY

After a two-week hiattus, press secretary Daniel Steinhardt returns to the Morgan campaign effective today. Steinhardt is expected to join the campaign today in San Francisco, where Morgan is addressing a noontime rally at the World Trade Center.

"Well, what do you think?" asked Molineaux. He and a bevy of Secret Service agents comprised the bulk of the advance team awaiting Morgan on the runway apron. Also on hand was Fallon's California field director and her minions, a number of Buford's bodyguards, several prominent Democratic fund-raisers and state and local officeholders, assorted Hollywood celebrities, and the local press. Dozens of police lined Morgan's pathway to the motorcade; others crouched on rooftops with walkie-talkies and high-caliber rifles.

What did I think? I'd had all night to decide what to do if Morgan reinstated me, in fact had argued it over with Kaya until nearly four A.M. She was angry that I'd even *think* of going back to the campaign, and issued an ultimatum: It was either politics or her. She wouldn't tolerate the role of part-time wife again.

I thought it was unfair to make me choose between the two great passions of my life right on the spot. Give me a week, I begged. She refused, saying that stalling was tantamount to choosing politics. At the very least it was a hedge on my commitment to her. Maybe so, I granted, but a new plan was forming in my head, and if I committed myself to her right then there'd always be a part of me that wondered whether I might have had a major impact on the country's—the planet's—future. I had to quell those doubts before I could fully give myself to our relationship.

What kind of plan? she asked. I couldn't say just yet; it wasn't fully formed. But it was ambitious, much more so than any scheme I'd hatched before, and right enough that it might even be worth risking our relationship for. I'd been a firsthand witness to the dying earth the last eight days, had learned how much it takes to rescue one tiny part of it. More than once I realized going one bird at a time was pointless. The only way to save the planet was to change the system that destroys it, and the only way to change the system was to work through people who could do it—like Jack Morgan. This time around I intended to use Morgan the way he used me. I just needed one more week to see if I could make it happen. Please, Kaya, give me that much longer.

Finally, reluctantly, she gave in, and relented also to my plea that she come along if I rejoined the campaign. She would be, as she always had been while I played politics, my link to the wild; and when I got caught up in the campaign, her presence would remind me that this time I had to work *through* Morgan, not for him, to achieve my ends. Besides, her leave of absence from the Lindsay Museum ran through November eighth.

But this is your last chance, she warned before we fell asleep, and I had no doubt that she meant it.

I reread Avery's press release. "What do I think?" I answered Molineaux. "I think I need a deputy whose first language is English, not gibberish."

"About the content."

"He makes it sound like I was out on drug rehab or something."

"Same self-righteous Steinhardt," Molineaux snickered, only half-joshingly. "You should be glad you're back at all." He looked through the viewfinder of his videocam as clouds gave way to sun. "When the old man saw you on the news last night he nearly split a gasket."

"How come?" Kaya asked. I wasn't going to inquire, partly because I figured Molineaux was exaggerating, partly because I *wanted* Morgan to be mad at me. That way he wouldn't have to make a big emotional shift when he saw Reed Gordin's stories and realized I'd sold him out.

"Dan-o here was still on payroll," Molineaux replied. "He had an obligation to clear public appearances with us."

"Well, if he was really pissed, he wouldn't have done this," I said, flourishing the press release.

"Yeah, but you stole his thunder. The whole reason he decided to come out here was to capitalize on the oil spill. When you beat him to it—with that heavy-handed stunt with the dead bird—I swear he would have killed you if he could've gotten his hands on you. I'm telling you, Dan-o, if Avery wasn't such a drip you'd still be cleaning ducks."

"So this trip has nothing to do with rallying the California faithful four days before the election?"

Molineaux grinned again, and winked. "Oh, no, and not with begging money from our northern California angels either."

"What are the polls like?" I asked.

"Gallup has us three points down. Harris has us two points up. All the others in between."

"Including Mitchell?"

"She says the real numbers are the electoral college. As of this morning we have the slightest edge, with eleven states too close to call, including this one. Talk to her this afternoon, maybe the other guy will be ahead."

"How is everybody handling it?"

"They're all tight as piano strings. Fallon hasn't slept in four days. And you should see Elena. She's been whiter than a southern country club since Jack decided to go out."

"That must have been a pretty tough decision."

"Not at all. The only one we needed to convince was him."

"That's surprising. I figured Fallon would object."

"You kidding? That guy lives for stuff like this. He was like a kid with all his toys back. I tell you, he was glad you weren't there when we discussed it. He was sure you'd rant and rave about breaking promises and all that shit. You know—self-righteous Steinhardt strikes again."

"Yeah, I know all about it."

"But just as a precaution, you'll be glad to know, we had Mitchell do a couple of TRACEs. It doesn't bother people. They know Jack's doing what he has to do to win. If anything, they admire him for being practical."

A Secret Service agent announced, "They're on the ground." Security people came together in a wedge. As the plane approached and swung around the tarmac, TV correspondents in the makeshift grandstand thirty yards away began to shout at their cameras, trying to be heard over the earsplitting jet whine.

The first ones off the plane were Secret Service agents and Buford's boys. National media people streamed in—the press plane had also arrived. When security and press were finally in place, Morgan, arm-in-arm with Elena, followed Buford and Fallon out the cockpit door. He raised his free arm in greeting.

It was the first time I'd seen him in two weeks, but it might as well have been the first time in two years. He was slighter than I remembered, the scar on his left cheek thicker and more prominent. And he looked surprisingly haggard for a candidate who'd only started traveling this morning.

"Molineaux filled you in?" he asked, shaking hands. I nodded. Then he shook hands and exchanged short pleasantries with Kaya.

"Listen, Steinhardt, I'm going to L.A. this afternoon and Fresno for a dinner speech, but I'm flying back here afterward to meet with some donors. How about we meet someplace, just you and me and the ladies, for a late meal? You can take me to one of those snooty Frisco restaurants you always brag about."

"Sure," I said. "What should I tell the press about my suspension? They're bound to ask."

"Tell them the truth—that you're delighted to be back."

He stepped up to a bank of microphones and gave a little statement.

"Mel!" I hissed at the sunglassed Buford. He stood directly behind Morgan, looking in all directions. He tilted himself slightly my way.

I cupped my hands around his ear so no one else would hear. "Find out who the mole is?"

He nodded.

"Who?" I asked, but he waved me away.

And then I heard my name. "We're thrilled to have him back on board," Morgan was saying, "and I'll let him have the mike for a couple of minutes in case there's questions for him. Dan?"

I figured I'd be pelted with embarrassing queries—like, if you didn't leak that campaign document to the *Times*, why exactly were you suspended?—but instead got only "In light of your reinstatement less than twenty-four hours after your private press conference, and Jack's appearance here today, weren't you selling us short when you told us your appearance yesterday had no relation to the campaign?"

"No, not at all. I didn't know Jack was coming to San Francisco until late last night, and didn't know that I was reinstated until just now. My wife Kaya here can vouch for that."

"Dan, should we address ongoing business to you, or should we continue dealing with Avery?"

"Continue dealing with Avery for the rest of the day. He'll bring me up to speed, and you can deal with me exclusively tomorrow."

And then off to the Fairmont for a fund-raising brunch. I hadn't been part of a rolling campaign since early June. Whereas then I was so sick of the touring that I devised a plan to end it, now I found it exhilarating. I remember days when our motorcade consisted of a pair of yellow taxis and we took an hour to cross town; today we swung onto 101 surrounded by light-flashing police cars and had five lanes to ourselves, the CHP having closed off all the access ramps. Our gleaming limos sped up the peninsula, past Candlestick Park, into the heart of the city at eighty miles per hour.

As Morgan held forth at the brunch, Avery told me what was happening in my department. The gist was that the media had latched onto the photo-finish aspect of the race, more interested in voting patterns and campaign strategies than what the candidates were saying. That was no surprise. What I really wanted to know was what was happening inside the inner circle, but since Avery lacked any sense of intrigue I got no clues regarding who was in Morgan's favor, who was out, and above all, who the snitch was.

We drove along the Embarcadero—again, sealed off—to the noontime rally, and that's when it hit us. All of us, even Morgan, had been living in a vacuum since the convention. Sitting in Toledo it had been impossible to realize how deeply Morgan had affected the electorate. But as we mounted the stage in front of the World Trade Center and heard the collective roar of people flooding Market Street as far as we could see, a rush came over every one of us. The PA system pumped out George Harrison's "Ding Dong Ding Dong," the same song used at the convention, and the crowd cheered even louder. The stage shook so much from the vibration that I wondered whether we were having an earthquake.

Morgan basked in the spectacle, raising his arms in a double wave, and then he blew the crowd away—and me as well. He gave the most impassioned speech of his career. Nothing scared him—not that the press would pick up a misstatement and make an issue of it, not that he might be called a radical, not even that he might lose. He came closer to telling the truth than I have ever heard a politician come, and after he finished, the response from the crowd hurt our ears. And, I had to admit, he thoroughly deserved the tribute. The man had his duplicitous side, that was for sure, but at moments like this he proved he also had the makings of a giant.

"Did you like it?" he inquired over the din.

"Didn't think you had it in you," I shouted back.

"That's gonna be my closing statement at the debate Sunday night."

They closed off 101 again for the ride back to the airport. "No matter how high this plane goes," chirped Molineaux, "it won't go as high as him." Indeed, Morgan was giddy, laughing and shaking hands with Buford's guards, even Buford himself. He wrapped his arm around the pale Elena and practically hauled her into the campaign plane.

"You do that to me and you're dead," Kaya warned.

"Come on, doll, our chariot's at the next gate," I said, pointing to the press plane. It felt good to have Kaya with me. She rarely saw me work, and I looked forward to joking with her afterward about the nonsense we'd encounter. If she was capable of humor, that was. Beneath her surface brightness lurked a crushing gravity of purpose; Buford never watched me so intently.

The reporters were as awed by Morgan as the crowd had been. "Did you get an official estimate of the turnout?" Sue Randall of CNN asked as she batted her story into a laptop.

"Quarter million," I replied, even though I'd heard no estimates.

"Morgan must be jubilant," speculated someone else.

It was the guy from NBC. I wondered if he knew what would be coming down from Gordin tonight, and was hoping for an unguarded statement implying the rally brought Morgan out of a deep funk. What a neat little coda that would make to the hatchet job they were preparing.

35

It was Claudio, the wise-cracking, native Italian waiter at the North Beach hole-in-the-wall I'd chosen for dinner who let us know that Gordin's stories hit the air. Seating us at the rearmost table at the insistence of the Secret Service—aside from Claudio and the kitchen help, they were the only other people in the restaurant —he took an admiring glance at Morgan, turned to me, and said with a wink, "He don't look crazy."

My color drained. I knew it was coming, but I wasn't ready for it yet. "Who said he was crazy?"

"You don't watch TV? Yeah! They say he was crazy."

"You're joking, right?" I leaned across the table toward Morgan and Elena. "He should be doing stand-up. We brought Kaya's parents here once and he had them rolling in the aisle."

"I'm not joking. You were on there too."

"I was?"

"Wit' that bird you let go. I was going to tell you we had duck on special, but maybe you get offended, eh?"

"You aren't kidding, then."

"Hey, if I heard about it, it was big story."

"What channel?"

"You know, the one with the guy who can't pronounce his *l*'s. What's his name?" Claudio snapped his fingers trying to recall.

"That's channel four. NBC."

I looked across the table, expecting to see alarm in Morgan's eyes. But he paid no mind to what he must have thought was harmless patter between old acquaintances. "What's easy on the garlic?" he asked, perusing the menu.

Elena, on the other hand, looked stricken. She sweated under her makeup, and her eyes darted this way and that.

Which, I suddenly realized, gave away the answer I'd been seeking.

"You like wine before your dinner?" Claudio inquired.

"None for me, thank you," said Morgan.

"Nor I," I shook my head.

"I want some," said Elena. "Bring me something dry and white and well-aged."

"Like me," piped Morgan, elbowing her. She didn't laugh.

"Actually, could I have a glass of wine also?" asked Kaya, as if she needed Claudio's permission.

"What is this, the men don't drink but the women do? What is this world coming to?" he asked, looking up to the plastic, autumn-colored leaves hanging densely from the ceiling. "You want me to bring a carafe?"

"Maybe half?" Kaya looked hesitantly at Elena.

"Bring us a whole," Elena commanded. "And tell me where the bathroom is." She abruptly pushed back her chair and rose.

"Straight through the kitchen, take the first right," Claudio informed her.

"Good idea," I said. "I have to go too."

There being only one bathroom, I followed Elena in.

"I beg your pardon," she huffed.

For a moment I wondered how I would apologize if I were wrong. Lord knows I've misinterpreted visual cues before. But there was little mistaking her reaction at the table. And if anybody had a motive, Elena Morgan did. "You're the one who told Reed Gordin about Jack's depression, aren't you?"

Wheeling on the toes of her high heels, she peered into the cracked mirror above the filthy porcelain sink and dabbed at her moistening eyes.

"You're also the one who leaked that master plan I wrote to the *Times*. But when that didn't do any damage, you pulled out the stops. You leaked the most damning information you had a week before election day."

She pulled mascara from her pocketbook and with an unsteady hand applied a fresh layer to her lashes. "I'm very sorry you were hurt," she said, "but I had to do something."

"Elena, do you really think if Jack loses it'll save your marriage?"

"It's worth a try, isn't it?" Her eyes blinked rapidly. Sooty tears ran down her face.

Even at my angriest I can usually maintain my self-control, but this time a spitefully cold cynicism slipped out. "Listen," I asked, "why don't you just give the man an ultimatum? Either politics or you. If he doesn't answer you the way you want, divorce him. It would serve him right."

"Go ahead, try to talk me into what you people want the most!" she fumed, too smart to take the bait. She unrolled a wad of toilet paper and cleaned her face.

"But really, Elena, why do you stay with him?" I pressed.

"Because I love him. I guess you wouldn't understand that, would you? For the longest time I thought you were the best of them. I thought maybe you understood, just a little. But you don't. You're a jackal like them all. You don't see people, you see obstacles or opportunities along your path to power. And Jack is one big shortcut on that road to glory, isn't he?"

"Elena."

"The worst mistake I ever made was letting him indulge this fantasy. He wasn't crazy when he was in business. He got depressed, but nothing like this. And don't say he'll be better if he wins. You told me that after the primaries, and he got worse. I know you people look down your noses at me, but give me this much credit: It's difficult to fool me twice."

Yes, Elena was the one who nearly cost me my career, and that gave me every right to continue twisting the knife in her heart. But a funny thing happened while playing Kaya's role in this exchange: I *did* understand just a little. And because of that, my anger rapidly unraveled.

"I almost didn't come back," I explained apologetically. "I wanted my humanity again. But I did come back, because the cause is too important to let all this effort, mine and Jack's and everybody else's, go to waste. We've paid such an enormous price, I want to salvage something."

Exhaling loudly, she gave a troubled shake of the head. "I don't think that's possible. But if you do. . . ." She shrugged. "You know, I really did come here to pee."

When I returned to the table, Buford was sitting in Elena's seat. I didn't need Kaya's furrowed glance to tell me that the prevailing mood had changed. "What the hell were you doing back there so long?" Morgan growled. "Take a look at what Buford brought."

He turned a miniature television my way. Buford hit the rewind button, and the tape he had inserted played again. It was Gordin's story about Morgan. It ran for only ninety seconds and didn't say much beyond the fact that two unnamed sources within the Morgan camp had confirmed that Morgan had an emotional disorder, probably chronic depression. Dingo Hutson, interviewed in Georgia, countered irascibly that Morgan had no mental problem "that in any way impaired his judgment or effectiveness."

Elena returned. Claudio, carafe of wine in hand, pulled up a new chair for her because no one else would.

"We know one source," grumped Buford, staring hard at her. She stared back without contrition. "What pisses me is now we have another squealer, and I'll have to do another inquisition."

It was now or never.

"No, you won't," I cut Buford short. "I'll make it easy for you. I'm the second source."

Morgan and Buford set their jaws and burned. Elena, suppressing laughter, nearly fell out of her chair. Kaya reached under the table and squeezed my hand, no doubt thinking I'd decided in her favor. What she didn't know was that this was the prelude to my plan, which now I set in motion.

"I didn't think that I was coming back, and Gordin put the screws to me," I explained. "So we cut a deal. For confirming what Elena told him, he ran that puff piece on me."

"You cocksucker," Buford pushed through clenched teeth.

"I'm not the innocent you think I am." I smiled, afraid, but for the first time feeling the equal of Jack Morgan and Mel Buford. I was playing in their league and winning. But I couldn't get too cocky; the game had just begun. "I hereby offer you my resignation," I announced grandly.

"Accepted." Morgan pounded the table.

"Although," I added after an appropriately pregnant pause, "once I'm off the campaign, I won't have any compunctions about confirming Gordin's story on the record. Because Reed was right. The people have a right to know *everything* about the man who may be their next president."

Morgan looked at Buford. Buford stared in disgust at the fake leaves on the ceiling.

I had them. And they knew it.

"What's your price?" Jack Morgan queried.

"First, I want to know the real reason you suspended me."

Morgan leaned back in his chair, stretched his arms straight up, then clasped his hands behind his head. "Because, your protestations notwithstanding, we thought you were the mole. You were angry that we went for style over substance. It embarrassed you, because you had promised I would talk about the issues. We figured one of your buddies in the press, probably the *Times* guy, got you bitching, and you handed him the master plan to prove your high-minded intentions. Probably you did it off the record, but he, being a journalist, couldn't hold to the agreement. He faxed the document to his pal in the other campaign, and the other guy broke the story so your buddy wouldn't get in trouble with us."

"Like Holmes and Watson, these two, aren't they?" barbed Elena, casting a mocking smile their way. "For their next trick they'll explain how come the earth is flat."

There was almost certainly more to it. I suspected that with the election this close Morgan hated being pinned so tightly on environmental issues, and blamed me for the votes he felt it was costing him. And then there was Kathy—but he wasn't about to bring that up with Elena around.

Hmm. Kathy and Elena. That was another card I could play if the game got rough.

"How come you didn't give the press a reason for my suspension?" I asked.

"We were protecting your reputation in case it turned out you were innocent—which, in that instance anyway, you were."

Uh-huh, right. And your grandma plays second base for the Mud Hens. "Okay, I'll buy that," I replied with the same sweet disingenuousness. "Now, the second thing I want—"

Morgan and Buford leaned forward.

"—is Secretary of Interior."

Had they food in their mouths they'd have spat it out like pellets from a shotgun. "You aren't qualified," Jack Morgan sputtered.

"Name the last Interior Secretary who was. And you'd better make sure I'm confirmed, because if I'm not, again, I won't hesitate to tell the press corps everything I know."

"You can't blackmail us," Buford said, so hotly I was afraid if I locked eyes with him I'd spontaneously combust.

"I'll be a good soldier as long as you play straight with me," I promised. "You don't fire me or hamstring me, I won't blow your credibility with the electorate. You end the sale of public land. Interior gets a five-percent budget increase above inflation each of your first two years, and inflation increases after that. You don't interfere with how I allocate my funds. I name my own subordinates. And you transfer jurisdiction over national forests to Interior. In exchange I play team ball. I'll be flexible. I won't embarrass you—politically, personally, any way."

They weren't buying.

"Look, I could really push this," I pressed, fearful that they'd call my bluff and everything would fall apart.

"I could insist on staying on as press secretary. Then what would you do, with me in your faces every day? At Interior you won't have to see me more than, oh, three times a month. And I'll also give you this. Keep me on as press secretary for the rest of the campaign and I'll clean up this Gordin mess. Or would you rather Avery took care of it?"

Morgan brooded heavily, his expression a mix of disbelief and hatred. Claudio brought bread. The presidential candidate ripped off a hunk, spread butter on it, and bit in.

"What kind of bread is this?" he asked querulously.

"Sourdough." Claudio shrugged. "You don't know sourdough?"

"He's from Ohio," I explained.

"Sourdough," repeated Morgan. "All right." He turned to me. "You've got a deal."

I whipped out my dictaputer. "See?" I said to Kaya as I turned it on, "I told you these things have their uses. Now, let's memorialize this agreement."

"No. First tell me how you're gonna handle Gordin's story," he demanded.

36

I HANDLED IT by lying.

"We expected late hits," I told reporters at an airport press conference Saturday morning in Minneapolis, the first stop of the day; we'd be in Chicago for a noontime rally, Milwaukee for an afternoon rally, and Des Moines for dinner. "This is one of them. We have two unnamed sources saying Morgan suffers from depression. No on-the-record sources. No documentation, except to note that Morgan underwent psychiatric counseling after he was wounded in action. Need I say that psychiatric trauma after being hurt in battle is not unusual, in fact, is a sign of normality? And that was twenty-five years ago. Today Jack Morgan is in perfect mental health. I repeat: perfect mental health."

"You'll pay for this," Gordin faxed. I'm sure he figured that I knew on Thursday night I'd be going back to Morgan and had deliberately set him up. Almost through the machine was my response—*"You understand the process"*—when I realized that anything I put in writing might be used against me.

Double-crossing Gordin reinforced the message to Morgan and Buford that they weren't dealing with a patsy anymore. For years I was their tool, harmless beyond my function, but no more. I'd finally realized that my words could kill; I nearly undid Morgan telling the truth, and then I went out and undid Gordin telling lies. I was a player, and they would have to reckon with me from now on.

They had but two ways to destroy my leverage. The first was to admit that Morgan had a problem, which they wouldn't do. The other was to kill me. I considered that a possibility, and still do, but it seemed further than Morgan was willing to go to win the presidency; he was, by his own admission, a softie, and didn't think any crime deserved the death penalty, much less a nonviolent one.

Melvin Buford, though, was another story. I didn't put it past him to have his boys toss me off a roof one night. Much as I was on my guard around them before, I was doubly so now.

In spite of fearing for my life, I was the happiest member of the Morgan camp. Reporters and fellow staffers attributed it to my "vacation," and I did nothing to discourage that impression. I had no need to flaunt my newfound sense of power; I didn't come back to fuck up the campaign. The exchange at the Italian restaurant remained a secret among the participants—so long as Elena didn't blab to reporters—and I did as I was told cheerfully and without so much as a cocked brow's worth of skepticism.

With the campaign coming to a tumultuous close, and with me suddenly having such a stake in its success, I worked harder than ever. I ran on adrenaline, coffee, and the energy absorbed from the people around me. Kaya, much less taken with my ambition than I'd hoped, tried to get me to sleep during plane rides, but had as much success as she did getting Nimby to sit through a combing. The minute I laid my head back I thought of something else to do, and jumped out of my seat to do it.

Morgan, for his part, was developing circles under his eyes. By the time we reached Des Moines he responded to every question by nodding slightly and curling his lips into a tiny smile, like an old man who can't hear. Elena cordoned off the first-class section of the plane, sequestered him within, and stood guard between the curtained entrances. She didn't even let Buford by; when he tried to zig around her, she kicked him in the shin.

After Des Moines we flew to Toledo for the night. The next day we'd be in New York, Baltimore, and Atlanta before heading to the debate. Rather than go all the way to Morgan's house we booked the presidential suite and adjoining rooms at the Toledo Airport Hilton. Once Buford's people had checked for eavesdropping devices, we held an inner circle meeting.

It was the first time I'd seen Mitchell, Ishikawa, and Kathy Cheng since mid-October. All of them looked as if they hadn't slept in weeks, which, given the late date and the close race, may have been the case.

Erika, as usual, was cordial. "Welcome back," she said, greeting me with a handshake. Spying Kaya in the hallway, she leaned over me and waved merrily. Ishikawa, to whom I became invisible the second I was suspended, nodded curtly, as if I'd never been away.

Kathy merely smiled. I smiled back uneasily, then quickly looked around for someone else to talk to.

"All right," Morgan commenced. "Where are we this minute?"

"Believe it or not, almost exactly where we were yesterday," Erika answered. "So far your travels haven't made a difference. Nine states still too close to call, including three of the big five."

"Which big ones fell into a column?"

"Pennsylvania and Michigan. We're going to lose them."

"Oh well. We knew that was coming."

"The biggest danger is the new commercials. That kind of economic scaremongering will cause a lot of last-minute defections."

"Their timing's perfect," Molineaux agreed. He and Mitchell were referring to the "It's Too Expensive" series of radio and TV ads, in which actors cast as ordinary citizens conjectured ominously about how much it would cost the average family to enact plans for sustainable technology and ecological renewal. "Just as you're ready to pull that lever," Molineaux frowned, "they grab you by the short and curlies and ask, 'Do you really want to make that leap?' "

"Any impact yet?" Morgan asked Mitchell.

"They're hitting us hard in New England, New Jersey, Maryland, and Georgia. We still have majorities there, but they're getting shaky. If we fall behind in those states, and the press picks up on it, defections could snowball."

"Any one of those states, except maybe Vermont or Rhode Island, could cost us the election," Ishikawa noted superfluously. We could all add.

"I'll have to counter at the rally in New York tomorrow morning. Steinhardt, Molly, I want phrases, paragraphs if you've got them, to the effect my policies will not cost money—even though they will. Anything else, Mitchell?"

She threw up her hands. "This thing is getting tighter. I've never seen anything like it, and I've been doing this longer than I care to admit."

"So, except for the commercials, nothing gives the other guys the impetus?"

"No. We're down to seven percent undecided among those who plan to vote. They're the ones who'll choose the winner."

"And they'll make their choice based on tomorrow night's debate," said Molineaux. "You don't seem in any shape for that, boss."

"I want the best makeup people you can find, to hide these bags under my eyes," Morgan responded. "I've already got my closing speech. Steinhardt tells me it's a winner. So I'll finesse the questions, and that'll be the end of it."

"Don't take it so lightly. You're vulnerable," Buford warned.

"What do you want me to do, Mel? I can't cancel those rallies tomorrow. I'm just as likely to let something brilliant slip out in the debate as something stupid. Now, Erika, who are those undecideds?"

She shrugged. "They're concentrated mostly in four NABR headings, but they're too diverse to send one message. Probably the best thing you can do is sum up your objectives in the clearest language possible."

"I can handle that. I've been saying this stuff long enough that if I haven't got it down by now, I never will. Ishikawa, how we stand on money?"

"As of tomorrow we'll officially be broke."

"I was afraid of that. You have a debt projection?"

"Two, three million."

"Thank God I'm rich. All right, subject to my approval cancel all expenditures you think are frivolous. Fallon, any news?"

"I'm tireder than a ten-point buck in hunting season."

"Besides that, Fallon."

"Everything's on schedule for tomorrow. We had to twist some arms to get the governor and mayor to appear together with you in New York, but we did it. Crazy New Yorkers."

"Hey, at least they don't tawk funny," needled Molineaux.

"And what about the weather?" Morgan asked.

"Chilly, but no rain anywhere on the itinerary."

"Good. How about the press?" he asked me casually, as if our relationship was just the same as it had been in June.

"I haven't had a chance to review the tapes of this evening's newscasts. Avery tells me all the networks covered the denial, but NBC took pains to note that *I* didn't produce documents to support it."

"Fine. As long as everyone's accusing and denying, the general take is it's a tempest in a teapot. Any polling on that story, Erika?"

"I'll have one done tomorrow," she promised, scribbling on her legal pad.

"All right. At this point it's better that we get some sleep. You all have your assignments. Those of you going with me, wake-up call is five-thirty sharp. We're on the plane for New York by six-thirty."

He reflected for a moment, pressing a hand to his scarred cheek. "Jeez Louise, everything depends on that debate tomorrow night," he murmured, as if realizing it for the first time. "I wish it hadn't come to that."

He sank into reverie. We didn't know whether to disband or wait for more.

"Oh." He noticed our hesitation and snapped back to attention. Staring directly at me, he said, "Good night, everybody. And pray that the debate goes well. Your futures hang in the balance."

37

MODERATOR : Senator Morgan, you have three minutes for your final statement.

Morgan: Thank you, Sarah. (Stares into camera, looks down and sighs. Begins to speak—and paces the stage. Camerapeople, caught by surprise, hastily follow.) Ladies and gentlemen, every country is run by an elite—the people who run the institutions that affect our lives directly. Here in America those institutions are the government, which makes the laws. The corporations, which supply our goods and services. And the media, which provide our vital information.

The people who run those institutions are the elite. I am part of that elite. The President is an even bigger part of the elite, given his authority. And the men and women who questioned us this evening are also part of the elite.

Members of the elite don't always act in concert. Anyone who's watched the Congress is aware of that. Their interests aren't necessarily the same. But there is one interest all of them do share, and that's to stay a *part* of the elite. I don't think I'm surprising anybody when I say that no one likes to give up power or authority.

(Stops for a moment, ponders, then turns in the other direction. Continues pacing as he speaks.) Initially elites become elites by serving the best interests of the public. For a period of time they continue their effective service, but the one universal on this earth is that things change. As things change, the best interests of the public change, and the elite has to adjust.

It can adjust two ways. The first way is to recognize the new reality and accommodate it. But very, very rarely are adjustments made this way. That's because changing means some institutions or parts of institutions lose their influence, and some of the elite lose power. That is not permissible, because, remember, the first rule is to stay a part of the elite.

So most elites adjust the second way, by consolidating power regardless of the consequences to society. We recognize this pattern right away when we think of failed dictatorships, like those of Eastern Europe in the nineteen-eighties. Like most irrelevant elites, they resorted to repression to maintain their power. They hardened, rigidified, until they didn't even serve their own needs, much less their people's.

We Americans have more trouble recognizing this pattern in our own elite. Every now and then we'll talk about it, like when we say the government's been bought off, or corporations care more about their profits than the welfare of humanity, or the media misinform us or don't tell us what we need to know. But after we say this, what do we do? Nothing, except become more cynical, more hopeless, more convinced of our powerlessness.

Ladies and gentlemen, the thing to do when your elite becomes irrelevant is to replace it. That's your only chance of living in a world you feel a part of. The President comes to you tonight as the leader of that ossified, irrelevant elite. A vote for him is for the same old thing. More disillusion, more cynicism, more powerlessness.

(Stops. Stares directly at the camera and jabs finger toward it on the accented syllables.) But I come to you tonight a renegade from the elite. I am the candidate of change. I am the candidate of hope.

(Looks down. Resumes pacing, hands thrust into pants pockets.) We all know what happens to countries where elites resist change for too long. They collapse, like England after World War Two and the Soviet Union in the nineteen-nineties. We also know that when we the people let elites go without challenge for too long, it takes extraordinary measures to replace them. Like revolutions. Two hundred and thirty-two years ago this nation was conceived in defiance of a bad elite. But it took eight years of war and hardship to replace it.

I don't pretend my challenge to the elite will easily succeed. As I push harder, it will resist with all the strength at its disposal. And that strength is formidable. I don't promise you an easy ride.

But I do promise you this: I will do everything in my power, to the last ounce of my strength, to restore *your* control over the institutions dominating our society. I will do it not through revolution, nor through repression of your rights, but through a top-to-bottom sweep-through of the government. I will yank the foxes out of the chicken coops. I will make sure that government enforces laws as they are written, for the protection and the benefit of us against the special interests. And I will push through campaign and electoral reforms that will force our representatives to represent the people, not whoever fills up their campaign chests.

And once control of government is back in our hands, we'll use it to cajole and, if we have to, legislate our other institutions into dealing with reality. We will finally deal with our deteriorating environment. We will finally deal with our sliding economic competitiveness, and with all the debts that hamper our recovery. We will finally deal with all the hopelessness and disillusionment that sap our energy like a disease. Again, it won't be easy, but if we take it one step at a time, with the tenacity we like to think we commonly possess, we will succeed. And our country and our world will be a better place to live.

(Returns to podium and stops pacing. Looks at camera, holds up hand.) Before I finish, I want to say one thing. What I've said may frighten you. Maybe you've heard that I'm a demagogue. Let me assure you that is not the case. My reforms are democratic with a small *d*. They're meant to open up the country, make the elite responsive. The fact that I want to be a Lincoln rather than a Coolidge is certainly in contrast to my rival, but hardly evidence I mean to run the country by playing to the mob's emotions.

Maybe you're afraid of what will happen if I win. Already there are rumors the stock market will collapse if I'm elected. In response to that I quote my favorite founding father, Benjamin Franklin, who said that anyone who'd give up liberty to obtain temporary security deserves neither security nor liberty. The stock exchange may plummet if I win, but you can rest assured that will be nothing compared with the crash that will come if we don't get our house in order now.

Maybe you don't want to take the chance. Yeah, yeah, everything I've said is true, but your life is okay, why make all these changes? Because if we don't act now, our children may not have the clean air, food, and water they need to survive. If you don't mind cursing your children with the hell of global ruin, if all you care about is whether you've got yours today, then don't vote for me. But if you want an America that cares enough about the future to take destiny into its own hands, an America that isn't passive or denying in the face of danger, then please, cast a ballot for me Tuesday.

You may never get another chance to vote for someone who will challenge our incompetent elite.

Thank you very much, and whatever the result of this election, may the Lord be with us all.

Moderator: Mr. President, you have three—

(Sudden shouts and screams. Two explosive cracks ring out, and then another. Secret Service agents in the crowd converge on someone in the audience. Secret Service agents from the wings behind the stage knock down the President and pile over him.

An instant later, Secret Service agents reach Jack Morgan. They are late: Buford is already there, straddling the candidate, who lies motionless behind the podium.

The right side of Morgan's face pours blood. The Secret Service agents bark into their radios.

Buford takes a closer look. "Can you hear me, Jack?" he cries above the din.

Morgan notes the black shoes all around him. "Cameras still on?" he inquires feebly.

Buford shoves the husky agents from his field of view. "Still on," he affirms.

"Help me up," Morgan commands. He raises an arm so that Buford can hoist him.

"Don't move!" a Secret Service agent orders.

"Fuck you," says Jack Morgan.

"You don't know how seriously he's hurt!" the agent pleads with Buford.

Buford pulls Jack Morgan to his feet.

"Fuck you," Morgan repeats at the agent, then starts to topple. Buford catches him.

"I'm all right," Morgan insists. Blood drips from the right side of his face onto his suit. "Got a matching set now, eh?" he jokes, pointing to his scar. "Loosen my tie," he orders Buford. "Give me your handkerchief." He dabs at blood and sweat. "Now show me the camera."

A Secret Service agent clutches Morgan by the

arm. "This way, Jack. Everything will be okay." He pushes Morgan toward the wing.

Morgan looks at Buford, who understands. So quickly that no one notices, Buford knees the agent in the groin.

Freed, Morgan walks to front and center stage. The members of the audience still in the auditorium give him a thundering ovation.

He raises both arms in the air. His eyes are wild and triumphant. He bellows something, but without a microphone his voice is drowned out by the claps and shouts and general tumult.

Seeing him onstage, the President returns, surrounded by a retinue of Secret Service agents. Morgan strides toward his opponent, parting the bodyguards like Moses. He wipes his cheek. He shakes hands with the President.

The President looks down at his hand and blanches.

Morgan faints.

The Secret Service bears him offstage on a stretcher.)

38

EVER SINCE THE first debate Jack Morgan had needed to show the public he could stand up to intimidation. That champeen-of-the-world bravado after taking a bullet in the face transformed him overnight into the tougher of the candidates and stemmed the hemorrhage of support caused by the "It's Too Expensive" ad blitz. No wonder, then, he seemed so happy in his hospital bed. It was for the rest of us to go back to Toledo and run around like headless chickens; having done all he could for the cause, he'd pass the last day of the campaign playing video games (a VR helmet wouldn't fit over his bandages) and drinking the twelve-pack of Stroh's that Buford snuck up to his room.

The near-assassination spooked us thoroughly, but Molineaux, ever mindful that politics was theater, admonished us that the show had to go on. So, starting at two A.M. Monday morning, I briefed the press hourly on Morgan's status. Will he live? (Barring unforeseen and drastic complications, yes.) Was his life ever in danger? (No.) Has he suffered brain damage? (None at all—the bullet grazed his cheek and ear and fractured the cheekbone. It had no effect at all on neurological functions.

301

We expect complete recovery inside a month. At worst his hearing may be just a bit impaired.) How long will he be in the hospital? (If all goes well, we may even see him at the victory celebration tomorrow night.)

On Tuesday there is little to do except wait for the returns, but even so, Fallon's on the phone to everyplace at once. I never thought I'd say it, but I give the guy a lot of credit. He won't quit chasing votes until the last precinct is closed; if I dare tell him about the little old lady from Bowling Green who called to ask for a ride to the polls, he'll need to be restrained from taking her himself.

Erika is tabulating exit polls. She's become so tired of us dropping by for the latest info that she's locked herself in her office and disconnected all but one line of her phone. At various times I've caught Molineaux, Ishikawa, and Joe Perez eavesdropping by her door.

As for me, with Morgan's condition stabilized there isn't much to tell the press. Consequently the reporters have dispersed to compose their final analyses (one for if he wins, one for if he loses) and gossip about their next assignment. TV correspondents call periodically to request a quote for a story that will run at slack times in the all-night coverage. Three so far have asked my estimate of the chance the electoral vote will wind up in a tie, throwing the election to the House of Representatives. They want to use this as a hook, to keep viewers watching the returns into the wee hours. I refuse to play along, saying that mathematically there simply aren't many ways the vote could come out even.

By mid-afternoon the calls stop, and for the first time since Yosemite I'm left alone to think. Kaya comes by and sees at once that I'm in trouble. She forces me to lie down on the floor, where she massages my furrowed brow. But for all her patient ministrations, my brain won't cease its churning.

Because despite the many flattering stories about

me since Reed Gordin's puff piece hit the air, I can't delude myself into believing it was my plan that brought Morgan close to winning. I kept him close until the first debate, yes. But after that it took what I can only call fortuitous disasters to keep his candidacy breathing. The oil spill brought public attention back from the "Call me a liar, Jack" sideshow and refocused it where it belonged, on the environment. And the near-assassination, as I already said, answered any doubts concerning Morgan's toughness.

I can't stop wondering whether these tragedies that worked so much to our advantage were just coincidences.

I go back to that night in the Reynolds Road motel, where Buford talked about the need to make Jack Morgan snap out in the second debate. When the necessary outburst didn't come, Buford must have realized that after years of repression it was impossible for Morgan consciously to expose his dark side. Only an unexpected and powerful assault, one that overwhelmed every defense, would unloose the Mr. Hyde from Dr. Jekyll. If the cynical obfuscations of the President couldn't do the job, something more drastic had to be provided. And no one was better positioned to provide something more drastic than Mel Buford.

Did Buford's reach extend into the bridge of the *Prince William Sound*? Not very likely. So far as I know he doesn't have connections in the oil trade, and I doubt he would have attempted such a bold stroke where his control was less than total. Besides, although the oil spill brought environment back into the campaign, it wasn't the sort of thing to set Jack Morgan off, even in private.

The assassination try, on the other hand, positively stank of Buford.

It wouldn't have been hard to arrange. Some former Marine or NSA associate would know a friend who knew a friend who knew a piece of walking shit who made a living knocking off priests and organizers in sub-tropical dictatorships. The shit would be handed a brief-case full of money, a ticket to the debate, and a gun sure to elude detection. But the sight wouldn't be true—off just enough so that a bullet aimed between the eyes would, in the distance of a hundred feet, shear three inches to the left. As the shit took aim, the money he was given would be retrieved and handed to his contact, who would immediately take an extended trip to Mexico.

After he was apprehended the shit would protest that someone put him up to it. But he would have no proof, and a public grown weary of conspiracy theories would readily accept that he alone intended to assassinate Jack Morgan. It wouldn't help when the district attorney in his home county announced that the shit belonged to a band of anti-environmental crackpots called the Sahara Club. (That came out this morning, much to Buford's professed chagrin; he wanted to encourage speculation that the would-be killer is a Republican.) So long as Buford's contacts honored their code of silence—which, from what I know of that crowd, was something Mel could take for granted—nobody would ever know the event was a gamble staged to provoke Morgan into performing for the bullies.

And now that I think about it, once the shots were fired Morgan did play his role perfectly, didn't he? Almost as if he was in on the plot himself.

But no. Stop there. This strains even my own credulity. Since when would a professional assassin shoot from a position he couldn't escape? And since when would Buford assume that within half a second, from dozens of feet away, amid a crowd of people, the assassin would take perfect aim and only graze Jack Morgan's cheek?

Well. If this is how I'm thinking now, what are the prospects for my sanity inside a Morgan administration?

I know I would make the best damn Interior secretary the country ever had. Absolutely incorruptible, devoted totally to preservation over exploitation. And I'd be a get-down-with-the-people sort of public servant, working side by side with trail-maintenance crews, sleeping on the ground at a campsite instead of on a four-poster in some luxury hotel, and chatting around the campfire with whoever paid a visit, even Good Sam Clubbers.

But how much would I really accomplish, and what would happen to me in the process? Because of what he sees as a betrayal on my part, a President Morgan would never invite me into his inner circle as candidate Morgan did. Indeed, because of his animosity I might actually be a liability to the cause. In my nightmare scenarios I see Morgan committing environmental outrages, then demanding that I publicly defend him because I promised to be a team player. Thus would he steal higher purpose from my lies and transform me into just another ambitious man of experience like himself—on top of provoking enough fear, through his henchman, to drive me beyond paranoia into madness.

So if we win, I think the first thing I will say to Morgan is *I quit.* Then I'll go home and stay there—act like a real husband—and become America's environmental gadfly. After all, if we win, a lot of reporters will feel indebted to me for their White House assignment. When I ask them for the favor of a sound bite, they will grant it, and from that spot on the wall beyond the reach of his swatter I will pester Morgan into living up to the promises he made. And he will have no choice except to do so, because thanks to Gordin the constituency that put him in the White House isn't really his.

It's mine.

ABOUT THE AUTHOR

ANDREW GOLDBLATT lives in the San Francisco Bay Area. He is co-author of *The Hamlet Syndrome* (1989).

The Turner Tomorrow Fellowship was created to encourage authors to write fiction that produces creative and positive solutions to global problems. Chosen from more than 2,500 submissions from around the world, *Ishmael* is the winner of this prestigious fellowship.

ISHMAEL
by Daniel Quinn

"TEACHER seeks pupil. Must have an earnest desire to save the world. Apply in person."

And in response, the narrator finds a massive ape named Ishmael whose thoughts he can read. In this extraordinary novel, man and ape embark on an intellectual journey that will redefine what it means to be human. It is a story of man's place in the ecosystem that extends backward and forward over the life span of the earth itself.

"*Ishmael* is a genuine discovery. It will be around for many years."—Ray Bradbury

"Quinn's smooth style and his intriguing proposals should hold the attention of readers interested in the daunting dilemmas that beset our planet."—*Publishers Weekly*

"By the end of the novel the state of the planet and what is probably the only way to its salvation are laid out for us with an originality and clarity few could deny."—*The New York Times Book Review*

Our Earth, Ourselves

The Action-Oriented Guide to Help You Protect and Preserve Our Environment

Ruth Caplan, Executive Director
and the staff of Environmental Action

With a foreword by Pete Seeger

Compiled by leading experts at the environmental group founded by the organizers of the first Earth Day, this comprehensive resource puts individuals and communities at the helm of the burgeoning environmental movement. A hands-on guide, it provides concrete, practical advice on what we can do to reverse the damage already done to our air, our water, and our land. Each chapter offers clear, up-to-date information, a point-by-point blueprint for action, and profiles of individuals who have made a difference. This book points us toward effective responses to such urgent challenges as closing the ozone layer, curbing global warming, and detoxifying our air, water, and food.

Available at your local bookstore or use this page to order.
❏ 34857-4 OUR EARTH, OURSELVES $10.95/$13.95 in Canada
Send to: Bantam Books, Dept. NFB 20
2451 S. Wolf Road
Des Plaines, IL 60018
Please send me the items I have checked above. I am enclosing
$_____ (please add $2.50 to cover postage and handling). Send
check or money order, no cash or C.O.D.'s, please.

Mr./Ms._____

Address_____

City/State_____Zip_____
Please allow four to six weeks for delivery.
Prices and availability subject to change without notice.   NFB 20 7/9